The Two Of Hearts

Part 7 of the Red Dog Conspiracy

Patricia Loofbourrow

Published by Red Dog Press, LLC

Printed in the USA

Praise for the
Red Dog Conspiracy

"Melancholy and loyalty. Blood and love. Violence and tenderness. They're all tangled together in this powerful series ..."

— OLIVIA WYLIE

"This very well thought out world is created with incredibly believable and realistic scenarios based on the best of steampunk, mafia family organisation, 19th century English living (not the nobles, but the real world of real people, similar to Dickens or Swift) and an intriguing dystopian future."

— LIN CRAN

"... intriguing in the many plot twists. Rival gangs, dishonest wealthy, and the grubby poor — all trying to make a living amidst a life-style that has fallen into ruins."

— MARILYN COATES

"Although it's an easy read there are twists and turns, dead ends and hidden meanings that help provide a wonderful dangerous complexity. For me the greatest meanings are in relationships and cultural distances. Things that are the heart of Jacqui's problems. That and love. A brilliant portrayal of flawed people caught in their own suspicion based traps."

— KAY MACK

"Even if you aren't a fan of steampunk, this series is a fun read! The author has created a unique world set far in the future where Victorian culture and steampunk technology are the norm. It is in this world that Jacq must try to make her way. Surrounded by enemies, married to a man she doesn't love, and every action by any person in her world could be an act of betrayal that will cost Jacq her life!"

— KEVIN SIVILS

For clues, backstory and more, visit JacqOfSpades.com

FICTION BY PATRICIA LOOFBOURROW

RED DOG CONSPIRACY

THE PREQUELS

THE COMPANIONS

OTHER FICTION

The Shooting

A hot rain battered my window-screen as thunder rolled overhead. I reclined upon the sofa in my parlor, gazing out past the screen to the narrow street beyond.

Jonathan Diamond sat in an armchair beside me, trouser-legs rolled up, his damp feet now resting upon a towel set on a chair. His boots and socks hung by the fireplace to dry. "The storm's only supposed to last another hour."

His hands shook, just a little. And I didn't like the way his feet looked, discolored and swollen. But he claimed that under the circumstances, they were quite well. "Is there anything I might have Mary get you?"

Jon grinned over his shoulder at me with a small shrug. "I'm wonderfully well-fed, warm, and dry, sitting next to the most beautiful woman in the world. What more might I need?"

My cheeks grew hot. "Since when have you become a flatterer?"

He reached over to take my hand, and I loved the way his dark, dark skin looked against mine. "Never."

We usually went out to luncheon, Jon and I, but I'd felt unwell — not ill, mind you, but that bleeding malady which strikes women monthly, like clockwork. And even so, he'd dared brave scandal and defy quadrant-folk custom to call on me.

A baby's wail came from far beyond the kitchen. Squeezing Jon's hand, I scooted up to press it to my cheek, eyes burning. "I don't deserve such regard, Jon."

He smiled warmly. "Of course you do."

My butler Blitz Spadros came in through the door to the kitchen wearing house clothes, carrying a tea-tray. "Care for some more?"

Our temporary housekeeper Mrs. Crawford must still have been at luncheon. It was the first of the month, and I'd given my lady's maid Amelia the day off, just as her husband and children back at Spadros Manor had. "I'll have some." I swung myself around to sit up, slipping my feet into my house shoes, which sat upon the floor. My back hurt, and my innards ached, but the doctor had said tea was good for my health. And I was a bit thirsty.

"No more for me," Jon said. "I've used my allotment for today." He grinned. "Have to leave room for my tonics."

Jon had a heart condition, which seemed to have worsened of late. The doctors had told him nothing more might be done, and even last week published a treatise upon his remarkable longevity. Yet despite his duties as Keeper of the Court, Jonathan took life in great ease and merriment those days, as if his ailment was merely an inconvenience. "Is your daughter well, sir?"

Blitz let out a laugh. "Being a newly-born babe must be a difficult matter, judging by the heart-rending nature of her cries. Yet the doctor claims she's perfectly well."

Ariana Spadros was only dealt in six weeks before, and seldom slept. I turned to Jon. "Your mother was an Apprentice and your grandfather an Inventor. Are you very good at fixing things?"

Blitz said, "What is it you need fixed?"

I unhooked the key to my dresser from my waistband and handed it to him. "There's what looks like a small hatbox in my top dresser drawer. Would you bring it to me?"

Blitz gave me a wry grin. "As you command."

Jon and I both burst out laughing.

Blitz left through the door to the front hall.

Jon said, "Did you see the special edition news? A copy arrived just before I left to come here."

I shook my head.

Jon shifted to face me. "You won't believe what Mayor Freezout said in his speech before the City Council today. He proposed that the Four Families should be sent to the Prison!"

"Good gods," I said. "Has he lost his mind?"

"There were several editorials asking the same thing. And that fool bill of Pike's is back —"

"Wait," I said. "Doyle Pike's writing bills now?" At one time, Mr. Pike had been my lawyer, until he tried blackmailing me.

"No, the young one. Thrace, I believe? The one with the District Attorney's office. He wants to make refusing to speak with the police a felony offense, rather than a fined misdemeanor."

I scoffed. "No one should be forced to speak with anyone, least of all one of those scoundrels."

Jon leaned back. "At least the Council's got some sense."

The City Council had kept Freezout from going to outsiders for help about the train crisis. The trains seemed to be in perfect order once again, which was reassuring. But there'd been rumors that Freezout still wanted outside laborers in to help with the continual power outages.

I never understood why Mayor Freezout would want outsiders involved with the city's repair. The only thing I might imagine was that bringing those people in would shame the Families somehow.

But with the Feds looking for any excuse to take the city, his actions endangered us all.

Blitz returned with my magnification spyglass case in his hand, peering at it. "What's this?"

I rose, taking it from him, then sat, taking out the spyglass. "It opens up, you see? Then when you look through it, small items are magnified." But it wobbled loosely these days, rather than opening straight. I'd paid a great deal for it, and it seemed more prudent to have it repaired rather than try to find another.

The sound of a carriage came clattering through the rain, which seemed odd. Our street was really too narrow to drive fast like that.

In the midst of handing my spyglass back to Blitz, he looked past me, eyes wide. "Get down!"

Jonathan lunged, knocking me to the floor. The spyglass hit the table, pieces of brass flying. The rat-ta-tat-tat of the Tommy gun sent bullets through my metal window-screen and into the room as glass shattered around us. The sound of the carriage continued on past through pouring rain and the angry shouts of men.

Jon lay atop me, face flushed, his dark eyes wide. "Are you hurt?"

"I don't think so." I felt, if anything, a bit squashed. "And you?"

His face was quite close to mine. "I don't think I am."

I felt a bit flustered. "That's twice now you've saved me."

Blitz came round then, pulling Jon to his feet.

Jon rubbed his side. "The table seems to have won this round."

The last time he'd tangled with my table, he'd been left with a huge gash in his side. I clambered to my feet, glass crunching beneath my house shoes, and opened his jacket.

Jon smiled. "I told you I wasn't hurt."

Eyes stinging, I threw my arms round him. "Oh, gods, Jon, if anything were to happen to you —" I felt his arm warm round me. He smelled good. I relaxed into his embrace, eyes closed, feeling safe.

How long had it been since anyone held me?

Blitz cleared his throat. "Mrs. Spadros —"

I let go of Jon, really looked at him. He'd drawn back, unsteady, shaken. "I'm sorry, Jon. You look as if you need a chair. Blitz, help Master Diamond to the kitchen."

My temporary housekeeper Mrs. Claudete Crawford rushed into the room from the hall. The ancient brown woman's eyes widened when she saw the damage. "Dealer preserve us." Then she looked at me and curtsied low. "My Lady, are you well?"

"So far." The rain had subsided, but we needed to take care of matters before my sofa was ruined. "Go to Mary and let her know we're all safe. Then the broom, if you please. Oh, and Blitz, after you send word to Master Jonathan's men, find a hammer, nails, and some blankets. We have to cover these windows until it stops raining or Mr. Howell's men arrive."

Mr. Eight Howell was the Family man for our street. I imagined he'd not be in a good humor at a carriage of scoundrels shooting up the place.

***

By the time Mr. Howell and his men arrived, the rain had slowed, and Mrs. Crawford, Blitz, and I had done a fair job of cleaning.

Mr. Howell wasn't too much taller than me, a pale man with a big bushy beard. "We stopped the bastards before they might clear the street." He scowled so fiercely that for an instant, I almost felt sorry for them. "We gotta take care of this before the police show up." He gestured to his men. "Start with the walls."

At once, the men searched the walls in the hall and front rooms for bullets. Fortunately, they got the last one out just as the police arrived.

When I opened the door, the rain had turned to gentle mist. "Thank you so much for visiting. How may I help?"

The young Constable scanned the outer wall, the window-screens. "What's gone on here?"

"I really couldn't say, sir. Some children with rocks, I imagine."

He began to laugh. Then he quickly recovered, pointing at the bullet holes piercing my thick door. "You want me to believe **rocks** did this?"

Blitz came up behind me. "Sir, this is the Lady of Spadros —"

The young man blanched, and he doffed his hat, bowing. "My apologies, mum —"

His partner, a man barely out of boyhood, stood frozen in terror on the sidewalk beyond.

"— so if she says it's rocks, it's rocks." He handed the man a dollar bill. "Most likely done by boys with slingshots. Got it?"

He gaped at the dollar. Then he glanced at the Family men around him. "Thank you, sir. You're too generous, sir." He bowed to me again. "Mum." The pair made a hasty retreat.

I turned to Blitz. "Did you have to give them a whole week's pay?" It was what I got from Tony to live on for a whole month.

Blitz shrugged. "I don't like scrabbling around for pennies."

Chuckling, I returned inside, Blitz following. Men were in my bedroom and the parlor, clearing the last of the glass from the frames to put new panes in.

Ever since I'd returned from the meeting with Cesare Diamond two months back, the Family men for my street had been particularly generous. I believe my cooperation in the matter improved the way Roy Spadros, our quadrant's Patriarch, now viewed me.

Of course, I'd not seen the man since then — he'd been somewhat occupied, if the papers spoke true.

For the past two months, massive negotiations had been underway between the Spadros and Diamond Families.

As a result, the South River between Spadros and Diamond was being dredged — which it sorely needed — to locate any remains that might still be there. People on both sides who'd lost friends and family in the first Diamond-Spadros War lined up for miles at various locations to be interviewed.

The process looked likely to take years to fully sort through. It was good for jobs, though, which pleased many, especially in the slums.

Jonathan sat at the kitchen table, still barefoot, sifting through the lenses and bits of brass now lying upon an old sheet of newspaper. "I think all the pieces are here." He looked up at me. "But this is delicate work. A watchmaker might be able to repair it, but I doubt I can."

I went round to sit beside Jon, facing the door to the parlor. "I should have asked Mr. Howell who the men were."

Jon raised his eyebrows. "That shot at us?" He let out a laugh. "I'm sure they'll figure it out eventually." His head turned towards Blitz, making a quick movement to the left.

Blitz said, "I'll see if your boots are dry yet."

As the kitchen door opened, daylight blazed into the room as a few men hoisted a window glass into place.

I gazed fondly at the pieces of my spyglass. It looked as though some of the pins holding the pieces in place had broken. "You remember when we went to buy this?"

Jon said, "There's something I wish to speak with you about."

"Oh?"

Jon slid the pieces of brass towards the center of the table and rested his arms upon it. "You're not safe here." He ran a hand over his face, the back of his neck. "This only proves it."

I shrugged. "We don't know this was about me. It could have just as well been aimed at you."

Jon stared at the table. "I've thought about this, Jacqui. The only way you'll be able to live in safety is to return to Spadros Manor."

Spadros Manor. It seemed my entire life's effort had been to leave that place. And now to return?

"My sister told me what you said to her at our Country House —"

Our enemies now know where you are. And they know my husband values you above all else. The longer you and my husband stay apart, the more you become a knife to his throat. Please, for his sake, for your son's sake, take Roland and go to him.

" — and it sincerely distressed her."

I felt somber, grieved. "I never meant to do so. Your people are so different, it seems like I'm in another city."

Jon tensed up, just a bit. "My people?"

I'd grown up in the Pot, and though it seemed they no longer wanted me there, I felt I'd never truly left them. "You know ... quadrant-folk."

Jonathan smiled to himself, relaxing. But underneath his smile lay sadness. "Your husband told me you thought he sent you off to die."

I did say so — I won't deny it.

"Jacqui, there's something you need to understand. Tony did fear for Gardena's life. But when he stops his agitation and thinks calmly, he knows we would do anything to protect her. His main and very reasonable fear was for his son. How can you fault him, when he had to choose between his wife's safety and that of his child?"

I snorted, feeling bitter. "And of course **I** was expendable —"

"No! It's killing him to know you think so. What choice did he have? Besides, if anyone could ensure Roland's safety it would be you. The boy knew you, trusted you. And Tony believed you cared for the boy. Yet if he misjudged you, he knew you'd die before letting harm come to any child, even your husband's bastard." Jon bowed his head. "Tony's done nothing but try to help you, Jacqui. In spite of all you've done, I believe he still loves you."

My eyes stung; I didn't know what to say. Tony trusted me with his son's life? "I misjudged him."

Jon clasped his hands together and swallowed, eyes still upon the table. "All he wants is for you to return home."

But it wasn't my home. It never had been. I felt shaky. "I don't know, Jon."

He rested his hand on mine. "I need you to be settled." He sounded weary. "I don't know how much longer I can keep on like this."

I whispered, "That's so unfair."

"Perhaps it is. But I must speak the truth." He withdrew his hand and shook his head, eyes still on the table. "All I've **ever** wanted for you was to be safe, and loved, and happy. You can find that there."

I bit my lip, blinking back tears. I felt loved here, and I'd been happy just an hour before, so much more so than there. And even at Spadros Manor, had I ever been safe? I pictured Tony's father Roy hitting me. "Let me think on it."

Jon nodded, eyes on the table.

I rested my hand on his. "I **will** think on it, Jon. I promise."

He gave me a fake smile. "I suppose that's all I can ask for."

The door to the back hall opened. Mary Spadros came into the kitchen wearing a robe, her long straight light brown hair down around her shoulders. When she saw us, she flinched, then curtsied. "I'm so sorry, mum! I didn't realize you were in here."

Jon said, "It's all right." He glanced at the clock. "I must be off."

Blitz came in at once, carrying Jon's boots and socks. "I have everything here for you, sir."

Jon scooted back a bit, glancing at his feet. "I'll need that towel again." He grinned at me. "It seems my feet water themselves now."

And so it was: his feet were positively moist.

Blitz knelt before him. "Let me help you." He dried Jon's feet and helped him into socks and boots.

Jon rose with some difficulty. "Have you seen my cane?"

Mary said, "I'll fetch it."

But Blitz stopped her. "You're not dressed, and the front hall's full of workmen." He left the three of us, returning a few minutes later with Jon's black and silver cane. "I had someone speak with your driver to have the carriage brought round front."

"That's very kind of you," Jon said.

Blitz said, "Not at all, sir. It's too far for anyone."

The rain had stopped. We got Jon out to his white and silver carriage, its mark of a Diamond Heir raised in real silver upon the door. Once he climbed the few steps, he sat heavily on the black velvet bench seat, eyes closed for a moment.

After his footman shut the door, I reached up through the open window to take Jon's hand. "I'll consider what you said. Please don't fret yourself on the matter any further."

Jon nodded. "I'll see you tomorrow for luncheon, then?"

"Hopefully I'll feel well enough to go out."

Jon shrugged. "If not, just send word. It's not too terribly far here." He turned to the footman. "The Courthouse, if you please."

"Right away, sir."

I waved as Jon's carriage continued down the narrow street. After fishing a bit of glass from my pocket, I lit a cigarette.

Tony had trusted me with his son's life.

His angry, stricken face in the meeting room several weeks before swam before me. *How can I trust anything you say again?*

A deep voice said, "I take it the Diamond wasn't hurt, then?"

I turned to Mr. Howell. The afternoon sun shone in my face; I held up my hand to shield my eyes. "Not at all. How may I help?"

He moved a bit to my left, out of the sun. "Thought you should see this." He presented me with a couple of plain white business cards. Upon them lay the stamp of a dog, in red. One had a dirty smudge upon it.

I handed them back. "The Red Dog Gang."

"They didn't put up much of a fight, so it's safe to say they intended on being caught."

"Or they were a couple of deuces," I tapped my temple, "not given instructions on what to do after shooting."

Mr. Howell frowned. "They'd send their own men to the torture?"

I took a drag from my cigarette. Everyone knew about my father-in-law Mr. Roy Spadros and his torture rooms. "It would fit with what we've seen from them before."

"What'd you tell the coppers?"

I smiled to myself. "Boys with slingshots."

He chuckled. "We should have this cleared up today, all but the screens. We'll patch them for now and order new ones."

"I appreciate that."

"We take care of our own, Mrs. Spadros. Mr. Roy said to tell you that personally."

"Did he send any other message?"

Mr. Howell hesitated, then shook his head. "I best get back to work." He tipped his cap and moved away.

"There is something you might do, Mr. Howell."

He faced me. "What?"

"That special edition of the news. I shouldn't have to learn these things from Master Diamond."

Mr. Howell nodded, his eyes wary. "It won't happen again."

I turned to survey my home. Men were replacing the siding below the signs upon the wall next to my front door, which read:

Kaplan Private Investigations

Discreet Service For Ladies

Below it hung another:

Studio For Hire — Inquire Within

Fortunately, the signs themselves were unharmed. But our little garden below the windows had been entirely trampled.

I finished my cigarette then went inside. The front parlor smelled of fresh paint and mortar. Mrs. Crawford worked a vacuum cleaner in the corners of the room. She glanced up, then turned off the machine and curtsied low.

"Where did this come from?"

"The men brought it, mum. Said to keep it as long as we like."

It seemed useful. But I'd already accepted more from the Family than I liked: I'd return it in the morning. "Very good; carry on."

Mrs. Crawford pointed. "You have a spot on your dress."

Had Mr. Howell seen it? Cheeks burning, I went into my bedroom. Someone had cleared the glass, patched the holes in the wall, remade the bed, and replaced the windows.

The wall still needed repainting, yet I felt grateful.

My insides ached. I changed my dress (which did have a spot on it), my closed-crotch bloomers, and the sodden rags held to it by pins underneath. After all the blood-stained clothing was set in my bathtub to soak, I got into fresh clothes.

After taking some salicylate, I lay in bed curled around a heating pad, feeling ready to cry. The Red Dog Gang, again.

What was going to make them stop harassing me?

What did they really want?

***

I lay there for some time, the pain rising and falling. There wasn't much I might do at present, and it irritated me. I had to endure this blood-soaked Queen's rite and learn what I might from here.

Despite what I'd said to Jonathan, I didn't think the bullets were meant for him.

But what had I done to these people to make them want to kill **me**?

I lay there, considering each action, the numerous times they could have murdered me and didn't. And I came to a conclusion.

They didn't want to kill me. The Red Dog Gang wanted something **from** me.

Each attempt on my life, the murders of each of my friends, felt like another message.

But what was the message? Why did they attack me **here**, rather than during one of the many times I'd been out on cases this month?

I wished they would just tell me what they wanted.

The sun shone golden upon my wall. A carriage pulled up in front of my windows, and a woman's boot-heels clacked up my front steps.

The bell rang. The sound of heavy feet, and the front door squeaked a bit as it opened. "She's lying down," Blitz said.

Then another, smaller squeak as my bedroom door opened.

Without turning, I said, "Hello, Amelia." No one else would dare to enter.

Amelia Dewey was my lady's maid. She curtsied there in the doorway, face flushed. "A thousand pardons, mum, I didn't mean to disturb you."

I smiled at her, held out my hand. "No harm done."

She came around to me, took my hand, and curtsied. Instead of her usual maid's garb, Amelia wore clothes best fitted for the street.

I sat up, dangling my feet over the side of the bed. "Why are you here, and not with your family?"

"Mr. Anthony came to our rooms and commanded I leave at once."

He went down to their rooms? Sent her here in a carriage?

She hung her coat upon a hook behind the door, surveyed the room, then went into the bath. "Very good," she said, as if to herself, then came back out. "How long have you lain there?"

I shrugged.

"It's almost time for tea. Let's see to your clothes — I'd rather catch the blood early than soak bed-sheets."

As it turned out, my personal storm seemed to be passing. Yet as I sat with Mary and Blitz for tea, I felt somewhat reassured by my body's orderly nature. After all that had happened, everything worked, and on time. And though I had my daily liver tonics to take, compared to my poor dear Jonathan, I was very well.

***

After tea, I sat curled up on an armchair in the parlor — a towel under me just in case — reading a mystery novel Mary had found at one of the poorhouse sales.

I wasn't particularly fast at reading, having come to it late in life, but I enjoyed it. Since no one would allow me to do a single thing more that day, it also helped pass the time.

Mary sat with me darning socks. Ariana nestled in a large, well-padded basket on the floor between us. The baby was a sweet little thing, when she wasn't howling.

The doorbell rang; Mrs. Crawford answered it. "May I help you?"

"I'm here to see Mrs. Spadros," Joseph Kerr said. "Is she at home?"

What could he want now?

"That depends. Which Mrs. Spadros are you here to visit?"

An edge crept into his voice. "Jacqueline Spadros? Your Lady?"

"She's indisposed, sir. If you'll leave your card, I'll send word when she's receiving visitors again."

Joe sounded annoyed. "Very well." His footsteps went away.

Mary and I exchanged a glance.

I hadn't seen Joseph Kerr since he'd shown up two weeks earlier at what was meant to be a celebration dinner for Blitz and Mary. My husband Tony had not been happy to see him there, and refused to speak to me for the rest of the night.

But then, I hadn't spoken to him either. The way Tony dismissed Joe when he seemed to be trying to apologize angered me. Yet the more I thought of it, the more I regretted leaving matters the way they were between me and Tony.

In spite of all you've done, I believe he still loves you.

Even with all the hate between our Families, Jonathan Diamond and Anthony Spadros were the best of friends. Jon called Tony his brother, despite how it enraged his quadrant and family. Many a time, I'd suspected Tony of sending Jon to plead on his behalf.

Yet it was no burden: in all the days before or since, I'd never had a friend like Jon. When I was with him, I felt as if we were always meant to be together.

Clearly, Jonathan felt I'd been in the wrong. He despised Joseph Kerr, a man I'd known since birth.

A man I betrayed my husband for.

I covered my eyes with a hand, unwilling to let Mary see my tears.

I loved Joe. I'd given up my position as the Lady of Spadros, my place at Spadros Manor, my marriage to the Spadros Heir, all for freedom. All for him. And he'd abandoned me.

Yet when I saw him after two years without a word, Joseph Kerr seemed to have every excuse for why I'd been left to die.

I felt sure it was only because of Tony's intervention that his father hadn't killed me for what I'd done. Tony had made some threat to Roy (I never learned what it was), and no matter what the provocation, Roy hadn't struck me for over two years.

Yet Roy Spadros still obviously felt as if he owned me. He'd said so to my face. My recent mediation on the Family's behalf — even though I'd been played into doing it — hadn't done anything to dissuade him from that belief.

Misery came over me. *All he wants is for you to return home.*

Deceit. Lies. Betrayal. Scandal. I had ruined my husband's life, hurt him over and over again.

How could I go back? How could he possibly have forgiven me?

The Police

The clock struck quarter past six when Mr. Thrace Pike arrived: I caught glimpse of him exiting his carriage. As he was with the District Attorney's office, I called to Blitz to let him in and sent Mary to the kitchen, thinking his visit pertained to the shooting.

As it turned out, it did, but not as I imagined.

Mr. Pike's position had improved somewhat since I'd last seen him. His suit, while still brown, was purchased at a reputable shop rather than the poorhouse, and his shoes were new.

I felt impressed to see him hand a topper to Blitz as I watched through the open doorway to the hall. "Come in, Mr. Pike, sit down."

He scanned the parlor then seated himself upon my sofa, puzzlement upon his face, probably wondering why I didn't rise to greet him. "I hope you're well."

"Reasonably so, sir. Would you care for tea?"

"No, thank you." He sat relaxed, gazing at me as if entranced.

The silence grew awkward. Finally, I ventured, "I presume this is an official visit?"

He appeared to be at a loss for words. But he quickly recovered. "Mrs. Spadros, I'm disturbed to hear of a shooting."

I smiled, amused. "Here?"

He leaned forward, frowning. "Don't bluff, madam. You may have cowed those boys dressed as officers, but you don't fool me."

This was new. "Is that a threat, sir?"

Mr. Pike blinked. "A what?"

"Will you charge me with a crime for not speaking to the police in the manner you wish me to? Is this what that bill of yours is for?"

"I don't understand."

"Do you mean to also target the young women who suffer unwanted attentions and attack by the police, and wish merely to be left alone?"

Mr. Pike gaped at me.

"Or is it rather their fathers and brothers, those men who come to their aid? Are those the ones that you wish to imprison?"

His face flushed red. "Mrs. Spadros, I mean nothing of the kind! You've just been shot at. What wise proclamation would **you** make upon the matter?"

"You might begin by considering what has happened to make it so people won't speak with the police. How we arrived at this point in the first place."

Mr. Pike said nothing.

"Do you not remember our conversation at the Plaza, sir? It wasn't even three years past. I can't imagine you've forgotten it."

He seemed to have nothing to say.

I sighed. Was he truly so ignorant? "You're a good man, Mr. Pike. A decent man. But you're not smart —"

He bristled.

" — at least, not in the ways that matter."

Mr. Pike frowned. "I want those men prosecuted, not torn to pieces below Spadros Castle! How can I protect you if you won't help me?"

"You have the matter directly in front of you, yet you fail to see it."

"I don't understand."

Of course he didn't. "In your world, warm and safe upon Market Center, men declare their cards boldly, for good or ill. But this isn't neutral territory; this is Spadros quadrant. We're playing poker with guns drawn. The loser doesn't have his day in court, sir. The loser dies, and so does his family. His friends. And his associates."

Mr. Pike appeared dismayed.

"I've had enough friends die. And I, for one, prefer to live. If you do too, I suggest that at least for your family's sake, before you continue your play, you at least learn the game."

He stared at me a full minute, then rose. "Good evening, then."

"Good evening, sir. My regards to your wife."

After a startled glance, Mr. Pike took his hat from Blitz and left.

Blitz said, "What was that all about?"

I shrugged, realizing that Roy, of all people, had been right about the man. "He's a crusader, Blitz. He's going to save Bridges from itself. A brave man."

Blitz let out a laugh. "For certain. By the way, dinner's ready."

Apparently Amelia had left to return to Spadros Manor while I'd spoken to Mr. Pike, because she was nowhere to be found.

Why did Thrace Pike even come here? Whatever the reason, I doubted he'd live to see the end of this. Sooner or later he was going to anger one of the Families, and that would finish him.

***

Halfway through dinner, the doorbell rang. Blitz answered it, returning with Master Blaze Rainbow, our only boarder and my business partner.

Master Rainbow (or as I thought of him, Morton) was in his later thirties. Only a bit taller than me, he had light brown hair, a nose that had been broken at least once, and poor skin. But he had a beautiful smile, a loyal spirit, and had been a great help to me in many a situation. "Come sit with us," I said. "Have you eaten?"

"Not as yet." Before Mary might rise to serve him, he waved her off. "I can get my own food, thanks."

Mrs. Crawford refused to eat with us. In her day, servants didn't sit at table with gentlefolk, even if one of the gentlefolk was a "Pot rag" like me.

Yes, she said it: Blitz might have been able to improve the soundproofing in the apartments, but you could still hear much of what was said in the other rooms. And the woman had no qualms about gossiping with Amelia when she thought I couldn't hear.

"You look well," I said.

After his narrow escape from death in Diamond quadrant, Morton had taken off for a visit to the countryside. He sat across from me. "The weather's nice in Clubb this time of year. I rented a room by the shore mid-countryside and did some fishing."

Blitz laughed. "Fishing? You're a man of many talents."

"Perhaps too much talent," Morton said. "I'm heartily sick of eating fish by now."

"Well, it's good we have none for dinner tonight," Mary said.

I thought it rather rude that he mentioned it yet didn't bring some back. "I'm sure by now you've heard about our adventure today."

"No," Morton said. "What happened?"

I watched as Blitz and Mary told him the story.

I don't know why I did. Sometimes I got the feeling that Morton wasn't always off doing what he said he was. Perhaps an overactive imagination, perhaps some intuition.

Or perhaps it was, for example, that after two weeks fishing, he wasn't the least bit tanned.

But he seemed to have no idea of the events here. "This is incredible. I'm glad no one was hurt."

People had been trying to kill Morton ever since he helped me on a kidnapping case almost three years past. Could this have been aimed at him? "Who knew you'd left here?"

Morton shrugged. "All of you, plus the driver who picked me up the day I left. Why?"

"I don't know," I said. "Just trying to make sense of what might cause someone to do this."

"Damn sloppy way to do it if they were after me," Morton said. "This smacks of intimidation."

Blitz nodded sagely.

I mopped up my gravy with the rest of my bread and ate it. "It'd be nice to know what I'm being intimidated about."

"Well, let's not worry about that now," Mary said. "There'll be plenty of time to figure this out in the morning."

The baby, off around the corner in Blitz and Mary's room, began to wail. Mary let out a sigh and went out into the back hall.

"Ah, yes." Morton's room was just across the hall from theirs. "I'd forgotten about our newest little tenant."

"She's sleeping better now," Blitz said. "But if she keeps you up, maybe we can play some dice."

Morton grimaced. "I still owe you for our last game."

I laughed. "How long will you be around?"

Morton stretched. "I should be here for a while, as far as dinner goes. I have some research to do, though, so I'll be spending my days upon Market Center."

"A pity," I said, thinking about the dreary government buildings there. "Do you already have a carriage?"

Morton shook his head. "Not as yet."

If anyone could fix my spyglass, it would be my friend Anna Goren. She was once a Tinkerer, and ran an apothecary shop there on the island. "I need to go to Market Center tomorrow. If you like, we can share the ride." Morton was still nominally Tony's man, so I reasoned that my husband shouldn't mind us riding together.

Blitz rose. "I'll call for the carriage. When do you need it?"

I shrugged. "After breakfast sometime. There's no hurry."

Once Blitz left, I said, "Any luck with the search?"

Morton speared a bite of chicken. "Not really." He chewed, swallowed. "I'm beginning to fear he's dead."

Morton and I had been searching for one of his informants, a former Detective Constable named Albert Sheinwold, for over a year.

Finding missing persons was how I began my business as an investigator some eight years before; it was something of a specialty. And up to then, I prided myself in the fact that I'd never once failed a case of any kind.

After some time, Blitz came in through the door to the parlor, smelling of the fresh night air. "Message sent."

"That took a while," Morton said.

Blitz let out a short laugh. "I don't use messenger boys anymore, not where Mrs. Spadros is concerned. I went to the Backdoor and sent a Family man over."

I nodded. "Good idea." The Backdoor Saloon was Mr. Howell's place, and where his men tended to congregate.

Ariana's little wails emerged from the back room. Blitz went into the hall.

The whole situation with Sheinwold disturbed me. Normally, I'd be the one out doing research and tracking leads, but I'd been beset by one problem after another along the way. "What topic are you researching?"

Morton set down his fork. "A police constable on Market Center has been granted permission to let me see Sheinwold's case files in the archives there. It's a building near to the main station by the Plaza. He's already gone through them, but perhaps I might see something he hasn't."

Excitement filled me. "That seems promising!" Some former case might have come back to haunt Mr. Sheinwold, instead of what we'd feared, that the former Federal Agent Zia Cashout had done him in. "Would you like some help? My errand won't take long."

"Sure," Morton said. "I'll let them know you'll be by."

For so long, we'd had few leads — even the police who might speak with us refusing to help at every turn.

This could be the break we'd hoped for.

The Mark

The next morning shone clean and clear, a coolness in the air which spoke of autumn.

Mary came in with my morning tea and toast, mail and newspaper, and set the tray upon my tea-table. "Good morning."

"Morning, Mary," I said. "How was your night?"

"Ariana's a bit fussy this morning, but last night she slept a whole three hours!"

I must have been tired: I slept through the screaming. "I'm happy for you."

Mary poured my morning tea, the bitter aroma filling the room. "My husband says the carriage will arrive at eleven, and —"

"So late?"

She shrugged. "That's what he thought as well." She let out a breath. "Is it important for you to leave earlier?"

"I suppose not. But I'd planned on riding with Master Rainbow, and I'm not sure he'll want to spend half the day here."

"I'll let him know," Mary said.

My tea tasted less bitter. I peered into the cup: the clear brown liquid looked the same. "Is this my morning tea, or the regular?"

Puzzlement came over Mary's face. "I made it myself." She lifted the teapot's lid and gave it a sniff. "Smells the same to me."

This particular tea was a blend sent by my apothecary friend Anna Goren. The formula was given to me by my mother for use in preventing children.

Not that I'd lain with anyone since leaving my husband Tony; it was more of a safeguard against sudden attack. While I had nothing against children, I had no desire to bear one of my own. "Put a bit of it in a sachet bag; when I visit Anna today, I'll have her test it."

Mary seemed confused. "Do you think it's gone bad? I don't recall that ever happening before."

We bought our supply a year at a time to gain the discount. But it was only September. "I don't know. I suppose it's better to be safe."

Mary placed her hand upon my shoulder. "Oh, mum. You worry far too much."

She seemed to hesitate then, and I said, "What is it?"

"Oh, I think sometimes — no, it's nothing."

"If you have something to say, Mary, I won't be angry with you."

"It's just — do you truly enjoy this work of yours?"

I considered the matter. "I do."

"It seems to bring you such anxiety, though. I worry for you."

This amused me. "What brings me anxiety are these men who shoot my windows." I put my hand on hers, thinking about solving puzzles, the joy on these women's faces when their loved ones were found. "My business is the least of my worries."

She seemed to relax, drawing back. "I'm grateful, mum. For that. And I'm grateful we can be here with you." She let out a breath, gazing about the room. "It's good to at least be able to pretend we're free, here in our little bit of home."

I smiled at her, feeling moved. "As long as I'm alive, you'll have a place here. I promise."

***

Amelia arrived soon after, in a hurry and a rush. Although she'd said a few weeks back that she'd be here at seven, my husband had forced her to take the taxi-carriage. And even though there were plenty now that the trains worked, at times she'd be delayed. "I'm so sorry, mum," she panted. "Please forgive me."

"Amelia, I don't care when you arrive. Go about your work."

Her cheeks reddened, and she curtsied. "Thank you, mum."

To my relief, my bleeding had vanished overnight. Jonathan and I had planned to meet for luncheon upon Market Center if I felt well enough, and after a few days abed, I was glad to get out of the house. I finished my tea and toast and took up the newspaper.

Amelia stood examining two of my four charcoal walking-dresses draped upon my bed. They were similar, with various differing details upon the collar and cuffs, perhaps a different flounce or two. She tended to be a nervous sort in those days, but on that day she seemed particularly distracted.

"Are you well?"

She turned to me and curtsied. "Entirely well, mum, thank you."

"And your family?"

"Yes, mum, very well." She returned a dress to the closet.

"I'm glad." Perhaps she and her husband had argued.

I unfolded the *Bridges Daily*. On the front page, it read:

MAYOR INSULTS DEALERS

In his remarks after a fundraising dinner last night, Mayor Chase Freezout referred to the Dealers as "grifters" and "fractious women." He also said "they should return to their husbands and fathers as the gods intended."

The Mayor attended a benefit dinner for the Plaza Business District on Market Center, which saw record losses during the train outage. Several in attendance, including this reporter, questioned the Mayor about his reason for making such remarks, whereupon Mr. Freezout abruptly left.

An organization calling itself "People For A Better Life" released a statement this morning calling for the Mayor's removal. "If blundering incompetence and ill health were not enough, antagonizing the religious heart of our city proves this man is unfit to stand as its leader."

I closed the paper. The name of this organization sounded familiar. Where had I heard it?

Mary came in with my liver tonic and set it down before me.

I showed her the paper. "Have you heard of this group before?"

"No, mum, but I can have my husband ask around."

Amelia looked up from where she sat beside my bed, mending a hole in my dress. "What group?"

"'People For A Better Life.'"

She shook her head. "Don't know it." Then she snipped the thread and stood. "Drink that down; it's time for your bath."

Amelia was old enough to be my mother, and as time went on she seemed to act as though she was. As I drank my thick, bitter tonic, I really looked at her. "Why are you still dressed for the street?"

She curtsied. "Forgive me, mum. It slipped my mind."

Since when did Amelia forget to change into her uniform? "Are you sure nothing's the matter?"

Amelia took up my dress and hung it on the closet door. "Yes, mum." She went into the bathing room; the sound of running water came forth.

I wiped my mouth, wishing Mary had brought in some regular tea as well, or at least a glass of water. I went to the kitchen glass in hand, bypassing the wails coming from the back rooms, then rinsed it in the sink and took a drink of water. A pan of shredded potatoes sizzled upon the stove, and the aroma of bacon arose from a covered pan.

The door to the parlor flew open and Amelia stood there in her maid's uniform, black with a white apron. "Mum, your bath's getting cold. Why are you out here?"

Right then, Mrs. Crawford opened the door to the back hall and curtsied. "My Lady," she said reprovingly, "you're not dressed."

I laughed at the absurdity. I was perfectly covered, in a robe that went to the floor. But I did have bare feet. "Very well, I'll behave."

I followed Amelia back to my bedroom, shut the curtains, and got into the bath, which was hot enough for anyone. But the mystery of the organization's name bothered at me as I scrubbed behind my ears and washed out my hair. It wasn't something I'd heard; it was something I'd read. But where?

"I remember!" I sprang from the tub, water flying everywhere, and grabbed a towel from its stand.

From the other room, Amelia said, "Remember what?" Then she came in. "Mum, you've made a mess."

"I'm sorry, Amelia." I dried off, then dropped the towel, using my feet to sop up the water.

Amelia let out a sigh. "Put on your bloomers — I'll deal with this."

Laughing, I went into my bedroom. On went some closed-crotch bloomers and I pinned in a folded rag, just in case. Then my chemise and stockings, a petticoat, and then I put my robe back on and began to search through my old newspapers and tabloids. I had a stack of them on the far side of my bed.

Amelia came in. "Let's get your dress — good gods, you've not combed your hair!" She grabbed my arm. "Stop that and comb your hair before it tangles!"

"Oh, very well," I said. "But I need a pamphlet out of there. It's by that group I was talking about."

"I'll find it for you."

But I could see her giving me glances, as if making sure I combed my hair. Which irritated me. I was four and twenty and the Lady of Spadros, not some child.

I twisted my thick curls into a bun and put on some makeup. I'd been doing my makeup differently, using the diagrams in the book Dame Anastasia had given me before she died. I wanted no one who had one of my portraits in their home to recognize me.

"Here you are, mum." Amelia handed me the pamphlet.

I didn't see much about the pamphlet that was unusual, until I looked more closely at the illustration upon the front cover. A tiny mark lay next to the illustrator's signature, the Holy Symbol used by the Hart Family.

The Harts. Why were they writing pamphlets?

***

After breakfast, I went to my study with some tea and examined the pamphlet more closely. But try as I might — even to exposing it to heat in search of any hidden writing there — nothing more appeared.

A knock at my door. "Come in."

Morton entered. "I'm off; just wanted you to know."

"I'm sorry about the carriage — I hoped we might ride together."

He shrugged. "No bother."

"And I do want to help with your files."

He grinned. "I should be there until tea-time at the very least. Just visit when you can."

Morton shut the door behind him, and I listened to the front door shut and his footsteps move away.

The mark could simply mean the man was from Hart quadrant, but it was more likely he was a Family man. And the more I thought about it, the more it puzzled me.

Etienne Hart and now-Mayor Freezout had conspired to frame me for the zeppelin disaster. So why now would a group associated with a Hart illustrator call for Mayor Freezout's removal?

Perhaps this Hart man was simply commissioned to draw the cover, I thought. Family men did at times take side bets, and as long as their Family got a cut, everyone was happy.

The front door-bell rang, and I heard Blitz walk past to answer it. Then he came back to my door and knocked. "Joseph Kerr's back. Should I let him in?"

Good gods, I thought. What now? "Seat him in the parlor."

Then I wondered whether something had happened. It seemed odd for him to come here in the first place, much less twice in as many days. I got up, went to my room to find my shawl, and crossed the front hall.

Joe didn't rise when I entered the parlor. Given what had happened the last two times he'd come here, this didn't surprise me. But I was reminded of the other times he'd sat there, the lies, the hurtful things he'd said. "Good morning. How may I help you?"

He seemed downcast, almost melancholy. "I'm sorry to intrude. Josie insisted I come here."

"Is there a reason she couldn't come herself?"

Joe rested his arms upon his knees. "That's what I'm here about."

The Betrothal

I glanced at the clock. "I have until half past ten."

He gave a small, distracted smile, not looking at me. "I wish I could have talked with you at the restaurant. Maybe this would make this easier to say."

I felt confused. "What's happened?"

Joe took a deep breath and let it out. "Remember when I told you my grandfather made a deal with Charles Hart to pay off our debts?"

"You mean your debts."

Joe flinched. "Yes, my debts. But my grandfather has some too."

"Go on."

"Well, my grandfather had to give something of value in return."

"I don't understand."

"Part of the deal is that my sister marries Etienne Hart."

"**What?**"

"She's asked for the standard two-year betrothal —"

"How could he do this? How could you agree to this?"

"— it'll give her time to secure a dressmaker, hire a lady's maid ..."

My vision blurred. "You can't give your sister to him: he's a scoundrel!"

"Josie feared this would upset you."

I rose, pacing. "Oh, gods ... Josie! How could she be sold like this?" I faced him. "I never in all my life thought you — of all people —

would sell your own sister to pay for gambling and whores. It's inconceivable!"

He looked up at me. "Jacqui, what do I have to do to convince you? I've never bedded anyone but you!"

I scoffed. "Stop with the lies. You were a whore, the same as everyone else in the Pot."

"Never anyone I loved, though!" He looked hurt. "How can you throw that back at me? And never since we pledged together. I love you, even still. Everything I've done has been meant to help my family prosper."

"How can I believe you, after everything you put me through? How can you let your grandfather do this to your sister?"

"He's old, Jacqui. Dying. All he wants is to see Josie settled. And when she bears the Harts an heir, our family will have a future."

Dying? I sat across from him. "Why now, Joe? Josie said he'd forbidden her from marrying so she might tend to his affairs."

Joe gave a little shake of his head. "Why would he do that? He has men who tend to his affairs already. He hasn't wanted her to make a poor match, that's all." Then he sighed. "I wish you might be able to offer congratulations and support, rather than upset. But I know your life in the quadrants hasn't been easy."

I leaned back, flabbergasted. I'd had my information about why Josie hadn't married from her own lips. Was he deceived, or had she been? "Why haven't I seen this betrothal in the papers?"

Joe glanced away. "We have to decide how to present it, her being from the Pot and all. When the papers learn of this, every aspect of our lives will be scrutinized."

They'd shielded me from much of it, but I remembered that time just the same. "Where is she? I must speak with her."

"At our home in Hart quadrant. Mr. Hart bought it for us as an apology, and a token of his esteem."

The clock struck ten. I rose, and Joe did too. "I'll visit, then." I had to stop this. "I'll send word before I come to call."

We walked to the front hall. Joe glanced down and laughed. "Is your 'spare jack' here, then?"

Jonathan Diamond's umbrella still sat in the stand: he must have forgotten it.

Then I realized what he'd said. "**Spare** jack?"

"Sick, hobbled — you know. Ruined. An extra card, when you can't get any good ones to play."

I gritted my teeth. "I will **not** have him spoken of in that way."

"I'm just making a bit of fun, Jacqui. Why are you so sensitive?"

"Get out of my house. Make your fun somewhere else."

Joe's jaw tightened. Under his breath as he went past, he muttered, "Crazy bitch."

I slammed the door. The nerve of that man!

In my room, I threw myself upon my bed.

I destroyed my husband ... for **that**?

Blitz spoke behind me. "What happened? Did he hurt you?"

Tony's haunted face swam before me, the hurt and horror in his eyes when he caught me and Joseph Kerr together. I sat up, tears cold on my cheeks. "Oh, Blitz ... what have I done?"

He leaned upon the door-post. I could tell by how he stood that he searched for something to say, and failed to do so.

The clock struck the quarter hour.

"I'm sorry, Blitz. This isn't anything of your making, and it wasn't fair of me to speak of it to you."

Blitz gave a small half-shrug. Ariana started to whimper.

I felt ashamed at slamming the door with a sleeping baby in the house. "Go on, I'll be fine. If you see Amelia, tell her I'm ready to get dressed."

He smiled. "Will do."

My rag underneath was still clean. So I changed into my split-crotch bloomers — essential when going out with a corset on, but fairly useful in other situations as well. I pulled off my house-dress, put on a robe, wiped my eyes, and re-did my makeup, finishing just as Amelia came in.

"Sorry, mum, I was helping Mrs. Crawford with the washing."

I picked up my under-corset. "Would you lace me?"

Then a petticoat, then the dress, then the over-corset. Why did women obsess themselves with fashion so? But if I was to dress in any way other than the current one, it'd end up in the papers.

After she got me dressed, as usual I strapped on my gun in its calf holster on the right. This made me realize — as it did every time I went out — that I never retrieved my boot-knife from the guard station from the last time I went to Diamond quadrant several weeks earlier. In the meantime, I'd gotten another. But I liked the one I'd left there: Jon had gotten it for me. I still wanted that one back.

Jonathan knows what it looks like, I thought. Maybe he could get it for me the next time he was there.

Out of habit, I secreted my lock-picks in the lining of my over-corset. Opening my dresser drawer, I took out the pieces of my spyglass (now safe in a smallish box) and the sachet bag of morning tea, wrapping them up in a bundle with paper, which I tied with twine. The day wasn't cool enough for a coat, so I sat waiting as Amelia gave my boots a final shine.

A carriage pulled up in front of my apartments, which irritated me, just a bit. My footman Skip Honor knew carriages weren't supposed to come down here unless absolutely necessary, and so did my driver. With a sigh, I went to the door, and Blitz opened it.

The carriage was piano black and silver, with black horses, black and silver tack, and ...

The mark of the Spadros Heir lay upon the side.

I turned to Blitz. "What the hell is this?"

Blitz didn't return my gaze.

I went down the steps, and the footman — Mary's brother Alan — opened the door.

My husband Tony sat beside the far window. "Get in the carriage."

So I sat diagonally from him, my tied bundle beside me. "What are you doing here?"

Anthony Spadros was an ordinary-looking man who normally tried ever so hard to keep his emotions from showing. Now, however, he made no attempt to do so. Frankly, he appeared annoyed. "Taking you to Market Center. Unless you're going somewhere no one's told me about?

I crossed my arms, feeling foolish. "So why are **you** taking me to Market Center?"

His lips twitched into a thin smile. "I'm going to get to the bottom of this mess, once and for all."

We rode along in silence for some time, my thoughts churning. Tony obviously didn't know I meant to see Anna, or if so, the entirety of what for. Yet I hesitated to ask.

And other thoughts plagued me. Why was Joe being so cruel?

"What was Joseph Kerr doing at your home just now?"

His voice startled me. "What?" I let out a sigh. "I don't know. He had a message from Josie." I felt glum. "She's been sold to the Hart Family. To marry the Heir."

Then I thought: Joe never did say why Josie couldn't visit me. But the situation did explain why she came to me veiled the last time she visited, and why she used a false name.

"I'm surprised to hear that," was all Tony said.

Perhaps Joseph Kerr's bad manners weren't entirely his fault. The situation must hurt him terribly. To have his own sister sold away from him! Surely he must blame himself, at the very least for causing his grandfather to be put in this position.

Polansky Kerr IV had grown up in the Spadros Pot, the same as I did. Yet he grew up knowing he was the descendant of the King, the heir to the throne: the man who should rightly be in charge of Bridges. For such a proud man to be bought a home on a low-card street and forced to sell his granddaughter to one of the Four Families to survive must feel devastating.

I recalled the luncheon Tony and I had with the Kerrs almost three years past. The way old Mr. Kerr's face glowed at the thought of his family's return to status and respect. And I felt sad for what the old man had lost.

The carriage moved onto the bridge to Market Center. The black velvet bench seat ahead of me was a reminder of all the hours Tony and I had spent together in this carriage. The arguments, the kisses. I leaned upon that very bench the day we were shot at and our former driver killed.

My husband stared out of the window, a hopeless loneliness radiating from him. And for an instant, I had the urge to speak, to hug him, give him some sort of comfort.

But the instant passed.

We were part way round towards the bridge to Clubb quadrant. "Where are we going?"

Tony didn't turn. "Not far. A restaurant. You've been there before."

"A ... but I'm having luncheon with Jon later."

"We aren't going there to eat, Jacqui." He made a dismissive sort of motion. "Just ... no one will harm you."

The fact that he said this surprised me. "I didn't think **that**!"

Tony sounded weary. "Things can't go on like this for much longer. If no one else will speak, I must. And this is the only way I can do so."

"Speak? About what?"

He didn't answer.

The carriage pulled up in front of a restaurant, and I had indeed been there before: the Kournikova. I'd had luncheon there several times, once with Jonathan Diamond, the others with Mr. Charles Hart. "Oh," I said, suddenly quite pleased. "The food here is good."

Tony snorted quietly.

His footman opened the door, helping me and Tony to the sidewalk.

Carriages from all Four Families sat in front of ours. I gaped at my husband. "We're to meet with the Families?"

Tony took my hand. "We're presenting formal protest to The Commission."

The Commission

I felt so taken aback that I simply let Tony lead me into the room.

The walls were two tones of mustard-brown split by a golden edging. Thick reddish-brown carpeting covered the floor. Round tables filled the room, surrounded by chairs upholstered in Paisley, woven in green, gray, gold, and brown.

As when I last dined there with Charles Hart, he sat facing us at a table in the center of the room: an overweight, white-haired man of three and seventy. However, instead of being set for luncheon, the oak-stained wooden table lay bare, without so much as a tablecloth.

And he didn't sit alone.

Alexander Clubb and Julius Diamond also sat, one on each side. Along the walls, armed men from all Four Families stood at guard.

None of the Patriarchs rose. "Come in," said Mr. Clubb. A handsome man, Mr. Clubb must have been at least eighty but looked a vigorous fifty, with golden hair and a disarming smile. Sitting to our right, he gestured with his mechanical left arm, only a bit of brass and steel visible where his glove and sleeve parted ways. "Please join us."

Across from him and to our left, Julius Diamond merely nodded. His son Jonathan resembled his mother more than his father, but they shared the same dark, dark skin and tight-coiled hair.

Tony and I moved to the table; I curtsied low.

Tony didn't bow. Rather, he took an envelope from his left inner breast pocket. "I won't waste your time." He opened the envelope, which contained a sheet of paper and a couple of business cards, which he slid into his right jacket pocket. Then he tossed the envelope on the table and opened the sheet of paper. "Spadros makes formal complaint against Hart for the following:

"One — the unprovoked and unsanctioned framing of the Lady of Spadros by the Hart Heir for murder, a dastardly and cowardly deed, which the Heir has confessed to in the presence of notable witnesses. Almost two years later, this attack has neither been addressed nor recompense made.

"Two — the concerted, repeated, unsanctioned attacks on said Lady and her associates by a group known as the Red Dog Gang. Spadros has evidence that this group originates within Hart quadrant."

He reached into his jacket pocket and threw the two cards upon the table, which landed face up, their dog stamps in red. They looked to be the ones Mr. Howell had shown me, as evidenced by the smudge upon one of them. "These were taken from the scoundrels who used Tommy-guns upon my wife's home yesterday. I might add, Mr. Diamond, while your youngest son sat there."

Julius Diamond scowled. Charles Hart stared at me, mouth open, turning so pale I thought he might faint.

Tony folded the paper. "Spadros demands action — or the right of action ourselves — against those who conspire against us."

The Patriarchs glanced at each other. Alexander Clubb said, "This is a serious matter, and we will take it under advisement."

Tony gritted his teeth. "Spadros quadrant demands justice! How long can we restrain our people from acting, when you won't?"

Julius Diamond's jaw tightened, but he said nothing.

"You must," Mr. Clubb said. "This is bigger than any of us, and your father knows it. What I don't understand is why he sent you here."

"He didn't send this boy here," Julius Diamond growled. He got up and ripped the paper from Tony's hand. Clicks came from around the room, as Spadros men tried to point their guns at everyone at once.

Tony raised his hands, taking a step back. The paper fluttered to the table, blank.

I gaped at Tony, stunned. "What the hell are you doing?"

Tony didn't look at me. Instead, he leaned over the table and spoke quietly. "I must speak with each of you, alone. This is the only way I might do so without drawing attention."

He didn't want Roy to know? Roy had to know at the very least that we were here. But perhaps Tony meant he didn't want the Red Dog Gang's spies — or Etienne Hart — to learn of it.

Alexander Clubb's eyes narrowed. Julius Diamond nodded slowly. Charles Hart bit his lower lip.

Tony straightened. "All is well," he said to his men.

The Patriarchs nodded.

The men around the walls lowered their guns, faces wary.

Charles Hart said, "Why bring her here?"

Tony said, "I thought that after we spoke, you two might have words for each other."

Mr. Hart frowned, his eyes narrowing.

What was Tony doing? It didn't make sense.

"Please," Alexander Clubb said to me, "sit down."

Charles Hart rose, and moved a few yards off.

I sat next to Mr. Clubb and watched them speak, but they spoke too quietly for me to hear.

"My father never trusted the Harts," Mr. Clubb murmured.

I blinked. "Why?"

Tony seemed to be pleading with Mr. Hart, who if I didn't know better, was doing the same with Tony.

Mr. Clubb gave a slight shrug. "He never believed their claims of innocence in sacking the Cathedral. He particularly distrusted," he gestured at Mr. Hart with his chin, "his great-uncle. The Cowboy's brother. By all accounts, a villainous-looking, conniving man."

Tony stood gaping at Mr. Hart in astonishment. For him to do that in public meant he learned something truly remarkable. Then the quiet words turned angry; Mr. Hart pointed at Tony, saying something which caused Tony to take a step back, eyes fearful.

I glanced between the two Patriarchs who sat beside me. If they knew what this was about, I could tell from their faces they weren't going to say it. "Will anyone explain what the hell's going on?"

Julius Diamond snorted quietly.

"My dear," Alexander Clubb said smoothly, "your husband is doing the best he can in a complex situation."

A mocking laugh burst from Julius Diamond.

Yes, Mr. Diamond, we all know you hate Tony. "You don't ever give him a chance, do you?"

Julius Diamond gave me a pitying gaze. "You're children. If it weren't for Roy shielding you, you'd both be dead ten times over. You think anyone ever gave **chances** during the Bloody Year? I was younger than you — had to fight and watch friends die to claw out the territory we have today." He snorted. "Coddled, the lot of you."

Roy, shielding us? Tony, and me? From what?

Tony came up to Mr. Diamond. "Might we speak, sir?"

Julius Diamond rose. "I've got nothing to say to you."

Tony said, "Please —"

Mr. Diamond waved to his men, and they left Tony standing there.

Mr. Clubb appeared then, taking Tony's arm. The two moved a few steps off and began to converse quietly.

Charles Hart came to me. "I suppose you have something you wish to say to me?"

I rose, faced him. "I do, as a matter of fact. Aren't you going to do anything about what my husband's said?"

Charles Hart's face turned red. "You want me to kill my son. Is that what you want?" Then his manner cooled. "I spoke with Etienne after the trial. I'd thought we'd gotten the matter resolved." His eyes fell, and he shook his head, a pensive expression on his round face. "To have men shoot at you?"

It hadn't been the first time, I thought. Jonathan saved my life from an assassin outside the courthouse almost two years back. "So you admit this Red Dog Gang is your doing."

Surprise crossed his face. "Not at all! I have no idea who would frame us in this way. If Etienne's at the root of this nonsense, I'll learn the truth of it." He seemed to hesitate. "But it makes no sense. He's got everything. Why would he want any part of that?"

"When I spoke to him a few weeks back, he said something strange: *my people play the long game*. Does that mean anything to you?"

Mr. Hart shrugged. "Not particularly."

I felt at a loss. What could Etienne Hart be up to? I almost mentioned Josie. But I feared his anger might fall upon her brother for sharing something with me which the Hart Family had to have declared secret.

"I wish you would come stay at the racetrack, just until it's safe."

The change of subject startled me. "What?"

"Or if you won't, then return to your husband's home. I can't stand the thought of you there in that ... hovel, unprotected."

"That 'hovel,' as you call it, sir, is my property and my home."

Mr. Hart raised a hand. "Forgive me: I don't wish to offend. But you must see reason!" His face turned pale, and he glanced away. "What if you'd been killed yesterday? I don't think I could bear it."

Mr. Hart had a long reputation as a philanderer. Despite the vast difference in our ages, I'd suspected he wished to seduce me for some time. But could he actually **care** about me? Why?

"I recall your wedding. When you emerged ..." He gazed into my eyes. "I'd never seen anything so," his voice broke, "so beautiful in my life."

Stunned, I recalled the tears upon his cheeks those long years past. He'd been **that** in love with me, even then?

"I know you feel staying separate from your husband is safer. And you think this can continue indefinitely. But —"

"It's not that, sir." Or was it? I no longer was sure. I leaned a hand upon the chair back beside me. "I'm not living where I am because it's safe, but because there, I've gained ... it's forced people to see me. To see who I am and value me, or not, for that, and that alone. In Spadros Manor I was merely a figure. A possession. No one truly **saw** me. Now, I may not be a fancy portrait in the shops to be worshiped, or even feared, but I'm respected — or vilified — for something real. The truth of who I am: a cast-off Pot rag still bound to a man who," at this, I faltered, "who'll neither forgive nor release me."

Mr. Hart's voice was kind, full of compassion. "My dear girl. Matters are never so simple! You are loved, yes, but for who you are.

And you're so much more than what you believe." He scrutinized my face. "Have you told him you still love him?"

This surprised me. "Joseph Kerr?"

"Your husband."

This rocked me on my heels. Did I love Tony? I didn't know. I shook my head.

"Perhaps in your case, the truth would be the best place to begin."

The Tea

I stared at Mr. Hart, some fear releasing inside me. He wanted me to be with **Tony**? What had changed?

It was then I noticed Tony standing off to the side, watching me. Mr. Clubb and his men had left. When did that happen? I curtsied to Mr. Hart. "Thank you for your kindness, sir."

He smiled. "My pleasure. And I will learn the truth of these attacks upon you; you have my word."

"Thank you, sir."

Tony took my arm, drawing me towards the door. "What did he say?"

"It may be someone in Hart quadrant, but I don't think he's behind this. He promised he'd find out why I was being attacked."

Tony let out a breath. "That's something, at any rate."

One of his men opened the door for us, and we went to Tony's carriage. He turned to me. "Where shall I bring you?"

"Oh." I gave Anna's address to the footman; we climbed inside.

Tony's glance went to the tied little package still sitting upon the bench seat. "What's this?"

I pulled my skirt-ruffles inside. The door shut. "It's an instrument I use in my work. I dropped it." I shook the package gently, a rattling sound coming forth. "I'm taking it to a Tinkerer to be repaired." Then a horrible thought occurred to me. "I hope Jon found all the pieces!"

Tony seemed distracted. "What sort of instrument?"

He'd never had much interest in my work before. "A sort of small spyglass." I chuckled in delight, remembering its tiny gears and lenses. "It fits into my handbag. I'll show it to you once it's fixed."

"I'm sure that if any piece is missing, it can be replaced," Tony said. "I wouldn't fret about it."

A spike of irritation came over me at his tone, and I crossed my arms, feeling melancholy.

"Forgive me," Tony said. "That sounded patronizing."

"It did." He often sounded so, yet I couldn't recall him ever apologizing for it before. What had changed?

We arrived at Anna's shop. I turned to Tony. "Thanks for the ride."

He gave me a small smile, yet seemed sad. "You'll still be having luncheon with Jonathan?"

"I will."

"I'll send your carriage there, then."

I hadn't planned to go home directly — there were still those files of Morton's to handle. But I said, "Thank you," and went to the shop.

Upon the front glass, the sign read:

Anna's Medicaments

Potions, Medicines, And Salves Of All Sorts

Supply To Hospitals And Clinics Our Specialty

The bell high on the door jingled as I entered the shop. Inside, arrays of glass bottles and jars full of pills, powders, and potions lined the walls.

Anna came forth from her back room, as usual, dressed in purple. She'd aged in the two years since I'd last seen her. She seemed smaller, her brown face more lined, the thick curls piled atop her head mostly white. But her enthusiasm for life hadn't waned. "Mum Spadros!" Tears came to her eyes as she took my face in her hands and kissed my forehead. "Oh, it's been so long! She went to the door and turned the sign to "Closed," then drew me aside. "I am **so** happy to see you!"

Feeling moved, I hugged her. "I'm so happy to see you, too."

"Let's sit in back," she said, "and you can tell me all the news." Then she seemed to notice the package I held. "What's this?"

"Oh," I said. "It's two things." I went to her counter and placed the package upon it, then drew out my boot-knife to cut the twine.

Upon opening the little box, Anna said, "Oh, dear."

"It's my magnification spyglass. Can you fix it?"

She poked around at the pieces. "I believe I can!" Anna clapped her hands, jumping up and down in glee. "What a marvel! I should ever so much enjoy this repair!" Then she sobered, placing a hand upon her counter. "Most are so terribly ordinary."

I chucked at her excitement. "I'm glad this pleases you."

Anna folded her arms upon the end of the counter and leaned on it. "That was one. What's the second?"

I held up the sachet of my morning tea. "It doesn't taste right."

She pressed the back of her hand to my forehead. "You have no fever." Then she cupped my cheek with her palm. "And you look well." She dropped her hand to her side. "When did this begin?"

"This morning."

Anna spoke carefully. "Taste is a delicate thing. Sometimes another malady, or even age can change it. Or it could mean nothing." She opened the small bag, sniffed it. "It smells right." She pondered this a moment. "Most problems with these teas don't change their effects. Perhaps it's just an off flavor, or in the worst case, a bit of mold." She peered inside the bag, sniffing it again. "I don't smell any mold. But I suppose it can't harm anything to make sure."

She pulled the drawstrings shut and wrote on a small tag, which she tied to the bag. She set the bag at the very back of a large tray full of similar ones. "I fear I've got enough analyses to last me a lifetime." Her tone turned conspiratorial. "I don't much care for doing them."

I looked at the tray and felt dismayed. There must be dozens of bags there. "I don't wish to be a bother —"

"No, no," she said. "For you, it is no bother." Then she took on a new energy. "I can't wait to get to work on your spyglass. And rest assured! I'll have your answer in no time." She placed her hand on my arm. "But I don't want you to fret one minute about the cost: I guarantee my work. If there's a problem with your tea, I'll replace the entirety at no charge."

I felt a great relief, and a great fondness for her. "Dear Anna. I'm so grateful for you."

"Now, we must sit, and you must tell me everything."

Most of "everything" was things I probably shouldn't tell her; they were Family matters. "First, you! Are you well?"

She folded her hands in her lap, beaming. "Entirely and completely." Then her face changed, and she leaned forward, eyes wide. "You will never guess who came to visit!"

"I couldn't possibly."

"Inventor Maxim Call!"

I sat back, surprised. But looking back, I don't see why I would be: the Spadros Inventor had told me he wanted to marry Anna once. And now that he was allowed to leave the quadrant, it made sense that he might come here. "What did he want?"

Anna gave me an amused grin. "Well ... he claimed he wanted my thoughts on those Steam Generators. But I think he still fancies me!"

"Really!"

"Yes! You should have seen him hem and haw and blush." She sat back with a smile. "Quite charming. We've gone to tea, and to luncheon. And we do talk of the Generators, for the most part."

"I see. Any progress?"

She leaned forward, elbow upon the wooden table. "I've done some research on the matter, but he's made it his life's work! The knowledge he has on the subject! It's fascinating." Then she leaned back. "But progress on fixing them? Not really. He seems to have some plan, though. I'm supposed to go with him this afternoon to speak with a woman at the Cathedral." The prospect didn't seem to excite her.

"You must tell me all about it when next we meet."

"I will!" Then she peered at me in some confusion. "I never knew the Lady of Spadros to have such interests! A brothel? The building, of course, is noteworthy. But I suppose it's a ruin, and I fear it to be a terrible dreary place, full of horrible sharpish women." Her face fell. "But he says I might be of help, so I'll endure it."

I laughed at her description. "Oh, Anna — you are delightful!"

"Why-ever do you laugh so?"

"I was born there."

Anna gasped, hands to her mouth.

"Whoever you speak with will probably be someone I've known all my life."

She leaned forward. "I never in all my days imagined —"

Evidently, she didn't read my testimony at the trial. "All's well." I put my hand upon hers. "I suppose we all have our little secrets." I smiled at her. "I think you'll be surprised by what you see. And most women are just like us, when you get to know them."

The Position

To my surprise, when I left Anna's shop, my plain carriage sat there.

My footman Skip Honor seemed ever so pleased with himself. "When Mr. Anthony told me he'd left you here, and you weren't yet at the restaurant, I had the driver retrace your path."

"Fine work," I said, "and I'm grateful." Although it wasn't far, I didn't fancy walking the distance. Ever since I'd broken a bone in my foot a year back, I tried not to overuse it, as at times it ached after too long a stroll.

Jonathan rose without much difficulty to greet me. He still had his cane, of course, but even so, his color was good and he seemed rested. "I'm glad to see you improved."

I smiled fondly at him. "The same."

A waiter brought tea. Once he left, Jon said, "How is your home?"

"Tony's man says they should be replacing the screens tomorrow."

Jon nodded. "And Master Kerr?"

I let out a disgusted breath. Not because Jon knew of it: he had spies out for my protection. But because of how Joseph Kerr had behaved.

Then I remembered. "Good gods! I forgot to bring your umbrella."

Jonathan laughed. "So that's where I left it!"

"I'll have someone send it over."

Jon shrugged and threw his hands into the air, a silly smile upon his face.

"To answer your question: he was rude." Recalling the scene angered me still. "But perhaps I shouldn't judge him so harshly. The news he received would trouble anyone."

"What news?"

I leaned forward, my voice low. "His sister Josephine has been sold to marry Etienne Hart. Traded, in exchange for payment of his debt."

Jonathan's eyes widened, just a little. "Well. This is unexpected."

"I never thought her grandfather would do this to her."

He let out a breath. "I don't know Miss Kerr all that well. But what I have observed of her makes me believe she wouldn't be in this position unless she wished it."

"What do you mean?"

His eyes fell; he chewed gently on his lip. "She's a beautiful, charming woman. But to watch her speak is like watching a zeppelin pilot at work, touching a lever here, a dial there. Every so gently, but each touch moves a vast number like they were dolls, entirely under her control."

"It sounds as if you've thought of her a great deal."

Jonathan laughed, and it was merry, full of joy. He sat his hand upon mine, his face earnest, his tone playful. "Never fear, my darling one. You are my best and truest love, and I shall never have another."

He could be so silly. "Where would you like to have lunch tomorrow?"

He chuckled, shaking his head, and picked up his menu. "Why don't we consider first what we might eat here, today?"

My cheeks burned, just a little. But it was more a fluttery feeling than any true embarrassment. "Very well," said I. "You do have the right of it. For today."

I selected roasted duck, Jonathan chose shepherds' pie. Once the waiter had left, Jon took out the many slim vials from the brown velvet bag he always wore upon his left hip. He chose out the ones with the number "1" engraved upon the glass, and measured out his tonics drop by drop into his tea.

This surprised me. "You can mix those with tea?"

He shrugged. "They all end up in the same place." He chuckled then. "Saves on my liquid allowance. Don't know why I didn't consider it before."

That did make sense.

"Have you thought about what we discussed yesterday?"

"What? Oh." I let out a sigh. "I suppose."

Jon didn't speak for several seconds. "I have a difficult decision to make, Jacqui."

"Something I might help with?"

"Well, it's not something I can share, but it involves you. And I'd feel better about it if I knew you were safe."

"Jon, I'm perfectly safe. After what happened yesterday, I doubt Tony will let so much as a fly come down the street!"

His eyes fell, his face uncertain. "I suppose." Then his eyes met mine. "But if something happens to me, promise you'll let Tony help you." His tone turned pleading. "Please, Jacqui. Don't keep pushing him away."

I grasped his hand. "Jon, what's wrong? What's happened? Why do you fear something happening to you?"

He took a deep breath, let it out. "I wish I could tell you, Jacqui. I truly do. But you know there are things I mustn't speak of."

I nodded. He was Keeper of the Court, a high position in Bridges. Not only that, he was a Diamond Heir, and our Families were, even still, technically at war. And surely a man kept many secrets or dealings in his life, ones which if revealed might harm another.

Jonathan seemed relieved. "Very good!"

The waiters brought our food. When they left, I said, "Something has bothered me."

"Oh?"

"Do you recall when we were young? How the man with the mask would bring you to see me?" I always thought of this gentleman — for clearly, he was one — as the Masked Man.

Jonathan nodded.

"Did you ever learn who he was? Why he brought you to see me?"

At the time, I was just an eleven-year-old girl in the Spadros Pot, the last person I'd think a Diamond Heir might visit.

Jon shrugged, but he didn't meet my eye. "He said that if anyone knew who he was, they might kill him. So I never asked."

Strange.

I began to eat, as did Jonathan, yet my mind was full of questions. Who was this man? Why did he hide? Why did he visit, and why did he seem so fond of me? And why, after my best friend Air's death, did he never return? My mother never would answer any questions about him, and now it bothered me.

Jon said, "I'll never let anyone harm you, Jacqui. Ever."

"You worry yourself too much on my account." Moved, I patted his hand. "But I do appreciate your regard."

Jon's cheeks colored, a small smile on his face.

After luncheon, Jonathan returned to his duties at the Court. I had Honor take me to the police station, which was across from the Plaza. "The building I need is supposed to be nearby."

Just beyond the station, Morton stood on the sidewalk smoking a cigarette. "There," I said through the brass tube, "take me to where Master Rainbow stands."

Morton tipped his hat when the carriage stopped in front of him. "Good afternoon. I trust your day has gone well."

Honor opened the door and I stepped onto the sidewalk. "Quite well." I turned to Honor. "I may be here some time; if you wish, you may amuse yourselves until my return." Then I said to Morton, "Shall we see these files of yours?"

I followed Morton into a white stone building. The inside, like most of the governmental buildings, was trimmed in wood painted black. We went across a narrow lobby then down two flights of stairs. Then left, to the third door on the right. The sign on its door read:

Archives Room A

This door opened onto a cavernous hall painted gray. Straight ahead, endless rows of shelves ran on either side of a narrow aisle. Each row held brown cardboard boxes with various labels upon them.

To the left sat a long table of unstained pine. An elderly uniformed man sat behind a counter to the right eating a sandwich, a mug beside him. He nodded to us as we passed. The aisle ran without break for thirty yards, then a space opened with a long table on either side.

Boxes sat piled upon and underneath both tables, many opened, with files and papers lying about. But not haphazardly: it appeared Morton had been hard at work.

A familiar-looking man sat at the end of the table to my right, his cap and jacket off, his tie loosened, his feet upon a chair. He stood when he saw us and bowed. "Good day, Mrs. Spadros."

The man was around forty, with dark hair. I peered at him, not recalling who he might be. "Have we been introduced, sir?"

"We have, yet it has been some time. Constable Paix Hanger, Mrs. Spadros, at your service."

The Outing

For an instant, I stood astonished. Yet once I'd recovered from my surprise, the story became clear.

Constable Hanger — he'd regained his title here on Market Center — had worked with former Detective Constable Albert Sheinwold. He'd been searching for the man himself, and felt glad to learn Morton had the same goal, if only to have some assistance.

"I felt surprised to learn you were Master Rainbow's business partner," the Constable said. "I recognized him from our unfinished business the day of the explosion."

My face grew hot as I recalled the chase, our deception on the train, the way I'd taunted him. "Forgive me for putting you to such trouble."

"After reading the account of your trial, your reason for fleeing became clear." He chuckled. "I should never have pursued you into Clubb, as my superiors made plain afterward. I spent six months on train station patrol for that one."

So that's why he was there the night I fled Spadros Manor. "If I may ask, sir, what are you doing here?"

He grinned, returning to his seat. "It's my day off. But Mr. Sheinwold helped me when no one else would, and I'd be glad to help him in return."

Morton gestured to the boxes on the left table, "Pick any you like."

So I set my hat on a chair and opened a box dating back some twenty years. Files full of petty crime. Reams of detail about walking the streets of Spadros quadrant. A portrait of a uniformed Probationary Constable Sheinwold barely out of boyhood.

I listed each name I saw there. Perhaps we might discern a pattern: a person who'd built up a reason to harm the man, or somewhere he might be hiding.

An hour later, Amelia arrived, and we set her to boxing up the files that we'd finished with. After several hours of work, I felt weary.

Morton rose. "Where's a good place to eat around here?"

We replaced our hats and the three of us went to a nearby stand which served tea and sandwiches. As we sat down, Amelia leaned over and said quietly, "Mum, if I'm to get home in time to get any dinner, I'll need to leave soon."

"Are the taxi-carriages that slow?"

"There's the checkpoint at Spadros crossing. They make people get out and account for themselves now."

Which my carriage wouldn't be subjected to. "Would it help to have me take you to my apartments first?"

"It would, mum."

"Then I'll do so. Don't you normally leave before dinner?"

"I do, mum. I normally get home well after, but Mistress Anne saves a plate for me in the oven."

"This won't do, Amelia — you should eat with your family! If I must go somewhere in the evenings — which up to now has been rare — Mary or Mrs. Crawford are quite capable of dressing me. From now on, you'll leave after tea. Is that clear?"

Her eyes fell. "Yes, mum."

Amelia hated for anyone to take even one bit of her duties, which she felt were her rights as my lady's maid.

We finished our tea, then I rose, as did the men. "Master Rainbow, Constable Hanger, I fear I must be off."

Morton nodded. "Tell your housekeeper I'll be there for dinner."

"I will, sir. And thank you for your assistance, Constable."

The carriage was close to where we'd left it, and Honor went to find the driver, who'd gone across the street to the Plaza. Amelia and I stood waiting. I said, "Do you ever go here on your holidays?"

"Sometimes, mum. It's been a while."

Honor and the driver, a swarthy man with white hair named Zeus, came hurrying back across the street. Jon had recommended Zeus to Tony after our previous driver had been shot by the Red Dog Gang. "My pardons," Zeus said, "Just went for a bite to eat."

"All's well," I said. "I thought we'd stay later, but as it turns out, I must return home."

We drove along the Promenade; I gazed at the couples strolling there. And it reminded me of a day several years before.

After luncheon, Tony and I had taken a carriage to the riverwalk east of our home, several of our men accompanying us for protection.

A lovely walk it was, although cold, overcast, and from time to time, rainy. The wind whipped up small waves in the river and created a chill which made me glad I had dressed warmly.

Tony had bought hot chocolate in small paper cups from a street vendor, which he and I sipped as we walked. The fine tall hedges which separated the Promenade from the railway swayed in the wind as a steam locomotive passed to our right.

It was a happy time. It felt innocent, clean, before David Bryce's kidnapping and all the ugliness which had plagued our lives since.

But I remembered how little we could say. Our secrets burst forth, it seemed, and each of the lies had torn at the other. But in spite of everything, I felt glad our cards were on the table. We stood before each other in honesty now, and at least to me, this seemed worth it.

I hadn't wanted to say so to Mr. Hart, but he'd been right. Jonathan had been right.

We'd gone home that night, Tony and I, then sipped brandy before the fire, warm and safe. That time together in Spadros Manor, in the evenings after dinner, had been my favorite part of the day. In those moments by the fire, Tony spoke to me like a person, from his heart.

No one shot through my windows there.

The lampposts along the bridge to Spadros blurred. So much had gone wrong in my life that it seemed insurmountable. I'd spoilt my liver; even if I did return to Tony, I could never sip brandy beside him again. And why would he want me by his side in any case?

I took a handkerchief from my pocket and wiped my eyes. I didn't know why Tony refused to free me from this ruin of a marriage. I felt like I didn't know anything, and even if I did, there was nothing I could do.

"It'll get better, mum," Amelia said. "I'm sure you'll find this man. You've always been able to."

A laugh burst from me at the absurd idea of sobbing over a man I'd never met. "It's nothing like that." I patted her hand. "I'll be fine."

"Yes, mum."

Ever since that day at the Diamond Country House, my emotions had been erratic. *They threw a grenade at us.* It angered and terrified and dismayed me.

Then they shot out my windows.

Was there nowhere I might live in peace?

But thoughts of Spadros Manor dimmed when I recalled the story of the shootout inside it, instigated by Tony's own men. Now all dead, if reports were true.

What caused this? What had we done to them? It felt so personal. I felt Tony and I were being herded towards the slaughter, towards some doom. The thought frightened me.

I arrived home. Blitz opened the door and I stepped into warmth, the smell of food, the smiles of my staff.

I'm happy here, I thought.

At the time, I believed I could fight the Red Dog Gang. I believed that if I just continued to fight, to refuse to leave, I could live free in my apartments, forever.

***

The next morning burned bright and clear, a slight nip in the air. Morton, Amelia, and I took my plain carriage to Market Center after breakfast, putting Jonathan's umbrella in the back.

Constable Hanger had duties elsewhere, but we three remaining continued to study files one by one.

I was to meet Jonathan for luncheon at a restaurant we hadn't tried before. I felt excited to see it, checking the time every few minutes. Finally, I gave up trying to work and took Amelia with me.

The exterior of the Rembrandt was white, trimmed in gold, with a runner leading up to the glass-paneled door a few shades lighter than the charcoal dress I wore. The door-man bowed as he opened the door for me and Amelia. "Welcome, ladies. Have a pleasant stay."

A man stood at a black podium, and I approached him. "I have a reservation for luncheon. I know I'm a bit early: it should be listed under Master Jonathan Diamond."

He checked a list. "Ah! Here you are. Master Diamond hasn't arrived as yet. But I can show you to the table if you like."

"Very well."

The man escorted us to the table; I chose a chair which gave me a view of the entryway. The man pushed in my chair for me and left.

Amelia said, "Would you like me to wait until he arrives?"

"I don't think it necessary. Do you?"

She hesitated. "If you're sure he'll be here soon. I'd hate for you to suffer embarrassment on my account."

There was that. I already was getting a few curious glances. "Very well, if you're sure you don't mind."

She smiled to herself, gazing over the crowd of diners before her.

A waiter came up. "Your drink order, mum?"

"Yes, tea service, if you please, for two."

He glanced at Amelia, who stood beside me in her maid uniform. "Right away."

I took up the menu. A simple, one-page affair, yet it took some time before I chose between two likely candidates. Then startled, I glanced up. "Where's Master Diamond, I wonder?"

Amelia shrugged placidly.

This wasn't like him. Jon had never once been late for luncheon — if anything, he'd been early, often with tea already ordered. But perhaps some work at the Courthouse had caused him to be delayed.

Could we have possibly come to the wrong place? I peered at the menu — this was the right name. I stopped a passing waiter. "Is there another restaurant in Bridges with this name?"

"No, mum." He rushed off.

Amelia said, "Is something wrong?"

"I'm not sure."

Just then, Inventor Maxim Call and Anna Goren appeared at the podium. Anna beamed, waving at me. The maitre d' headed our way, and they stopped at my table. They were both dressed for the street, but a bit shabbily for the caliber of the restaurant.

"Good gracious!" Anna said. "I never expected to see you here!"

"This is my first time to visit," I said. "Would you care to join me?"

Inventor Call's eyes narrowed, just a bit.

Anna said, "I would love to!"

With that, the pair sat, about the same time that the waiter came with tea. "Would you care for honey?"

"Oh, yes," said Anna.

"No thank you," I said. When I was brought to Spadros Manor to stay, back when I was sixteen, for months all they gave me to drink was thickly honeyed tea. I now preferred my tea without.

The waiter nodded. "I'll bring another cup right away."

"Make that two," I said. "One more is yet to arrive." I turned to Amelia. "You may go to your own luncheon now."

I turned to my guests. Seeing the two beside each other for the first time, it struck me how similar in appearance they were. Both white-haired, with wizened brown skin. Their main difference was Inventor Call's piercing blue Spadros eyes.

And Anna's boundless energy. "Oh, my dear girl, are you well?"

"Very! And you?"

"Indeed I am!" She turned to Inventor Call with enthusiasm. "We should tell her about our outing yesterday!"

I'd forgotten about her trip to the Cathedral.

The waiter set down two cups with their saucers and poured three, leaving Jonathan's untouched.

Once the waiter left, I said, "I would very much enjoy that. What did you see?"

"Oh, my dear, it is an utter ruin, as I feared. And the women were rather snappish, particularly the one in charge."

Inventor Call snorted quietly. "Worse than the last one, to be sure."

"Wait," I said to him. "You went there before? Tell me everything."

Apparently after the meeting two months back, the Inventors conferred. Inventor Call was asked to approach the Dealers about the Magma Steam Generators.

He'd spoken to the Dealers at the Spadros poorhouse over on the East side, and was told he must speak to the Cathedral. So the next day, he went there. "I was brought inside to speak to an elderly woman with long white hair."

My great-grandmother, who the Dealers' Daughters called Eldest.

"But she told me that ... let's see, how did she say it? 'The Dealers' Daughters are forbidden to discuss the Cathedral's affairs with men.' The whole matter seemed quite odd to me."

"You were given quite an honor. Did she look well?"

"She was ancient," he said, with an awe to his voice which almost made me laugh, given his advanced age. "She never rose." He considered this soberly. "She looked tired to the bone."

I marveled that she still lived. "And you saw her again yesterday?"

Inventor Call shook his head in disgust. "That fool Freezout! He's given us a dire setback. Instead of greetings and smiles, a bevy of tattooed-up thugs stood outside scowling. I begged them to let me speak to the woman I talked with before. Finally, a much younger woman emerged."

"She was very rude," Anna said.

"Yes," said the Inventor. "She just appeared, looked us over as if we were last week's fish, said, 'The question hasn't been asked,' and went inside. As if that explained everything!"

The Eldest had said this many a time. *Only if the question is asked, the woman provided, and the room cleansed, should the sacred Heart of Bridges ever be exposed.* "What did she look like?"

Inventor Call's face twisted in distaste. "A girl, really. Perhaps forty? Black hair, brown eyes. Short, and hardly wore a thing. Just some shift you could almost see through."

"Not properly dressed at all," Anna said with a nod.

This sounded suspiciously like my Ma.

The waiter came up. "Would you care to order?"

Jon still wasn't here. Where could he be?

We gave our orders. I ordered lamb chops for Jon, his favorite.

Inventor Call said, "We're working on several lines of inquiry —"

What did "the sacred Heart of Bridges" mean? No one had ever explained it.

"— but it keeps coming back to the Cathedral. Mrs. Spadros, do you have any idea why they won't talk to me?"

"What? Oh, I don't know." I had a few ideas, but I was in enough trouble with the Cathedral already.

Anna had been sitting unusually still, which normally meant she pondered something of great importance. "Do you know what she meant by 'the question'?"

I shook my head. "I don't." I'd often wondered at that. "I was never really part of the Cathedral's inner workings. I suppose if I hadn't gotten tangled up with the Family —"

Then it came to me. The Eldest was, even though technically an Initiate, still one of the Dealers.

Both of them said, "What?"

I shook my head. "No, it's nothing."

Inventor Call leaned forward. "If there's something which might help us, please."

"It's not that." But my mother owned the Cathedral.

What did that make me? If anything happened to Ma, would **I** own the Cathedral? "Just something — nothing to do with this." An embarrassed laugh burst from me. "Forgive me."

The waiter brought our food, set it down. Jon still wasn't here? I raised my hand. "Excuse me, sir. Would you fetch my maid from downstairs? Mrs. Amelia Dewey."

"Right away, mum."

When Amelia came out, I said, "Would you check out front for Master Diamond's carriage? And make certain with the driver that we're in the right place."

After a few minutes, she returned. "The driver assures me this is the address Master Jonathan gave us, mum. And there aren't any Diamond carriages on the street at all."

"Thank you, Amelia."

Anna said, "Is all well, dearie?"
"To be honest," I said, "I don't know."

The Worry

The food was delicious, yet I looked round for Jonathan the entire time. After our meal, I sent Jon's plate down for the servants and said farewell to the others. And to this day, I regret that my farewell to Anna was more than a bit distracted.

When we returned to the Archives building, I told the driver to trace the route from the Courthouse to the restaurant. Then if they didn't see Jon's carriage, to return here. "I worry his carriage might have suffered mishap. They may need help."

The driver chuckled. "I imagine them Diamonds have the matter in hand, but if it'll make you feel better —"

"It would."

He grinned. "Off we go, then."

Amelia and I returned to the Archives room. Morton sat hunched over a file, glancing up when we arrived. "Good, you're back. I —" He closed the file and stood. "What's wrong?"

"Master Jonathan never arrived for luncheon. He's never been so much as late, ever."

Morton considered this for a moment. Then he picked up the file. "Let's put all this away and look into it."

By the time we got all the files back in the boxes and the boxes put on the shelves, my carriage had returned. "No sign of him," Zeus said.

I felt a bit turned round. "Which is closer: the Keeper's quarters, or the Courthouse?"

"The Courthouse," Morton said, before Zeus might speak.

A bit of fear rose within me. "Let's go there, then," I said. "Perhaps he's just been delayed."

The streets were serene, with light traffic. We passed a large park with a fountain and many trees before arriving at the Courthouse.

A white stone building upon a base of red brick, with white steps up. When we stepped onto the street, a vision of screaming angry crowds stopped me.

Honor said, "Are you well?"

A few passers-by gave me curious glances. Heart pounding, I said, "I'm fine. Master Rainbow?"

Morton and I left the carriage and climbed the wide marble steps, Amelia trailing behind. Men dressed in navy with buttons of real silver stood guard. "What's your purpose here?"

Morton said, "Master Blaze Rainbow and Mrs. Jacqueline Spadros to see the Keeper."

The guard tipped his hat to me. "Of course, mum. Sign here."

Once we'd done so, he pointed into the golden lobby. "First hall on the right, then to the end."

Jonathan's secretary, a youngish pale man with brown hair, seemed surprised to see three at his desk. "May I help you?"

"Is the Keeper in?"

The secretary said, "He's not back from luncheon yet."

Now I felt concerned. "I was to meet him for luncheon. He never arrived. Did he look well?"

The man raised his eyebrows. "As well as he ever does. But he seemed distracted today."

"Hmm." I didn't know what to make of it. "Thank you."

"If he's fallen ill, he may have gone to his quarters here on the island." The man gathered together the papers on his desk and stood. "Let me know if you can't find him there. In the meantime, he has two cases still today. I'll notify the Court that he's been delayed."

I nodded. "Thank you."

From there, we went to Jonathan's quarters as Keeper of the Court, a half mile east of where we'd been.

His butler was as mystified as we were. "Since returning to Diamond Manor, he only comes here when too ill to travel. I feel fortunate not to have seen him in over a week."

"That is fortunate."

"But this isn't like him. He's never late: it's almost an obsession."

Not knowing what else to do, I said, "Thank you, sir." Then I went to the carriage.

Honor said, "Any luck?"

"No," I said, "and it worries me."

Morton nodded. "I don't like this either."

I went round to peer up at Zeus. "Take us to the Diamond Bridge." I turned to Morton. "His father needs to know about this."

The Disappearance

Matters at the bridge to Diamond had improved since my last visit there: they let us through to the Diamond shore without much trouble. But as had happened the time I went there before, we were asked to exit the carriage. This time, though, Morton, Amelia, and I were escorted to the guard station, rather than the search house.

Two very dark-skinned guards dressed in the white and silver livery of the Diamond Family stood behind a counter. "What's your business here?"

I said, "I am the Lady of Spadros. And I have urgent message for Julius Diamond regarding his son."

"What's this urgent message?"

"That's for his ears alone. I can go there, or you can summon him: it matters not."

This sent the pair into some discussion. They asked us to sit upon some silver-toned chairs upholstered in black leather while they might decide their course of action. After perhaps ten minutes or so, one of the guards went into a back room, emerging twenty minutes later. "You may wait here, or in your carriage, if you prefer."

"Is he coming here, then?"

"Yes."

Mr. Diamond must be somewhere on Market Center, I thought. Close by, to get a message back so soon. "I left a boot-knife at the search station the last time I was here. May I have it?"

"We'll send someone," the guard said.

Morton whispered in my ear, "Never thought I'd see Julius Diamond respond to a summons by anyone."

The scene in the restaurant with Tony a day earlier came to mind. "We shall see."

But then I had a dilemma: stay here, or in our carriage?

I weighed the risks. Our obviously Spadros carriage had our men around us. Yet what might be so secure as a guard station?

But the thought of someone recognizing me — particularly someone selling the story to the tabloids — made me return to the plain carriage.

Zeus had parked the carriage around the corner in a narrow street next to the stables. For some time, I reclined upon the bench seat. Morton sat across from me fiddling with his pocket-watch for a while then took out a cloth from an inner jacket pocket and wiped down his shoes. Then he sat glumly, hand to chin. Amelia sat beside him, alternating between examining her fingernails and peering outside.

Many came passing by the sheer curtains, giving the carriage curious glances. Zeus walked past, from the set of his shoulders carrying something heavy. The sound of water splashing onto pavement followed him. Our horses whinnied, slurped and lapped, Zeus murmuring to them in a kind tone.

While we sat, I thought about what I might say to Mr. Julius Diamond. Yet my thoughts were about more than where Jonathan might be. This could be my opportunity.

Tony and Jon's sister Gardena had a child together. Despite their protests, they loved each other. They belonged together.

Tony and I had been forced together. I'd disgraced and embarrassed my quadrant, and had brought Tony nothing but trouble. He certainly didn't need to be burdened with me, no matter what either of them thought about it. Maybe if I spoke to Gardena's father, I could make him understand.

All I wanted was to live my life at my apartments, free of the Family. I'd tried to talk to Gardena, get her to see how much Tony loved her, how important it was to her and her son's safety for her to go to him. But she wouldn't hear of it. If her father could be persuaded to approve the match, perhaps he might be able to sway her.

I looked at Morton and Amelia sitting there. Could I possibly speak about what I wanted to in front of them?

Perhaps I might be able to persuade them to step outside for just a moment. Or if Mr. Julius refused to sit with us, I might ask to speak with him outside the carriage.

Yes, that's what I would do. And if that went well, I might even ask about the Masked Man.

Julius had to know him: Jonathan was only fifteen the first time we'd met. Whoever this man was, he had to be well-trusted indeed, to bring a Diamond Heir into the Spadros Pot!

With this plan in mind, I felt eager to speak to Mr. Julius. Yet we sat there an hour before a white and silver Diamond carriage pulled up beside ours.

I sat up, arranging my dress around me. I felt ready.

The door next to Amelia opened.

But instead of Julius Diamond, his oldest son Cesare stood there.

A man in his early thirties, Cesare Diamond shared the same dark, dark skin of his youngest brother Jonathan. Yet, although taller, he most strongly resembled his father.

Cesare climbed in next to me, handing me my boot-knife. "Have you found him?"

Given his usual demeanor, this surprised me. "So you've heard." I tucked the knife into my hand-bag. "Unfortunately, no. We've spoken to his secretary and his butler, but neither has seen him." I felt dismayed. "I'm sorry you've come all this way for nothing."

"Wait," Cesare said. "Which of my brothers do you refer to?"

Morton said, "Young Master Jonathan. Who did you **think** we referred to?"

Cesare's jaw dropped. "Jon's missing? Since when?"

Now I felt entirely confused. "Who did **you** mean?"

"My brother Jack," Cesare said. "He's gone missing, too."

***

Jack Diamond. Though identical in appearance to his twin Jonathan, the two could not be more different.

Jack's voice was much deeper than Jon's, and Jack kept his head shaven, which in Bridges was odd for anyone. Even from boyhood, he'd earned the name "Black Jack." Whispers said the other children feared him, and he'd been expelled for stabbing one.

Despite the name, he seemed to have an obsession with wearing white, which in Bridges was reserved for Diamond livery — certainly nothing a gentleman would wear, much less an Heir — and maidens at their weddings. Everyone said that even as a boy, he couldn't stand to wear any other color, even to the soles of his patent leather shoes.

As a man, he'd been made Keeper of the Prison. Yet the most terrible rumors followed him: violence, torture, murder. Jack had declared vendetta against Peedro Sluff, the man who claimed to be my father, and had publicly threatened me more than once.

Most said he was mad.

Madness did run in the Diamond Family. Jack's sister Gardena had told me of his strange behaviors: speaking incessantly for days, then sleeping just as long. He came to a Grand Ball a few years back, shouted at Tony, and even tried to assault Jon.

I felt bound to Jack Diamond through my nightmares.

I'm not certain whether the malady I faced had been caused by seeing my best friend Air murdered before me, or Jack's mad ranting after his manservant was murdered shortly before — both deeds done by my father. But apart from a short, blessed week after I'd rescued David Bryce, every night since had been filled with terror of Jack Diamond's revenge.

Cesare had told me Jack wandered in the forest like an animal. But to everyone's surprise, Jon wouldn't hear of anyone restraining his brother. "So someone's been tending to him."

Cesare nodded. "After we spoke several weeks ago, I sent my men to find him. He visits certain places quite regularly. But a few days ago, he vanished. We've tried to keep it quiet, so my father was surprised at your message."

I forced myself to chuckle, heart pounding. "As I am at yours."

Dismayed was more like it.

Jack hated me with passion. If he found a way into Spadros quadrant again, he was a definite danger to my person.

"Tell me about Jonathan," Cesare said. "What happened?"

"He was to meet me for luncheon and never arrived." I felt unsettled, suddenly close to tears. "We retraced the route from the Courthouse with no sign of his carriage. His secretary told me he seemed well, if distracted. His butler at the Keeper's quarters hasn't seen him in over a week."

"He stays at the Manor most days," Cesare said. "Due to his duties as Keeper of the Court, he takes breakfast before us and leaves early. Today his schedule was as usual."

"Did you see him? Was he well?"

Cesare shrugged. "As well as he ever is." He seemed to consider his words. "The last few days, though, he has seemed ... distracted, as you say. Yes, that's the best word for it."

Amelia gave me a quick glance.

I pondered this. "Yesterday, your brother told me he had a serious decision to make. Do you know anything about this?"

Cesare shook his head. "He never spoke of it to me."

"He said yesterday, 'if something happens to me' —"

Morton and Cesare jerked, exchanging a startled glance.

"— so I worry that something **has** happened, as he feared."

Cesare sat for a while, elbows on his knees, hands barely touching. Then he took a deep breath. "This could be your father-in-law's work. A way to stop the accord?"

"I don't see why he'd want to. The accord was Roy's idea in the first place." And why take them both?

"I must inform my father," Cesare said.

"We'll continue to look into his movements upon Market Center," Morton said. "But it'd be good to know whether he crossed the bridge onto Diamond."

Cesare's eyes widened, as if he hadn't considered that.

I don't know why I hadn't thought of it before then either. "Or Spadros," I said to Morton. "Well done."

Morton grinned. "Seemed obvious."

"Thank you for telling me of this," Cesare said. "Good day to you." He opened the door and was gone.

Amelia's eyes were red, and it surprised me: I didn't think she felt so attached. "Never fear; we'll find Master Jonathan."

Then I saw her hands. In them, she held her handkerchief, twisted so tightly that her fingers were red, the folds white. "Oh, mum," she said, her voice breaking, "what if it's that Strangler?"

The Search

The Bridges Strangler? Jon was well past the age of men taken. And I'd never heard of that fiend taking someone upon Market Center.

Although one of the tunnels under the island was where the body of young Stephen Rivers was found.

Morton's eyes were wide, his face paler than usual. "This is bad, Mrs. Spadros. We have to get the police involved."

Why in the world would he want that? Sometimes I felt like he wasn't even from here. Maybe he'd been spending too much time on Market Center. "Not without knowing what the Diamonds want. This is a Family matter, and it has to be handled properly." I felt certain both Zeus and Honor had heard everything. So I purposefully looked Morton in the eye and glanced at the brass tube.

He leaned over and whispered, "At least bring me to the station. Perhaps our Constable might be willing to help discreetly."

"I must speak to the Spadros crossing guards, and with Master Jonathan's secretary. Want us to return you to the Archives?"

Morton nodded slowly. "If you don't make it back by tea-time, I can get a taxi-carriage home."

"Sounds good." I took up the brass tube which extended from the carriage's ceiling. "Zeus, take us by the Archives, please."

His voice sounded tinny. "Yes, mum."

***

Jonathan's secretary was gone when Amelia and I returned to his office. A peaked sign of thin cardboard sat upon his desk. It read:

Back In A Few Minutes

Indeed, after a minute or so, he returned, evidently surprised to see us again. "He's still not arrived. And I haven't heard from him."

"Well, we haven't found him, but his Family's been notified."

The man's eyes widened, his face turning paler than it already was. "They don't know where he is either?"

I shook my head. "Did anything unusual happen when he left?"

The man's ears turned a dark pink, as did the skin around his eyes and neck. "I didn't actually see him go. I stepped out, and when I returned, his hat, overcoat, and cane were gone."

I pointed to the hat rack in the corner. "They hung there?"

The man nodded.

Nothing at all hung there now, nor did anything lay upon the floor. "Might I see his office?"

I had Amelia wait by the secretary's desk. Jon's office was close by, sporting a large window facing the alley alongside an equally large desk. A brick wall showed through pale tan wooden blinds.

The man said, "That's odd: normally those blinds are shut." He shrugged. "Feel free to look around." He returned to his desk, which was in view of Jon's desk, and pointed past Amelia. "You're welcome to sit over there if you like."

I stood in the midst of Jon's office. Cabinets lined the walls. A chair sat in front of Jon's desk. Below the windows to the alley and hall, low bookshelves of legal books. A framed document certifying Jonathan Courtenay Diamond as Keeper of the Court hung upon one wall. Family portraits rested atop the bookshelves, cabinets, and much of the neatly-arranged desk.

The top drawer held pens, pencils, paper-clips. A large side drawer held files. Something lay behind the files, and I had to pull the drawer all the way open to reach them.

Two photographs, both framed. A rather plain, very young woman, with straight blonde hair strewn around her bare shoulders, and a formal portrait of me.

I felt touched by Jon keeping a portrait of me close by, very much so. Yet I wondered who this young woman was. The girl was quite ordinary, yet the photo was intimate, her expression one of great fondness. I'd never once seen her, nor had Jon ever spoken of her.

I slid the glass from the frame, took out the photo, and looked at the back. No inscription lay there, so I replaced the photograph and its glass, put both portraits where they were, and closed the drawer.

It's none of your concern, I thought.

Might this woman know where Jon was? Who was she? Without a name, she was impossible to find.

Perhaps one of his family might know her.

I opened the bottom drawer and found more files, an empty hot water bottle, a pair of dress shoes, and a small box holding silver cufflinks and a neatly folded white cravat.

The cabinets were stuffed full of files. Behind his door hung a brown leather satchel holding brushes, watercolors, a tightly capped bottle of ink, two pens, and a folder containing several drawings of birds, each signed "JCD".

I never knew Jon liked birds. Or to draw. Or to paint.

What else didn't I know about him?

I looked round the room once more.

No signs of a struggle.

No clues to where he might have gone.

And other than my revelations, nothing out of the ordinary.

Amelia watched me from the hall. "Are you well, mum?"

"I find nothing to tell me where Master Diamond might've gone."

The secretary came by with a teacup and saucer and resumed his seat. Then his face turned surprised. "I do recall something strange!"

I went to his desk. "Anything at all might help."

"I don't normally leave my desk when it's near time for him to go, in case he needs assistance. So I was surprised to see he'd left."

"Go on."

"Perhaps twenty minutes after, a Court driver asked about him. At the time, I thought nothing of it. Sometimes the schedules get mixed up. But now I wonder."

"Where's the schedule office?"

He set his peaked sign upon his desk. "I'll show you."

I followed the man to a small office across the hall with a door labeled, "East Security Station." There behind a counter stood a short man with curly red hair and big eyes.

Jonathan's secretary said, "This is Mrs. Spadros with a question about today's scheduling for the Keeper's carriage."

The red-haired man said, "Oh?"

"Yes," I said. "He left, then a second arrived to collect him. Were there two carriages scheduled by accident?"

"If there were, it weren't by me." He took out a ledger and opened it. "These are all the calls, carriages, and drivers sent." He glanced at me, then back at the ledger. "We got to document every one. Like I got to write you came here."

I nodded. "All's well."

"So ..." He ran a finger down the ledger. "Call for carriage at nine forty-seven for half past twelve to the Rembrandt. Here's the assigned driver: he come back reporting call canceled by secretary," he glanced up, "that'd be you."

The secretary nodded. "The Keeper had already left."

I leaned upon the counter. "So no other calls came before?"

The red-haired man ran a finger down the ledger, flipped the page, then ran his finger down once more. "Last carriage call was for yesterday luncheon. Call at ten oh two for half past twelve. Brought back at two forty." He leaned back. "Pretty regular, that one. Docket starts at three, he's never late."

It was close to five. "He's late now. And no one's seen him."

The red-haired man's eyes widened. "You notified the Court?"

Jon's secretary said, "I told the judge." He let out a breath. "I better contact the Clerk. They're not gonna be happy."

"One more thing, sir," I said to the red-haired man. "I was curious about your uniforms. Have any recently gone missing?"

"Not that I know of. Each man gets two, but they're not the same shade. That's so they make sure they're rotated and cleaned proper. Wrong one'd stand out in morning lineup. The cost is taken from your pay if so much as a button goes missing." He chuckled. "Those buttons cost a whole day's pay. We're real careful with them."

"I imagine. Thank you for your help, sir. We'd appreciate it if you didn't speak of this to anyone just yet."

The man nodded quickly. "Best way to get in trouble is to start flappin' the jaws."

"One more thing," I said. "Where's the carriage office?"

"Outside and to the left. You'll smell the stables 'fore you see it."

"I'll escort them," Jon's secretary said.

Amelia and I followed Jon's secretary through the other door ahead, then right past a guard outside —

The man fell, blood spraying behind his head, a bullet-hole under his chin where it met his neck —

Amelia's voice startled me. "Are you well, mum?"

Everyone stood looking at me with concern.

The day Jon had saved me from the assassin, right here at the Courthouse. Not this alley, the one around the corner. Why did I think of it now? I nodded, heart pounding.

We went to the left through the alley, which did smell of horses. The door to the carriage-office stood on the right.

A raised table holding a large ledger and a pen sat to the left of the door; a desk lay straight ahead. A brown-skinned man with straight black hair sat behind the desk writing. He glanced up as we entered. "Can I help you —?" Then his face lit up as he focused upon Jon's secretary. "Hey, Cinco! You still on for tomorrow night?"

"This is Mrs. Spadros, and —"

The man rose and bowed. "My apologies, mum."

I waved him off. "None needed. I had a question: have any carriages or horses gone missing?"

"No." He peered at me. "What's going on?"

"It's not something I can discuss. Thank you for your help."

Jon's secretary escorted us through the security room and back to Jon's office. "Is there anything else I might do for you?"

I couldn't think of anything else to ask. "I'll let you know. Thank you for your kindness."

Amelia and I returned to the main lobby, then down the front stairs to the carriage. Honor asked, "Where to now?"

"The Spadros Bridge guard stations," I said.

None of the guards at either end of the bridge to Spadros quadrant had logged Jonathan's carriage going into the quadrant that day.

I spent the ride home pondering the matter. Jon left early, without telling anyone. Yet the call to the Security Station hadn't been canceled. Why not? He could have simply walked across the hall. So he must have planned to return in time to use it.

There wasn't time to go all the way into Spadros and back, not if he intended to have luncheon with me. I imagined Cesare would inform me if Jon had gone into Diamond, but again, there wasn't time, not if he planned to take the Court carriage he'd ordered.

Where could he have gone? Twenty minutes wasn't long. With the amount of time it took him to do anything these days, Jon had to have gone some place not more than a few minutes away. City Hall, the Opera House, the Ball House.

Jonathan could have sent a messenger, or even asked his secretary to get anything he needed. So it must have been some personal matter. A face to face meeting?

It had to have been something that he hadn't felt right about using a Court carriage on, such as Diamond Family business.

Which, when I considered it, was strange. He'd always used the Court's carriage for our luncheons upon Market Center. Up to then, I'd never thought anything of it.

But the bigger question was who drove him? From all I'd observed, he went willingly. His office was immaculate, without even a piece of trash upon the floor. And Jon wouldn't have left with just anyone. So either he already knew his driver, carriage, and footman, or they'd appeared convincing enough that he'd been fooled.

Hmm, I thought. The Red Dog Gang had faked Spadros livery before. Could they possibly have faked a whole carriage, horses, tack, footmen, livery and all?

I remembered the attack outside the Courthouse during my trial. They faked Court livery then. And I'd met the man who'd shot at me.

All they'd have to do was to get him out of the Courthouse.

We're going to have to go back. I almost grabbed the brass tube, then I noticed we were turning onto my street.

When Amelia spoke, it startled me; I'd forgotten she sat there. "Do you know who took him?"

I remembered her fear of the Bridges Strangler. "No. But even if this **is** the work of the Strangler, he holds men for weeks. And Master Jonathan's Keeper of the Court." I reached over to pat her hand. "We have the whole city on our side, Amelia. We'll find him."

The Alley

When I got inside, Blitz stood waiting, a letter in hand. "This came a few minutes ago," he said.

The letter was on Diamond stationery, white edged in silver:

> Our mutual friend did not pass the Diamond bridge. I've had men to the Families for permission to investigate the other two.
>
> Please advise.
>
> Cesare, Diamond Heir

The manner of his signature amused me. Using letters was dangerous, but I went to my study at once to write a letter in reply:

> Sir,
>
> The Spadros bridge is clear. Yet smugglers rarely keep a prize in view.
>
> The Court has been informed. No struggle was given.
>
> I fear deception. Others fear villainy. Silence may not be the best course of action.
>
> We await word on how we may assist you.
>
> — JS

Blitz stood there, peering at me. "What's happened?"

I stood, putting the letter in my pocket. "Jonathan Diamond never arrived to luncheon. From speaking with his secretary and examining his office, I suspect someone passed themselves off as a Court driver and lured him outside."

Blitz turned pale. "Good gods. Any idea where he went?"

I shook my head. "So far as we can tell, he didn't go to Spadros or Diamond. But to smuggle him off the island —"

"They'd only have to give him a good whack on the head and hide him under a blanket in the back," Blitz said. He gave a wry grin. "We used to do it all the time." He sobered then, and stood for a moment, hand to chin. "The Family needs to know about this —"

"You're right," I said. "If only to deny responsibility."

Blitz glanced at me, face startled.

"It's already been voiced by the Diamonds. All our work will be undone if another war breaks out."

Blitz dashed for the door.

I went to close it, watching him sprint towards the Backdoor Saloon. Remembering the letter, I turned on the light for a messenger.

The day was cool and quiet, with lights coming on here and there in windows, the smell of cooking in the air. I stood in the open doorway savoring the clear blue of the sky, the stars appearing one by one through the faint shimmer of the dome.

Jon was out there somewhere. He might be right now looking at this same sky through some dismal barred window. The thought made my heart seize up within me. *I can't lose Jon. Not him too.*

I wiped my eyes just in time to greet the messenger and hand over the letter. "It must get there tonight." I handed over an extra penny.

The boy was missing a front tooth. "Yes, ma'am!"

As the messenger boy sped away on his bicycle, Blitz came walking up. "Mr. Howell has sent horsemen to Sawbuck, the Manor, and the Castle. Until we hear back, there's not much we can do."

Sawbuck, of course, was Ten Hogan, my husband Tony's first cousin, right-hand man, and enforcer. Tony lived at Spadros Manor, and my father-in-law Roy lived at Spadros Castle. On the same street, but some ten miles from each other.

I wished it were a thousand. "I need to go back to the Courthouse." I suddenly felt weary. "But I suppose that can wait until tomorrow." By the time we got back to the alley outside the Courthouse it'd be full dark, with no one to escort me.

"That seems for the best," Blitz said. "Perhaps Master Rainbow can be of assistance as well."

Right then, Morton came walking up the street from the other direction, not looking particularly happy.

I called out, "Is all well, sir?"

Morton shook his head, rolled his eyes, and moved past us into the house. We followed, I for one curious as to what might have upset him so. Morton went to his rooms, then turned round. "I was seen going into the police station to inquire after our Constable. I've spent the entire day with goons following me."

"Goons?" I'd never heard the term before.

"You know, hoodlums. Thugs. Some attacked me, asking if I'd turned informant." He seemed disgusted at the notion.

"I'm so sorry, Master Rainbow."

"Well, if you were hiding that we worked together, it's no longer a secret." He seemed to be embarrassed. "I had to use your name to keep the Hart men from killing me."

Blitz and I exchanged a glance. "Good grief," I said. "Didn't they know you and Mr. Hart are friends?"

Morton shrugged. "I did do some work for him, before I ended up staying with you. That, and Mr. Roy marking me as off-limits, may have made him less kindly disposed towards me."

I hadn't considered that aspect of the situation.

Yet it surprised me that Roy would do so. He'd done several things in the past year or so which seemed out of character for him. Jonathan's mother had suggested that Roy now regretted some of the things he'd done. Could he possibly be trying to win me over?

A calculated kindness would be just like him.

"Never fear, Mrs. Spadros," Morton said, his voice kind. "It was my choice to go there, and I knew what might happen. It's not your fault if I suffer because of it."

Blitz said, "Would you like a late tea, or early dinner?"

"Dinner," Morton said, "if that wouldn't cause too much trouble. I need my bed more than anything."

The man did look weary. "The same," I said. "But if you already had tea set up, that would do just fine."

Blitz smiled; he looked tired, too. "Mrs. Crawford would be grateful. She hasn't been well the past few days."

I said, "Oh?"

Blitz lowered his voice. "She doesn't complain. But she sighs, and holds her back, and sits with her head in her hands when no one is looking. At least, that's what my wife tells me." He gazed down and to one side. "She's well past the age to have her own home at the Country House. She's earned it, her late husband being one of Mr. Acevedo's men and all."

Mr. Acevedo Spadros was Roy's father, until the man was murdered by his own men. Her Mr. Crawford had died before this occurred, but perhaps Roy still laid some blame upon him and was treating her poorly in return.

Morton sat on his bed. "You didn't plan to keep her more than a few months. What will she do?"

Blitz shrugged. "We can help her find a position when the time comes." He turned to me. "I'll get something together for you. They've eaten, but Mrs. Crawford is lying down and Mary's feeding the baby."

I followed Blitz into the kitchen. "Let me help you."

We found a large leg of roasted meat hanging in the pantry, sandwiches left over from their tea, and quite a few vegetables which needed eating. I chopped the vegetables and set them in the oven to roast while Blitz sliced the meat, set it in the oven to heat up, and arranged the sandwiches. That with some tea made a fine dinner.

In the meantime, Morton had cleaned up, changed, and sat at the table, looking glum.

I put a heaping of roasted vegetables, two slices of meat, and two sandwiches on a plate and set it before him. "Were you at least able to find the Constable?"

Morton smiled to himself. "Thank you. I was. Yet he didn't want to do anything until a report had been filed." He let out a breath. "Can't say I blame him."

I made up a plate and sat across from him. "We can still get into the Archives room. Perhaps some old case —"

Blitz let out a laugh. "Someone take a Diamond Heir? The Keeper of the Court? They'd have to be mad!"

Morton had been in the midst of cutting his meat, but he set the knife and fork down. "You never know what desperate circumstance might drive someone to. It's as good a place to start as any."

I speared a roasted carrot. "Well, the scoundrels will be in touch with the Diamond Family with their demands soon enough." A small dread hung in the back of my throat. Then I recalled the brown velvet pouch he kept upon his left hip wherever he might go. "He has his medicines with him, at least."

Morton went pale. "How long do you think those will last him?"

I pictured the slim vials, and the number of drops he used of each. "Three days, maybe four. But he **must** have them." I glanced between the two men. "He's barely holding out health as it is."

Blitz began to pace. "His family knows this. They'll be setting out a search for him." He stopped. "I wish we might do something."

I did too.

Come on, Jacqui, think. I'd been a private investigator for eight years now. Finding people was my specialty. "We must first deduce why someone might take him. Otherwise, we might search forever." Bridges lay under a dome six hundred miles across. Vast areas of city and countryside lay before us, too much to search even if the whole city did so. "Thank gods for the Travelers' Board."

Morton nodded.

The Travelers' Board still searched every container, every bag since the zeppelin bombing two years back. So we had a fighting chance. If someone were to take Jon out of the city, we might never find him.

As I ate, I pondered what might be going on. Could this be the work of the Bridges Strangler, as Amelia feared? It seemed unlikely.

Could the Red Dog Gang be behind this?

It was the sort of organized torment directed at me that they'd done so often over the past few years.

Signs of them would be the first thing I looked for upon going back to the alleys around the Courthouse.

***

In the morning, I called for the plain carriage as usual.

Morton and I went to the Archives building. But when we arrived, I said, "I have a few visits to make first."

"Very well," Morton said. "I'll look into Master Jonathan's cases, if I can find them."

First, Amelia and I went to the Courthouse. Jonathan's secretary hadn't heard from him, but he'd received a message from the Diamond Family to clear Jon's schedule for the morning: matters would be taken care of.

Just then, who should walk in but Mr. Beloty Diamond!

Beloty Diamond was Jonathan's brother, just a year older, a thin man with very dark skin and large mournful eyes. He seemed surprised to see me. "Good morning. What brings you here?"

"Two things," I said. "I'd first like to look along Master Jonathan's possible routes from this room to a carriage, to see what I might find." If Jon had been taken by the Red Dog Gang, they might have left one of their cards stamped with a red dog, or a stamp of a red dog upon the wall, as they often did to taunt us with their actions.

"Sounds good."

"Second, might we look at any his cases which involved threats?"

Beloty hesitated. "I doubt I can have those released, since you're not part of the Court. But as I've been appointed Acting Keeper," at this, he gave a mischievous grin, "I might be able to collect them for you to look through here."

"That would be most helpful."

Beloty turned to his secretary. "Mr. Hardeman, would you escort these ladies for me?" He began hanging up his hat and coat.

"Certainly, sir." He turned to me. "Where first?"

"Just the route he normally took to a carriage."

We stepped into the hall. "By the way," I said, "what time did you notice him gone?"

Mr. Hardeman considered this. "About a quarter past twelve."

"And how long were you gone?"

"It was just after noon. I went to the legal library to fetch a book he wanted. It took some time to find it, but I returned straight-away."

"So he asked you to get the book right then, at noon?"

"He did." This seemed to dismay him. "But the Keeper wasn't scheduled to leave for a while, and had everything out. He appeared to be in the midst of work."

So sometime between five and ten after twelve, the other driver arrived. A half-hour before he was supposed to leave, yet Jon had to have made ready: his desk was in perfect order. He went with the driver peacefully, and was entirely gone in less than fifteen minutes.

I pictured Jon watching the clock, noting when his secretary left.

Yet would he just leave without telling anyone? That seemed so out of character for him.

We walked down the hall and out to the main lobby. "This is the only way he could have gone?"

"I suppose he could have cut through the East Security Station and out, but the guard would have seen him." The lobby was busy, with dozens of people going to and fro. Mr. Hardeman looked around. "He might have taken the front door. But he doesn't much care for stairs these days, so I imagine he'd have gone this way," the secretary pointed to our right, "and then around to the side entry. It's only a few steps down to the pavement, with a good strong railing."

The way in question passed through the hall I'd first gone down during my arraignment. But few people were there, and we went to the door without trouble. Just before the door, the East Security Station entry was to our right.

A guard stood outside in the alley.

I said to him, "Are you here every day?"

"Yes, mum. I get off at two."

"Did you see the Keeper leave for luncheon yesterday?"

"I did, mum, with his driver."

"Did they seem in any distress?"

"Not at all. He smiled right at me. They both tipped their hats, nice as could be."

"Did you recognize the driver?"

"No, mum, I just started here."

"What did the driver look like?"

He hesitated. "I didn't get a good look at him. A crowd of toughs tried to get in, and we're only supposed to let out at this door. I had to whistle for help."

Right at the same time. "So where was the carriage?"

He pointed to his right. "Parked down at the end."

"Did you notice anything strange about it?"

He considered the matter for a moment. "I do remember the footman — for an instant when the carriage passed by, I thought he was a woman." He gave his head a shake. "Of course, it couldn't be ... but that was the **prettiest** man I've ever seen."

Amelia and I exchanged a glance. "Did they wear Court livery?"

He hesitated. "No. Wait." Surprise filled his voice. "I **knew** there was something wrong. It wasn't navy. The footman wore black!"

That fake Spadros livery again. This had to be the Red Dog Gang's work. Why hadn't Jonathan noticed? "Would it be all right if we went to where the carriage parked?"

The man looked to Jonathan's secretary.

He nodded. "It's all right; they're with me."

The guard said, "Go on then."

Why would they park way down there? Wouldn't it have been better for Jon, more usual for him, for them to park right at the entrance? Scanning both sides of the narrow alley, we walked along to its end.

Partially-dried mud, cigarette butts, cobblestones, brick.

To my right, Jon's office window stood where the carriage would have parked.

With the blinds open, he could have seen the carriage arrive.

Almost to the street, a business card lay stuck in the mud.

Blank on one side, but on the other lay something I did not expect: the letters "LB."

The Doubt

Amelia said, "What does it mean?"

The strike of the typewriter's keys had pressed through, making raised marks on the other side. And the card had just the slightest curve to it. "I have no idea."

Who would do this?

Who had cause to take Jonathan Diamond from the Courthouse?

Who had cause to do anything to Jon?

People liked him. Jon was steady, thoughtful, kind.

Everyone loved him ...

Everyone except Joseph Kerr.

Or I might say, the two hated each other.

Jonathan believed Joe to be a cad, an utter scoundrel who'd cheated on me with dozens of women. Joe named Jonathan an untrustworthy liar, a man who planned me and Tony harm, only by my side to spy on us.

In all the years I'd known him, Jonathan had rarely lied to me, and the few times he had it was only to protect his family.

But even if Jonathan had lied about it all, would Joseph Kerr seize a man in failing health, just because he lied about him?

I'd known Joe since I was born. At first, I didn't want to believe he'd do any such thing. But standing at the mouth of that alley, card in hand, I began to doubt.

Who benefited by Jonathan being absent? Why, Joe. With Jonathan gone, Joe would no longer have him telling me anything.

I put the card in my pocket, desperately gazing out at the carriages passing by.

Joe couldn't have done this.

Joseph Kerr had behaved horribly at his last visit, it was true. His words were hurtful, cruel. But who knows what I might have said or done if one of my family were sold to a vile slug like Inventor Etienne Hart? The man was well old enough to be Josie's father, near blind, a repulsive fat man who'd confessed to trying to have me killed.

This didn't ease my doubts, though. Perhaps Joe had asked to meet with Jonathan …

Then what, refused to let him go? Why would he do such a thing?

But I could envisage the scenario, and it bothered me.

Joe didn't know about Jonathan's illness. If they'd argued, fought … Jonathan had his pistol with him, certainly, but in a fistfight, he didn't have a chance.

Perhaps they'd gone to that park close by. That would have left enough time for them to speak and for Jonathan to return. Perhaps something happened — Jonathan became injured, unconscious, and Joe feared reprisal from his Family.

But Joseph Kerr didn't know about Jon's medicines. Joe wouldn't know how to tend him. And Jonathan wouldn't last long without help.

I couldn't let Jonathan die, even unintentionally. And I couldn't stand thinking Joe would do something like this. "Thank you, Mr. Hardeman. That will be all."

I brought Amelia to my carriage and said to Honor, "I wish to call on Miss Josephine Kerr." I opened my handbag and gave him the card her brother had left when he called at the house a few days before.

He peered at it for a moment. "Right away, mum."

Amelia and I got into the carriage and the door shut. She said, "You're going to see them?"

"I am." I had to know whether Joe did this, once and for all.

***

The brownstone building with the wrought-iron fence round the back hadn't changed since Tony and I went there on New Year's Day almost three years back. But a different woman answered the door: an older woman with white hair and gray eyes, perhaps eighty. "Miss Kerr will see you in the parlor." She turned to Amelia. "Would you care to join me for some tea?"

Amelia looked to me, a question in her eyes, and I nodded. So the two of them left, and I stood looking about the room. It hadn't changed: the same portraits, the same rug, the same ... everything.

Tony's cousin Sawbuck had told me that when he came to search for Joe and his family the night I fled Spadros Manor that the place had been cleared out.

I didn't know what it meant. And it bothered me.

The parlor door opened, and Josephine Kerr came in.

Blonde curls caught up in fresh flowers, pale skin, eyes of clear blue. She smiled and came to me.

But behind her was her brother Joe. I stormed past her to face him. "What have you done? Where is he?"

Joe stopped, a baffled look upon his face. "Where is who?"

"Jacqui," Josie said, her voice entirely surprised, "what's wrong?"

"Jonathan Diamond is missing," I turned to Joe, "and I want to know what you've done with him."

Joe took a step back, hands up. "Wait. I didn't do anything. I haven't seen him in ..." he frowned slightly, blinking. "Since that Grand Ball we all went to, the one where his brother showed up."

Josie said, "Why would you think Joe took him?"

I pointed at Joe. "Because you hate him. He told me about all your women, and your gambling, and your lies, and the children you have out there, and when I confronted you with it, you shouted at me." I felt close to tears. "With him out of the way you wouldn't have any opposition. If you asked him to meet you and you argued, or fought ... I don't care. But please. I must know where he is. He needs his medicine. Please let me go to him."

Joe shook his head. "Jacqui ... I don't know what to say!"

He took a deep breath, let it out. "I suppose if I were that sort of man, it might be in my advantage to harm Master Diamond. But I didn't!" He stared at me a long moment, mouth open, then his face fell. He shrugged, casting his arms out a bit to fall to his sides. "I don't know where he is. I haven't seen him. I don't know what I can do to make you believe me."

Josie said, "I didn't know Master Jonathan was sick."

I turned to her. "He is, dreadfully sick, and —" I couldn't help it: all the terror and grief came upon me, and I began to cry.

Josie put her arm round my waist. We sat upon their sofa. "There, there," she said. "All will be well. Joe, have Susan bring some tea."

I leaned my face upon her shoulder as I wept. The door opened and shut, and the room became quiet.

Josie handed me a handkerchief; I wiped my face. "I'm sorry."

"Shh," Josie said, her arms round me. She began to rock me like a child. "All will be well. You'll see."

The Suggestion

After a bit, the housekeeper brought in a tea-tray. Josie took up her cup and drank a bit.

I had no idea what to say or do: I'd just accused Joe of the most horrible thing. And now I didn't think he'd done it.

Josie set her cup down. "I'm sure Joe's not angry at you. We want to help, if we can."

I put my face in my hands. Josie was going through a terrible trial, and I'd come in and made things worse.

"Talk with me, Jacqui. What can we do?"

"I don't know. And now I'm sorry that I came here."

Josie took one of my hands off my face, and when I peeked at her, she gave me a warm smile. "Don't be. We all make mistakes." She rested an arm around my shoulders. "We're sisters, remember? Or as close as we might ever be to it. You're having a difficult time, and we want to be here for you."

I took her hand. "I feel awful, Josie. Here you're being forced to marry, and I've —"

"None of that, now," Josie said. "I knew it would upset you. That's why I wanted Joe to have you come here, so I could explain." She let out a small ironic snort. "But it sounds like you two argued instead."

"He was cruel, Josie. He cursed me and stormed out." The memory upset me still.

"He told me. He regrets what he said." She took her arm off my shoulders and turned to face me, taking my hands in hers. "He doesn't understand my decision either. It hurts him. He can't help but compare my situation with yours."

"So, wait ... you're **choosing** to marry Etienne Hart?"

"Of course, Jacqui: it was my idea. It's the best play under the circumstances."

She seemed entirely candid. "But ... do you love him?"

Josie laughed. "Of course not. But I can endure anything to make sure my grandfather is cared for. Just think! I'll be the Lady of Hart."

At the time, I supposed she must know even better than I about what marriage entailed. Unlike me, Josie had no wealthy Masked Man to forbid her from becoming a whore — she worked, just like all the other children in the Pot.

"I heard about the shooting at your home," Josie said.

"However did you hear about that?"

"Etienne and his father had a terrible argument about it. I'm not sure why his father blames him."

I wasn't sure how to tell her this. "Josie ... Etienne Hart confessed to framing me for the zeppelin bombing. In front of all the other Inventors and Heirs." Not to mention that Inventor Hart was, if not the ringleader of the Red Dog Gang, firmly encased within their deck.

I pictured his pale gloating face and shuddered, squeezing her hands. "He frightens me."

"You let your imagination run wild." She patted my hand. "He's a harmless old man who fancies himself a revolutionary. I encourage him to think so."

"But Josie, it hurts me to see you tie yourself into a loveless marriage. You deserve better."

She smiled warmly. "Women must consider what's best for ourselves. I carefully considered my family's position and where I might do the most to further it. For me, that's this match."

Josie hesitated for a moment. "What hurts is to see you alone and endangered because of a misunderstanding. Joe has behaved badly. But he loves you. He doesn't seem to be able to speak of anything else but you. I know that if you could put aside your fears and talk with each other, you could find a way through this."

"I don't know if I can."

She sat quietly for a time, then said, "Stay with us. We have an extra room. Or you could stay with me, in my room, if it makes you feel safer. Anything to keep you from harm's way."

"Your betrothed has tried to kill me! How could I —"

"Would he possibly do anything to you here? I would never forgive him!"

"And I'd be in Hart quadrant. His mother hates me, not to mention Roy Spadros would —"

Josie squeezed my hands. "You forget, Jacqui, our home is under Hart Family protection."

"Did Hart Family protection help you when Mr. Hart let you live for two years on the street, running from the Families?"

"This is different. We are entirely safe, Jacqui, I swear. Could Roy Spadros actually come into Hart quadrant? He wouldn't get past the guards at the bridge."

I didn't know what to do. The thought of living in the same house as Joe ... being free to see him, love him ...

But I wasn't free. For better or worse, I was still the Lady of Spadros. Hiding here was no different than hiding with Charles Hart at the racetrack, or in Mrs. Diamond's cottage behind their Manor.

Just as I'd told Mr. Hart and Mrs. Diamond a year earlier, hiding would open up a whole new set of troubles. My quadrant would be thrown into turmoil. And I'd lose my business — the instant I stepped back into Spadros quadrant, I'd be taken as a traitor.

"We have a place for you here, Jacqui. You can leave the Spadros Family and never look back." She patted my hand. "You don't need to decide now. Just promise me you'll think about it. Think about what would truly make you happy."

The Breakthrough

I stayed for luncheon. Joe was quiet, Josie chatty. But all I could think of was how Jonathan and Tony would feel when they learned I'd come here.

When I left, Joe said, "I'm sorry if I upset you. Please forgive me."

I nodded, feeling bleak, and went down the stone steps with Amelia, not knowing what else to do.

The entire trip back, I pondered Josie's offer. I didn't understand why she'd think staying in Hart quadrant with her was a good option.

Normally she was so skilled at understanding the correct play. Could she possibly not understand the situation?

If I refused to return from Hart quadrant, my status would either become that of traitor or kidnap victim. In either case, Roy Spadros would be forced to invade Hart to retrieve me or face yet another uprising amongst his men. Either way, it would start a war, right when things were peaceful again.

Could Josie not be thinking straight? For a while, it bothered me. Then I realized she was so desperate to get me somewhere safe that it had clouded her judgment.

And Joe seemed to be changing into a hard, cruel man, so unlike the carefree boy I once knew. I didn't know what was happening to him. I didn't know what to do to help him. We'd been apart for so long that I didn't even know where to begin.

We returned to the Archives room, where Morton sat poring over Sheinwold's files. "They won't let me anywhere near Master Jonathan's cases." Morton seemed more than a bit discouraged by it.

I sat across from him. "Beloty Diamond has taken over as Acting Keeper. He'll let us look at the files there in his office."

Morton's face brightened. "That's wonderful! Shall we go there?"

I hadn't considered doing that, but it seemed a good idea. "I suppose we'd better. Amelia, help us put these files away."

The three of us returned to the Courthouse, where Beloty Diamond had everything ready. "I've had all his cases put into the workroom. You're welcome to come here any time we're open."

The workroom was small, with light shelving from floor to ceiling around an equally small table. Both the table and room was now entirely filled with boxes of case files. Setting this up must have taken him a good part of the day.

Morton went into the room and took a box from the pile, setting it upon the table. Still standing in the hall with Amelia, I turned to Beloty. "Thank you."

Beloty sobered. "No, thank **you**. This is an immense help, one I don't have time for and none of my brothers would have considered. Your generosity is —" he faltered then, but quickly recovered. "It shows a true regard for my brother, which I deeply appreciate."

"It's no trouble, sir. Jon is my best, dearest friend, and a true ally. I have no other goal than to find him, if I can." I smiled then, and took his hand. "I have been an investigator for eight years now, and I specialize in finding those missing." Morton's eyes met mine, and I realized I spoke as much for him as for the Acting Keeper. "I have never failed to find who I search for."

Morton nodded, his face dubious, and then focused upon the file in his hand.

But I felt determined. I would find Jonathan Diamond and Albert Sheinwold, even if those were the last things I did.

Then I remembered the "LB" card. I took it from my pocket and handed it to Beloty. "Do you recognize this?"

Beloty shook his head, handing it back. "Should I?"

"It was outside in the alley, where the carriage which took Jonathan away was parked." I hesitated to mention the false Spadros carriage and livery, if only because it would take a great deal of time to explain. I couldn't recall if Morton already knew about the false livery situation, and if he didn't, I didn't want to speak of it in front of him. And it might cause Beloty to suspect us. "A guard to the East Door saw your brother and the driver walk past. He said your brother smiled and tipped his hat."

Beloty touched his chin. "So he went willingly. And the driver?"

I returned the card to my pocket. "The guard is new and didn't get a good look at the man. I have reason to believe the driver and footman were false, possibly impersonating members of the Court."

Morton glanced up. "Oh?"

Beloty raised his eyebrows. "That warrants investigation. The guards are supposed to check the identity of those entering." He gave his head a quick shake. "I'll have Mr. Hardeman look into that."

I said, "No Court uniforms, men, or carriages have gone missing, so all I can surmise is that this was planned well in advance."

"Why would my brother go with these men? And why take him in the first place?"

Morton said, "That's the real question. And why now?"

"Now doesn't matter," Beloty said. "What's vital is that we find him, and soon."

So Beloty had come to the same conclusion as I did.

"My father has ordered all off-duty Court and police in Bridges to search every inch of Market Center for my brother by tonight, including Mayor Freezout's residence." Beloty gave me a delightfully evil grin. "I wish I could see that scoundrel's face when they do."

Amelia looked scandalized. Morton chuckled.

I said, "Well, we best get to work."

We set Amelia to noting the names and places listed in the files. First we separated out those involving kidnappers, murderers, and men who performed outbursts against the Court during their trials. These files we set to one side. If there were any involving trouble of a desperate nature involving great sums of money, or vendettas against the Diamond Family, those we put in their own pile. The rest we returned to their boxes, as they seemed much less likely to be the cause of this sort of trouble.

"I've marked the ones in the Prison now," Amelia said. "Can't capture a man if you're confined yourself." She seemed quite pleased with herself.

"Unless you have men do it for you," Morton said.

Amelia drew back, cheeks coloring.

I gave her a warm smile. "It's helpful, Amelia, and in most cases, correct. The ones to worry about are those with ties to other Families, or street gangs with a great deal of Party Time sales." I fished out one such case. "This one, for example. Leader of a gang in the Diamond slums who deals in Party Time and threatened the judge when he was sentenced. He threatened members of the jury as well."

Morton said, "Not a Family member, I take it."

I snorted, putting the file away. "Sounds like even their Acey-Deuceys didn't want him." There were always men who thought they could rise up and take over their quadrant's Family. Since the quadrants had been controlled by the Families, those who tried usually died.

Morton said, "Acey-Deuceys?"

"Roy's enforcer training program. The roughest, most violent of the young ones. He mostly uses them to terrorize those in the slums who don't pay their Family fees. But a lot of what they do is to root out any other gangs taking hold in the quadrant. If they survive to adulthood and settle down a bit, he puts them to whatever they're good at. Assassination, dragging in men for torture, beating merchants who don't pay ..." I shrugged. "It seems to work. We don't let guys in Spadros build up enough cash to create their own Businesses."

"Wow," Morton said. "You people take this thing seriously."

You people? He did say he once lived in Hart quadrant. Or did he say he grew up there? I couldn't remember. "Well, it's worked so far."

Being chosen to the Acey-Deuceys did encourage some violent behavior, but after a kid's first time seeing a man beaten half to death, most went back to being a messenger boy or money runner. Some loved doing it, though, and this was a way to use them.

Beloty came in holding a page, which he handed to me. "The log of those coming in the front door yesterday around noontime. This handwriting ... I've seen it before, but I can't place it."

Jonathan Diamond, two past twelve. "This isn't Jon's signature. And surely the guards would have known him."

Beloty shrugged. "Both of those on door duty were new."

Good gods, I thought. This had to have been planned. "So the scoundrel just walked right in."

"He did," Beloty said, "yet my brother went willingly." This seemed to trouble him. "I don't know what it means."

We spent the rest of the afternoon sorting through files, leaving to return home for tea. Beloty wouldn't let us put anything away; he simply locked the workroom door. "No one uses that room. Just come back and start where you left off."

When Morton, Amelia, and I got back to my apartments, Blitz said to me, "You have some mail; I put it in your study."

Amelia got me changed into my house dress. I put the letters on my desk into my pocket, then went into the parlor. Morton sat there already wearing a soft tan sweater and trousers, reading a book.

Mary came out from the kitchen. "Tea's ready. Would you like it out here, or in your rooms?"

"The kitchen's fine," I said. "No need for a fuss."

Morton chuckled. "I like the way you do things."

Amelia sniffed disdainfully. She never liked Morton from the first time she saw him.

I said, "You may join Mrs. Crawford upstairs for tea if you wish."

Amelia gave me a startled look, then went out into the hall and up the stairs, chin high.

Mary and Mrs. Crawford had made finger sandwiches of creamed chicken mixed with dill pickles chopped fine. They tasted delicious.

As we sat eating, I asked, "I hope Ariana is well these days?"

"Right now, she's sleeping," Mary said. "But she smiled today!"

"Perhaps she's finding life more pleasant." I certainly hoped so — her cries might wake the household at any hour of the night. It wasn't that I disliked babies; we certainly had many dealt into the Cathedral when I was young. But they seemed more trouble than I cared to take on, particularly in the situation I found myself in.

The front door-bell rang. Blitz said, "I'll see to it."

Mary said, "Any word about Master Jonathan?"

"His Family plans a search of Market Center tonight."

"That sounds good," Mary said. "I'm sure they'll find him."

Blitz came back, letter in hand. "It's for you."

I set it to one side and took a drink of my tea.

"The messenger said it seemed urgent," Blitz said. "He came from Market Center."

Had they found Jon? I grabbed my butter knife, wiped it on my napkin, and opened the letter. Inside lay Anna's spidery writing, and it seemed I could hear her voice inside me as I read it:

> My dear Mum Spadros!
>
> I have Tidings! I have Learnt a Way to Repair the Magma Steam Generators! It was more a Deduction than a Learning, forgive me for Misspeaking. But it is MOST EXCITING.
>
> The Explanation would take much too long to Write, and might require more Explanation of its own. So once You Receive this Letter, come Visit at once so I may Tell you!
>
> I have also made Invitation to our mutual Friend, the Esteemed Inventor. I'll meet You at my Shop forthwith. Please if you can, Visit Tonight. I simply would Burst with the News otherwise!
>
> In all true Enthusiasm for Your Arrival,
> And all my Love,
> Your most Loyal Friend,
> Miss Anna Goren
> Proprietor, Anna's Medicaments

I smiled at her note fondly. "It's a friend, asking me to visit her on Market Center. I believe she has some good news." I turned to Blitz. "Do you think we can get the carriage back so soon?"

Blitz shrugged. "We can certainly try." He got up and went towards the front door, presumably to call a messenger.

"No, Blitz, wait." I got up and went to him. "It'll be an hour at least, perhaps two, before the boy gets there. Another hour at the very least to get a carriage ready and here, then a half hour or more to Anna's shop. It'd be much quicker to take a taxi-carriage!"

Blitz hesitated. "I don't like you going alone, and Amelia will want to leave soon."

Morton said, "I'll escort her. I have nothing better to do."

I turned to him. "Oh, would you? I know you'd like Anna, she's the most brilliant woman in the city. And such a delight to speak with."

Morton's eyebrows raised. "She does sound interesting." Then he smiled warmly. "I'd be honored."

I called for Amelia, and after going through the other letters, I went into my bedroom for her to dress me. "You know," I said to her, "I wish I could wear a house dress everywhere."

Amelia chuckled. "It's that Pot upbringing, it is." She pulled the laces on my outer-corset tight. "We'll make you into a proper lady one day, you'll see."

I felt miffed. "Is that your idea of a 'proper lady'? Done up like a stuffed turkey?"

Amelia curtsied. "Forgive me, mum. I didn't mean to offend."

"Oh, just truss me up so I can get out of here. I'm sure Master Rainbow's been dressed a half hour already."

Indeed, he sat in the parlor dressed for the street, shoes shined and hair immaculate, again reading. He wore an entirely different set of clothing, all in shades of brown, the chain of his brass pocket-watch lying upon his chest. He'd lost most of his clothes when he fled the trap in Diamond quadrant several weeks back, yet the new ones he'd purchased were just as fine.

He glanced up and set the book aside. "Are we ready?"

"We are," I said.

Hats on, we went out like any high-card couple on promenade, and I admit we made some stare as we got onto the taxi-carriage at 33rd Street bound for Market Center.

After many stops, we arrived at Anna's shop. Inventor Maxim Call stood outside.

I got out of the carriage, went to him, and curtsied. "Good evening, sir. This is Master Blaze Rainbow, one of my husband's men."

Morton removed his hat and bowed low. "A pleasure to meet you."

Completely ignoring Morton, Inventor Call said, "She's not here." He gestured at the sign, which read:

Open

Then he said, "Door's locked."

"That's odd," I said. "She must have stepped out for a moment." Then why would she leave the sign to Open? "Let's go to the back: she never locks the back door."

But when the three of us went round to the back, that door was locked as well.

"Something's wrong." It only took a moment to retrieve my picks from the lining of my over-corset, and soon the door was open.

"Nice work, that," Morton said as we stepped inside.

I snorted in amusement, recalling the day Morton and I first met.

The room was dark. A feeling made me draw my gun from its calf holster. "We need a light."

A sound, then Morton appeared, holding a small lit match. I grinned at him, then turned on her lamps at the switch.

The place seemed empty of people, yet every possible surface save the floor was covered with articles and books, mostly about the Generators. "Anna? Are you here?"

But then I recalled her hidden wall closet, clicked that open, and felt round for any other secret areas. Nothing.

I searched round her room with my eyes, knelt upon the floor to look under the bed. Nothing.

Then I knelt upon something hard. "Ow!"

Rubbing my knee, I pushed the rug in front of her bed aside; a trap door lay there. To my horror, blood lay upon the ring handle.

I reached forward, but Morton stopped me. "We don't know what's down there. And you can't be seen to have any part in this. So before we look, we need a plan." He considered this a moment. "Inventor, open the door, if you please."

Inventor Call gave us a penetrating glance, then pulled at the door with all his might. A wooden stair lay below, descending to a lit room. Bookshelves, equipment, and Anna.

She lay on the floor, clearly dead.

The Anger

The gun dropped from my hand, and I myself would have fallen if Morton hadn't caught me.

"Oh, gods," the Inventor moaned. "My poor Anna."

She lay upon her back fully clothed. Blood congealed between her breasts around a large knife, but she had other cuts as well. Her eyes lay open, staring.

My vision blurred. Who would kill Anna? Why?

But for the sound of Inventor Call's weeping, the room was quiet. Yet the lights were on.

Anna had customers, deliveries. Sooner or later someone would knock as we did, see the lights, deduce that someone must be inside.

We couldn't be caught here. I couldn't be caught here. I couldn't be involved in yet another murder.

I dashed tears from my eyes. Why would they cut her? I remembered Madame Biltcliffe, her horrible wound, the blood.

And then I realized the truth. "There's not enough blood."

Inventor Call's voice was anguished, angry. "Why would you say that? Weren't you her **friend**?"

"I was," I said, feeling bleak. "But whoever did this ... they did it for a reason." Why stab her? Why do it down there? "They cut her."

"Ohhh," Inventor Call cried out. "Oh gods, Anna."

"Here," Morton said. "Come away from there and sit, sir." After helping Inventor Call to a chair, Morton picked up my gun and handed it to me. "You're right. Those cuts were made after she died."

I remembered a man back home, one of Acevedo Spadros II's men who murdered him. Roy had cut out the man's tongue, tortured and mutilated him, left him to die in the Pot.

But he didn't die.

I remembered that man. I remembered his scars. I put my gun in my pocket. "Someone wants people to believe Roy Spadros did this."

"Good gods," Morton said.

Inventor Call jerked as if stabbed, his eyes wide. "What is it?"

I took a deep breath, let it out. I had to think. "Inventor, here's what we do. You open the front door and shout for help. Tell the police you came to the front but it was locked. She always keeps the back door open, so you came in and you found her down there." I grasped his shoulders, looking him in the eye. "Can you do that?"

His eyes were wild, but eventually he focused on me. "She always keeps the back open. I found her. Down there."

I let go, moved away. It might work. No man in the city was more respected than an Inventor.

Morton placed a hand on his shoulder. "And you were alone."

Gradually, the old man's breathing slowed. Clarity came to his eyes. He nodded. "Yes. Yes. I was here. I knocked on the door, and a young couple came up to ask if she was here. I didn't know them. I said, no, the door's locked. They left. I went round back. The door's always open round back." He nodded. "She always keeps the back door unlocked. I thought I'd wait inside for her. But something made me look. Down there." He began sobbing, burying his face in his lined hands. "Oh, gods ..."

"We need to go," Morton said. "Can you call for the police?"

Inventor Call nodded, his face still in his hands. Then his hands dropped to his lap and he took a deep breath. "I can do this."

"Thank you, sir."

The old man rose. "I can do this." Without looking at Anna, he moved past her equipment.

Morton grabbed my arm. "We have to go."

I gave her a final glance, eyes stinging. *Goodbye, Anna.* We hurried out her back door and away from Inventor Call's screams.

"We didn't touch anything," Morton panted, almost as if to himself. "You had your gloves on. I can't believe I'm doing this."

I put my hand on his arm. "Slow down. Let's get to a street." I pulled him to our right, to a more populated area, moving into the crowds on evening promenade past the shops. "Give me your arm." I took hold of his arm and slowed our pace. "There."

"I'm sorry." Morton's voice shook. "I've never covered up being at a crime scene before."

Oh, Anna. I grasped his arms, people streaming past us on both sides. "We didn't do it," I whispered. "Now let's figure out who did." I took his arm and kept walking. "We must go to Mr. Roy —"

Morton stopped, eyes wide. "Are you certain?"

"He has to know someone's framing him." I must admit, if I didn't know Roy except by reputation, I'd be afraid to go see him too. "You find Constable Hanger. Tell him this wasn't Roy's work, and that the police mustn't say so. Then go to my husband and tell him what happened. I'll deal with Roy myself."

Morton said, "Let me get you a taxi-carriage."

A taxi-carriage pulled up to the stand, empty. To my surprise, Morton pushed to the front of the line. "I'll give you a dollar to go straight to Spadros Castle."

A woman standing beside Morton cried out, "What? You can't do that! We were here first!"

The driver looked at the crowd. "Make it five and you got a deal."

A man behind Morton said, "This is unfair!"

Morton opened his wallet. "Three's what I got. Take it, or I find another cab." When the driver hesitated, Morton said loudly, "Hurry, if you will — this is Family business."

That seemed to quiet those waiting. The driver glanced at me then took the three.

Morton brought me to the carriage through the grumbling crowd and got in as well. "The Family can talk to the police if they want. I'm not going anywhere near there right now."

I crossed my arms, trying to ignore the glares of those standing nearby. "Very well."

As we crossed the river and moved past the Hedge surrounding my homeland, tears ran down my cheeks. *Anna.*

She did work for me without charge, gave me luncheons and teas without number. She hid me from the police when I was on the run after Zia betrayed me. She'd kiss my forehead when I left her.

I bit my lip, gripping my hands together to keep myself from sobbing. *Oh, Anna.*

Her entire delight in life was to know, and to understand. I'd never met anyone before so joyful, so alive. So giving of herself simply for the happiness bubbling from inside.

Was this murder for no better reason than to torment me? Had she been killed, like all the others, because of me?

"I'm sorry," Morton said. "I can tell she was dear to you."

"She was." Anna had been more than dear. She'd been a mother to me, just as Madame Biltcliffe, and my friend Vig's little mother, and Marja had been. All dead.

And we were no closer to finding Jonathan than yesterday.

By the time we got out of the taxi-carriage at Spadros Castle, the sky was darkening and the street-lamps were on. To my surprise, Tony's carriage, marked with the seal of the Heir, sat in front of the so-called Castle. Tony's footman, Mary's brother Alan, stood nearby.

Morton drew back, eyes wide. "I'll stay out here."

So I went through the gate and up the steps alone as the taxi-carriage pulled away.

The front hall stood as before, pale gray and chill. The servants never spoke, never met my eye.

I was shown into the parlor. Tony and Roy stood there, and by their stances, they'd been arguing. Tony turned to face me. "What are you doing here?"

I went to Roy. "A merchant on Market Center has been murdered. From the look of it, you're meant to be blamed."

Roy took a step back, eyes wide. "Which merchant?"

"Anna Goren. She's an apothecary —"

"I know who she is," Roy said, going even paler than he was already. "How do you know this?"

"We're friends. She invited me and Inventor Call to visit. Her letter said she'd discovered a way to fix the Steam Generators." The image of her lying dead swam before me. "When we arrived, the door was locked, so we went round to the back. We found her. Stabbed." It took me a moment to speak. "But she was cut up after she died." I focused on Roy. "After. But it was just like what you do."

Roy stood very still. "Market Center is neutral ground. Someone wants to bring the entire city upon us."

Tony snapped, "Why didn't you tell us she was your friend? We could have protected her!"

Roy's voice was stern. "Anthony —"

Tony flinched, just the tiniest bit. He hated being called that.

But my outrage overcame any pity. "Are you now blaming **me**?"

"I want a list of everyone, Jacqui. Everyone. All your informants, all your friends, every one of them, so I can keep them safe!" Tony's face grew fierce. "Stop with these secrets! What will it take for you to see they only cause more grief?" He shook his head. "What are you so afraid of? Why do you not trust me?"

I turned away so he wouldn't see my tears.

"I give up," Tony said to Roy. "Perhaps you can make her see reason." He strode past, and was gone.

When the door slammed behind him, I leaned on the back of an armchair and began to cry. He hated me. And that hurt as much as anything else.

When Roy touched my shoulder I jumped, heart pounding.

"Sit down," Roy said. "I won't hurt you."

I sat in one armchair, he in another, and we looked at each other.

Roy said, "You left Anthony because of what I've done to you. You fear to return because you believe your life will return to what it was. I believe you told him you felt as if in a cage. Yes?"

I nodded.

He leaned forward, elbows on his knees, thick hands clasped before him. "I hurt you. I was wrong to do so."

I stared at him, so astounded by this that I couldn't speak. Roy Spadros, admitting he was wrong?

He gazed towards the thick carpet of pale blue and gray. "For far too long I've been full of anger ... at everyone, I suppose." His tone grew cold. "Only one man deserves my hate, though —"

I nodded. Mr. Charles Hart.

"— I've let that hate spill over every part of my life. I gave the anger which belonged to him to you, and you didn't deserve it."

I had never learned what Mr. Hart had done to Roy. I feared to ask.

Roy looked up at me. "I swear that if you should choose to return, you may order your home as you wish. No more interference. I won't harm you." Our eyes met. "You have my word."

I had no intention of returning. But hearing this did make me feel better. "And if I should choose not to?"

Roy scoffed, tossing himself back in his chair. "This isn't some veiled threat! I want to help you make an actual choice." He looked at me. "Anthony loves you more than I could have ever imagined."

Roy was wrong. I knew Tony. He may have loved me once, but now? He hadn't forgiven me. He looked at me with disgust and disdain. I'd publicly betrayed him. How could he ever do otherwise? "I must find my friend, and learn who killed another. That's all I want." I pushed grief aside. "But I thank you for your apology."

Roy let out an exasperated sigh. "How much longer will you go on like this? You're not safe there. You have a place in this city, yes, but in your home, at your husband's side."

Anger rose within me. "I came here as a courtesy." I stood. "But I won't be lectured on morality, least of all by a Family man."

With that, I left. Morton stood outside smoking, but dropped his cigarette and stepped on it when I emerged.

And in spite of how awful I felt, I laughed: we had no carriage.

"Well," I said, "I suppose it's time to find ourselves another taxi."

The Gratitude

We began walking down the right side of Book Street, Spadros Castle glowering at our backs. The night was overcast and cold, but not overly so. Morton strolled along beside me, hands in his jacket pockets, head down, as if lost in thought.

Tony had been right about one thing: anyone associated with me could be the next target, for the Red Dog Gang or whoever else was doing this. As much as I hated to lose that last bit of privacy, I had to make sure they were protected.

I'd lose some informants, true. Many only helped me on the condition that the Family wouldn't know they did so.

I sighed. Many of the others would likely begin reporting to Tony to gain his favor as soon as they realized he knew of our arrangement.

As the taxi-stand came into view far ahead, a carriage pulled up beside us. "Was wondering where you'd gotten to," Zeus said.

Honor got down off the backboard and opened the door for us.

"You're up late," I said.

Honor chuckled. "It's my job, mum, and I'm grateful for it."

I got in, Morton climbing in to sit across from me.

The carriage moved along. I hadn't ever considered whether some might actually like or even be grateful to be servants. Amelia had said so, but before Roy's mother had taken her on she'd been in a dire situation. What did I know about men like Skip Honor, who'd sworn to me at possible cost to his life?

Honor had been caring for little Pip Dewey ever since his parents abandoned him. He and Tony's manservant Jacob Michaels had been together for I didn't know how many years and obviously loved one another. Honor was with me when I found Madame Biltcliffe dying in her shop, and had pulled me to safety.

He was a good man. I owed him a great debt.

As the carriage trundled along, I felt discouraged, weary. Anna was dead, and her death brought back all the grief from all the others.

Madame Biltcliffe, Dame Anastasia, Marja. Women I looked upon as mothers. Women who helped raise me, made me who I am today.

Then there was Maria Athena Spade. Major Blackwood. Stephen Rivers. Herbert Bryce. I didn't know those ones well, but I couldn't help but think that they'd been killed because of my actions.

And Air, my best friend in the whole world, murdered in front of me when I was twelve, just for trying to stop me from being sold to the Spadros Family.

Then there were those ruined lives. The whole Spade family, left bereft after they trusted me to find their girl. My friend Vig, likely still grieving his mother, who died a few years back after Roy destroyed his saloon. Again, because of me. Little David Bryce, Air's younger brother, taken by the Red Dog Gang as bait to lure me then left unable to speak. The burden his mother Eleanora and her new husband faced in caring for the boy.

What had been done to him?

I couldn't even make myself think Jonathan Diamond might have fallen into the Red Dog Gang's clutches. Their man Frank Pagliacci, who'd lured Maria Athena to her death, who I felt certain to be the Bridges Strangler ... if he had Jon ...

I covered my face, trying my best not to cry. Yet I failed.

Morton's voice startled me, but his words were kind. "Perhaps you should take a few days' rest. I can work on those files on my own."

Up to then, I hadn't known how seeing the faces of men who might want to kill Jonathan had affected me. "Thank you."

For a long while I sat, a vast blank emptiness pulling at me.

I can't live if Jon is dead.

A liquor store passed, and I desperately wanted to stop, buy a bottle, start drinking.

No. I couldn't die. Jonathan Diamond was alive. He had to be.

I felt on the edge of myself, desperately trying to believe it. Somehow, someone would find him.

But I couldn't rely on anyone else. I had to do whatever it might take to find him.

"We all want the same thing," Morton said. "We each have our own part to play in it. Right now, you need to get your strength back."

Anna was dead. Jonathan was missing. I lifted a shaking hand to wipe tears from my face.

"All will be well," Morton said. "I want to find Master Jonathan as much as anyone." The passing lights played across his face, moved him into a dark silhouette. "You've helped me more than you know. Let me help you for once."

It was then I realized I hadn't responded to his words, so I nodded.

"Take tomorrow off. Two days, even." He smiled, seeming to relax. "As much as you need. Rest will do you some good."

The Rest

Morton left before I awoke, or so Mary told me.

The morning paper had this as its headline:

KEEPER OF THE COURT MISSING

Massive manhunt finds no trace

Overnight, hundreds of off-duty police searched for Master Jonathan Diamond upon the island of Market Center. Master Diamond, our Keeper of the Court, went missing two days ago. A survey of his family and friends has not found him.

The Keeper of the Court, a position required by Merca Federal Union law, provides an independent opinion in case of appeal. Mr. Beloty Diamond has been appointed Acting Keeper until Master Jonathan can be located. Mr. Beloty has acted as such in the past, and is considered well-qualified for this post.

Mr. Cesare Diamond, the Keeper's eldest brother, is expected to hold a conference for the press later today as to what further steps will be taken.

Wait, I thought. Cesare told me that his brother Jack — the Keeper of the Prison — was missing as well. But no one had remarked upon it as yet. What did it mean?

A portrait of Jonathan Diamond lay upon the right side of the news column. But in the portrait, as with all portraits done in Bridges, Jon didn't smile, and he looked so much like his twin Jack that a chill came over me.

Where was Jack Diamond? Why had he gone missing right now? Could the same people have taken them both? I pictured Jack at the Grand Ball, so wild, so angry, so full of violence. The news report said it'd taken all five of his older brothers to drag him from the room.

A large group must be involved with this, I decided, if Jack were missing as well.

For a full day, I tidied my rooms, went through my files, made notations in my accounts, all while Amelia darned the many holes and thinning spots in my dresses. Every so often, she'd remark, "You're supposed to be resting," as I'd pass by.

I never could rest properly that day: too much filled my mind.

Anna's face, her eyes wide with what I couldn't tell was surprise or horror. If I stopped, I might see it too closely. I might fall into the reality that she was dead.

I feared it might kill me.

I couldn't stop, I couldn't think, I couldn't breathe. I found myself in the bathroom, sitting on the edge of the tub, weeping.

Mary knelt before me. "Oh, mum. I'm so sorry."

I cried on her shoulder, great sobs of grief, my heart a vast hole of bitter pain. Little Ariana wailed far off, as if feeling my grief and wishing to share it.

Mary glanced up and to the side. "You go on; I'll care for her."

Footsteps went away as wails of my own came forth, even while little Ariana's subsided. And after what seemed a lifetime, the dark, bitter tide drained away, left my heart dry.

I lay my head on Mary's shoulder. "I'm sorry."

I didn't realize she had her arms round me until then. "Never be sorry for grief, mum. It means you cared."

I suppose it did. I nodded.

"It's what my Ma told me," Mary said, as if far away. "I've not lost anyone, well, not that I remember — but my husband's brother Mr. Theodore lost two of his sons to measles when they were small."

I sat up. "Good gods."

She slumped onto the floor. "It's times like that make me wish we lived in Azimoff — the children dead of things we aren't allowed the tech to cure."

"Why is it like this here? I never understood it."

Mary shrugged. "It's the law; I don't understand it myself. Like the Telephonic Telegraph Mr. Anthony set up for us. Why must we hide it? Isn't there some way that all homes might send messages?"

"The Cultural Correctness Committee might not want that, though." I wished I knew more of their law here, what we could or couldn't do. "Besides, then how would the messenger boys help feed their families?"

"It seems wrong," Mary said, for once seeming downhearted, even angry. "All of it." Then she let out a sigh. "But it's the law: I suppose someone thinks it's for the best." She stood, took my hand. "Let's get you something to eat."

***

The next morning, I woke late.

My curtains were open, the sun streaming through my new window-screens to fall into gentle patterns upon the wall. The noises of the neighborhood were soft, muffled outside closed windows.

Cold tea and toast, paper and mail sat upon my table.

I smiled to myself: Amelia probably hadn't wanted to wake me.

From the kitchen came the sound of running water, the clink of dishes. A faint smell of food lay in the air.

My stomach rumbled. I sat up, stretched, put on my robe.

When I opened the kitchen door, Blitz and Mary stood there dressed for the street. Little Ariana lay bundled up in her basket, which sat upon the table. A picnic basket sat next to her.

"Oh, good, you're up," Mary said.

I yawned. "What-ever is going on?"

"We're going to the river for the day," Blitz said. "My brother Theodore will guard the house from this side, and your husband's men guard the back. Of course if anything should happen, Mr. Howell has his men out."

This late, Morton would be at the Courthouse. "Where's Amelia?"

Mary said, "Mrs. Dewey's little daughter isn't well, mum."

Blitz glanced away. "Mrs. Crawford's out shopping." He gave me a wry smile. "At least, that's what she told me. I have a feeling she's running personal errands as well, but don't tell her I said so."

I let out an amused snort. "No matter. She's earned a day off. Did she say when she'd be back?"

Mary said, "Around tea. But I have your breakfast in the oven and food for luncheon and tea set in the pantry."

"That's very kind of you." For an instant, I felt an expansive freedom. I raised my hands high. "I have the whole house to myself!"

Blitz chuckled. "Master Rainbow thought you needed some rest, and I agree. Enjoy your day."

"And yours too. I wonder what Ariana will make of the river!"

Once they left, I locked the back door, then ate breakfast and drank my morning tea and tonic. When finished, I cast myself upon my still unmade bed, wondering what I might do. I came up with many ideas, yet set them aside as they too much involved work.

I'm here to rest.

I made the bed, bathed, put on a house dress, and after putting my mail in my pocket, straightened the room. The *Bridges Daily* sat upon the kitchen table, the marks of Ariana's little basket still pressed upon it. A few areas had been smudged, but it was mostly readable.

I got a cup of tea. The headline read:

SEARCH FOR THE KEEPER

The Court asks for your help

The article held no surprises. The hunt for Jonathan had expanded into the Pot, yet the searchers were finding the people there resistant to strangers in their land, no matter how good their intent, and violent clashes had developed.

I put the paper aside. After over a hundred years of abuse and betrayal, they couldn't possibly expect the Pot to welcome quadrant-men searching their homes — could they?

A knock at the door: Mr. Theodore Sutherfield stood there.

Now that I knew Blitz was his youngest brother, the resemblance showed plain, despite Mr. Sutherfield's dark skin and eyes. "Good morning, sir. How may I help you?"

"We have a man calling himself Joseph Kerr at the east corner. Mr. Anthony says no one can come here today without your say-so."

I sighed. "No, I don't want to see him. Not today."

"He's brought flowers. Do you want them?"

I shook my head. Accepting flowers from gentlemen had gotten me into a mess once already. "Sorry to put you into this position."

He shrugged. "Better than digging ditches." He grinned cheerfully. "Something my Ma always said." Then he tipped his hat. "I'll move him along, never you fear."

"Thanks." I closed the door, returned to the kitchen, and made myself more tea. Then I took up the news:

Farther down the front page, it read:

RESTORATION HELPS POLICE

Many old cases solved, Chief says

Bridges Chief of Police Geofrey Schwimmen released a statement today that the joint effort by Diamond and Spadros quadrants to restore unidentified remains to their loved ones has been a great help to law officials. "We're finding many a missing persons case or suspected murder to be solved, some stretching back fifty years."

The effort comes from an agreement between the quadrants brokered late last month, ending the conflict between the two. As part of this agreement, dredging of the South River has begun, starting near the Suction. Due to the full assistance of the Clubb quadrant's river-men —

I chuckled to myself at the mention of Clubb quadrant. After our discussion a few weeks back, Lance Clubb had gone to his parents with the list of demands I'd given him. They'd turned them down flat. And as I suggested, he'd gone to his sweetheart Gardena Diamond — Jon's sister — asking her to leave Bridges with him. As I knew would happen, she'd turned him down flat.

As Jonathan described it, Lance and Gardena had a huge argument on the topic. Now their courtship was broken, which couldn't have pleased me more. Maybe now Tony would feel free to speak with her once again.

At the time, I clung to this bit of hope that Gardena and Tony at least could live happy through the devastation that the feud between their quadrants had brought. But looking back, I believe it was just a fantastical dream, like so many others I'd indulged in.

But in that moment, I felt encouraged. I had a plan of the next step I might take in this matter, when next I had the opportunity: speak with Gardena's father.

I continued to read the article:

> Due to the full assistance of the Clubb quadrant's river-men, a full forty yards of river have been cleared in this mighty effort. Although numerous remains have been returned to their loved ones, many still lay unidentified.

> Now the City asks your help. Please contact your local officials should you have anyone missing from the vicinity of the South River to see if the descriptions match those found.

> The city's Head Engineer reports that due to the length of the South River, this is likely to be a years-long endeavor. He begs your patience.

It was good that Blitz and Mary went to the river today. At this rate, by Yuletide the nearest shore would be filled with investigations and bones. Would the crowds and commotion help or hurt our Riverfront shops?

As I pondered this, I realized that I should have asked Blitz to speak to our mutual friend Vig Vikenti to see if he'd heard anything about Jon's disappearance.

Vig's saloon had become a popular spot for those who didn't like the Families — particularly the Spadros Family — and Vig might have heard about something which might help us find Jon.

I still had my mail in my pocket. I turned over one of the letters, taking a pencil from the small holder which sat upon the counter beside where Mary's clipboard hung. I made notes:

Ask Blitz to speak with Vig about rumors of Jon

Speak with Mr. Julius about G & T

I put the mail back in my pocket. Then, tucking a foot under my other leg, I turned the paper over. A smaller headline lay there:

NOTED APOTHECARY DEAD

Market Center Apothecary Miss Anna Goren, aged 81, was found dead in her home the day before yesterday.

The Apothecary belonged to the Tinkerer's Board from the age of ten, rising to the rank of Under-Apprentice. She opened her shop, Anna's Medicaments, in 1852, which has since then provided tonics and other medicinal supplies to hospitals and clinics across Bridges.

Apothecary Goren leaves behind her betrothed, Inventor Maxim Call of Spadros, as well as a host of friends and associates. Already, news of her death has spread, and the area in front of her shop is filled with flowers and messages of sympathy.

When had this betrothal taken place? And why had Anna never mentioned it?

As far as I knew, she'd always considered marriage more of a burden than it was worth. What happened to change her view?

So many questions. Yet now the extreme distress of our Inventor became clear. He loved her. And she'd loved him.

Grief rose within me once more like a wave swelling over the shore, leaving my face wet, my heart heavy. *My poor Anna.* Who came into her home? Why had she brought them to her basement?

What had she meant to tell us about the Magma Steam Generator?

She'd treated me like a daughter, sharing her food, her clothing, her excitement about her discoveries. Night and day, all she ever wanted to do was to know, and understand. My question to her about the Generator must have filled her mind with desire to learn more.

Had she learned something which others might kill to silence?

This felt disheartening. I couldn't help but think that Anna's murder, just as I went to visit, was too much of a coincidence. She wouldn't have known someone was opening my mail — most likely the Red Dog Gang.

Tony had been right: I'd left her helpless, not even aware there was a danger. And he didn't know to protect her.

It was times like that I most wanted to rush to the Saloon, grab a bottle of anything and just start drinking. I felt as if my life teetered on an edge, and I wasn't sure if I cared whether the drink killed me.

But then I thought of Jonathan, alone, trapped perhaps just as poor little David Bryce had been in some dank forsaken basement, without medicine or hope. And in my heart I pushed forward.

I couldn't die. I had to find him. I couldn't let him die, if it was in my power to stop it.

And to let my beautiful Anna, so full of years and life, go unavenged and forgotten seemed unthinkable.

Grief filled me once more, and I lay my head on the table and wept. Oh, my Anna! Why did you have to die?

***

I lay there, face upon the newsprint, and I must have dozed, because I woke with a start.

The rest of the news was rather ordinary. But on the fifth page, there lay a short announcement:

> The District Attorney's Office
> Announces The Promotion Of
> Mr. Thrace Pike
> To Assistant Deputy Prosecutor
> Our Congratulations For
> Work Well-Done

Well, I thought. It hadn't been that long since he was hired on as clerk! He must really have impressed someone.

The man was a crusader, no doubt about it, and I could see how his zeal to free Bridges of crime would serve him well as a prosecutor. I only hoped he kept his crusading to the common and petty criminal, and stayed away from harassment of the Families. Mr. Pike might be naive and foolish, but I didn't wish harm upon him.

On the last page, a small article ran:

Young man found dead

Strangler, or "copy-cat"?

Master Clover Stevens, age 20, was found dead in an alleyway near East 14th Street and Canasta, Spadros quadrant. Our sources in the Coroner's Office reveal that the signs and markings indicate the death is remarkably similar to those perpetrated by the Bridges Strangler, who was hanged for his crimes earlier this year.

But there are a growing number who believe the scoundrel has what the young people call a "copy-cat" — a man masquerading as the dead villain to continue his work.

The police and the Mayor's Office have declined to comment.

I recalled the gangly young man named Clover with the eye-patch, that friend of Morton's. One of his Aces, if I recall correctly, part of that original children's gang, the Red Dogs, which the vile and vicious Red Dog Gang tried to frame for their crimes.

Clover was a common enough name, particularly amongst the Clubbs. But the particular Clover I thought of would be about the right age for this report, and he lived near where the body had been found. I hoped that the dead man had the same first name as he did was merely a coincidence.

Could this be the Bridges Strangler once again at work? Or could this possibly be a "copy-cat"?

I seriously doubted that the Bridges Strangler — who had to be the villain Frank Pagliacci — would tolerate another man taking credit for his deeds. If someone did try to copy the scoundrel, he'd be wise to watch his back.

If, on the other hand — as I believed — the Mayor and the police had colluded to hang an innocent man, then their lack of comment on the matter made entirely too much sense.

But someone was still out there murdering young men. And reading this article reminded me of Jonathan, still not found, who might be now held by the Strangler, as so many feared.

I had to find Jon. I needed desperately to find him. But I had no further ideas as to how to go about doing so.

The doorbell rang. I put the paper aside and went to answer it.

Tony stood there.

The Feelings

"Good morning," I said. "I'm astonished to see you."

"You didn't get my letter then?"

"Oh. I haven't yet opened my mail."

For an instant, our eyes met, and I felt flustered. But then I remembered my manners. "I'm sorry. Would you like to come in?"

He hung his coat upon the stand by the door. Then he gave me an amused smile. "There's ink upon your face," he pointed at my cheek, "just there."

"Oh." I'd laid upon the newspaper! "Please excuse me." I went to wash my face; letters from Anna's article lay upon it, reversed.

Somewhat embarrassed, I returned to the hall, where Tony stood, top hat in hand, as if I'd never left. "I hope your sister's well?"

He shrugged. "As well as she ever is these days." He put his top hat upon the stand. "I hope she's learned something, at any rate."

His little sister Katherine had almost started a war.

But some good had come of it: the accords, the restoration of bodies. And maybe her parents would talk with her for once, rather than at her.

Tony had been surveying the hallway, yet his demeanor was full of interest, not the disdain I'd feared. His voice held pleasant surprise. "I haven't really looked at the inside of your building since before you moved here."

Our eyes met; his gaze was kind, gentle.

I'd been so angry at him before. Why had I been so angry? I closed the front door. "Would you like a tour?"

Tony didn't move. "I'm sorry I shouted at you."

This surprised me. Yet he seemed sincere.

"I — oh, there was no call for it. She was your friend, and now she's dead." Pain lay in his voice. "I should have stood beside you as comfort, yet I only caused you grief."

Oh, Anna.

I didn't want to cry in front of him. So I went to the parlor, and he followed. I tried to keep my tone light. "Any news about Jon?"

"None, sorry to say. I wish there were."

We moved to the kitchen. "Would you care for some tea?"

"No, thank you."

Not knowing what else to do, I went through the kitchen door into the back hall. I showed Tony the piano Jonathan had given me, that I had sanded and stained. "I'm finally learning how to play properly. Blitz is a good teacher."

"Is the arrangement working well?"

"It is. He and Mary take such good care of everything — I hardly have to direct them. And it's good to have them around, so I'm not alone here."

I faced him, back to the piano, and with my left hand, pointed towards Blitz and Mary's rooms. "They stay there. They're at the river today." I felt foolish: of course, Tony knew that. "It's been difficult with the new baby, but she's beginning to sleep more."

Tony smiled to himself.

Then I gestured to my right. "This is Master Rainbow's room. And upstairs is where our temporary housekeeper is." I led him down the hall, past the little closet under the stair and towards the staircase.

"Where **is** Master Rainbow today?"

A hint of something lay in Tony's voice. Jealousy? Fear? "At the Courthouse, I'd imagine. Jon's brother Mr. Beloty is letting him look through the old cases, to see if anyone might have wished Jon harm."

I smiled at Tony, feeling a great wave of fondness for him. On impulse, I took his hand. "Master Rainbow's always been a perfect gentleman."

Tony gave me a startled glance, then we climbed the stair.

I moved the curtain at the top of the stair aside, then went in to show Tony our large upper room.

Furniture had been set up: an elegant sofa, a screen behind which models might change, an empty clothes-rack, a writing-desk. A stool and easel stood in the far right corner near the plate glass window.

Tony appeared puzzled by them. "These are for the artists?"

"Yes, although many bring their own easels. Not that we've had any of them scheduled since the baby was dealt in."

Without making any move to open it, I pointed out the curtain covering the far corner of the room beside the bath, which we'd designated as Mrs. Crawford's quarters. "She's rather old and set in her ways, but she's been so helpful with Ariana. We'll probably keep her another few months, just until the baby sleeps through the night."

I considered what Blitz had said a few days back. "Her husband was one of your grandfather's men. She deserves to be at your Country House in her own little cottage there, not out having to look for work all the time. Can't you speak with someone about that?"

Tony just nodded as he surveyed the room.

Outside, the sun stood high, bathing the garden on the rooftop across the street in brilliant light. All was quiet, peaceful.

To the east, hundreds of rooftops and buildings stretched toward the merchants' area, and much too far off to see, Spadros Manor itself. "When I first noted Jon missing, I looked through his office."

Tony seemed surprised. "Oh?"

"I found a portrait in his desk of a young woman. Paler even than you, with long straight hair. Blonde. Has he ever spoken of her?"

"Never once." He fell silent for a moment. "I wonder who she is?"

"I wondered that too."

A soft chuckle came from him. "Are **you** jealous, then?"

This entirely surprised me. "Jealous?" Was I? I didn't know. Yet this disturbed me. My people felt jealousy to be a childish weakness, rather than a mark of love. No, I couldn't be jealous: that's what quadrant-folk did. "He's never spoken of her. Yet her portrait lay in the drawer beside mine. So I was curious."

Tony's eyes widened. "Oh." It seemed he felt as puzzled as I did.

"Let me show you the rest." I led him downstairs and to my study.

Tony stared, mouth open, at the nameplate on the door, my study, the cabinets and papers there. "This is like a real office."

Normally, I would have been upset by this, but that day it amused me. "It **is** a real office. I don't have any clients at present, but some weeks I have two or three at once."

"So it's done well." A tinge of pride lay in his voice.

"Yes, it's done well." I didn't really even need his dollar a month anymore, but it helped: Blitz ate a great deal. I gestured to the door. "Would you care to see my bedroom?"

We went into there, looked around. And I realized how safe, how settled I felt here. It felt good. It felt like home.

"Your rooms are lovely," Tony said. "So different from our own."

"I suppose they're more suited to my tastes. I prefer bright colors."

Tony sounded shocked. "Why did you never say so? We have all the money in the world —"

I turned away. "I never had a say in anything, ever. Why should anyone listen to my tastes, my whims in furnishings?"

"Because it's your home," Tony said, as if stung by my words. "But then ... it never was your home, was it?"

Tears suddenly came to my eyes, and I stood unmoving.

Tony came round to me, just as Jonathan had that night long ago at the Grand Ball.

Moved by the memory, I put my face in Tony's chest. He smelled good. His arms around me were warm, gentle. "I'm so afraid, Tony ... I can't bear to lose him."

Tony froze. "You love Jonathan, then."

The bitter memory of Jon pushing me away the day I tried to kiss him wrenched at my chest. I scoffed, pulling away to reach for my handkerchief. "Of course not. I mean, I do, but not like that. He's my dearest friend. I care for him more than anything." Was he even still alive? "I would die, right now, if it would see him happy and well."

Tony watched me as I wiped my eyes. As I returned my handkerchief to my pocket, he reached out to touch my face, hand trembling, and kissed me.

My life with Tony came rushing back; I wanted him near me again. I flung my arms around him and kissed his lips, running my hands through his hair. I took his face in my hands. "I'm sorry, I'm so sorry."

"Oh, Jacqui, I've missed you so," Tony said, and oh, it felt so good to be touched, to no longer be afraid and alone, to have someone desire me again.

I kissed his face, his neck, his mouth, yearning for his touch. We moved to my bed, and he pulled me to him. I felt his desire for me hard against my body, and oh, it made me want him even more. I ran my hands over his back, his legs, and he moaned as we kissed, his fingers in my hair. I ran my hands around him, undoing his trousers and letting them fall, and he laid me in bed, moving my dress aside, and entered inside me.

Desire overwhelmed me as he moved, as he kissed my breasts, my face, my neck. He didn't fumble, didn't falter. How had my Tony been so skilled and yet I never knew it?

And I realized that all the years we lay together, while I'd imagined it to be Joe, that it was Tony who lay with me, who loved me. Who knew my body and what it wanted, because he wanted to please me. And as we cried out in our passion, it was Tony, my Tony, he alone, not some fantasy that I loved.

Tony fell upon my chest. "I love you so, Jacqui."

I stroked his hair and kissed it, utterly spent, tears in my eyes as I held him in my arms, as he rolled gently beside me. I gazed at his face, his dear pale face and closed eyes, and I wanted to love him in truth.

But something held me back.

Tony caressed the side of my face, the naked raw love in his eyes tearing at my soul.

My desire for him was plain; what held my heart from him?

What was **wrong** with me?

I began to cry, throwing myself into his arms. I felt utterly lost and wicked, ruined, unworthy of any man's love. I sobbed until exhausted, as he held me and smoothed my hair.

Tony kissed the top of my head. He caressed my face, gazing at me as if viewing pure beauty.

"How can you look at me so?" *How can you ever forgive me?*

He smiled. "I can't help myself; you're so beautiful."

I lay my head on his chest and wept.

The Bond

When I woke, I lay under the covers, my hair loosened and combed out, my slippers and stockings laid neatly on the chair. I rose to find the doors locked and the room straightened.

Tony was gone.

I sat in a chair by my tea-table, grief overwhelming me. After everything I'd done to him, Tony still loved me. Passionately, tenderly he loved me.

I couldn't bear it. I couldn't face it. I didn't understand it.

And yet again, I sat alone.

A note lay upon the table:

> Jacqui,
>
> I didn't come here intending to seduce you. I have never felt happier than when we were together today, yet now I feel I have caused you pain. Please forgive me if that is the case. I love you beyond all bearing, but if you say the word I will never return here again.
>
> I want to help in any way I can to find Jonathan. He and I share a bond that compels me to rescue him from whatever has befallen him. I have no memory of my brother, but I think of Jon as such and feel great distress when I consider his disappearance. I'm not skilled in such matters, so I await word of how I can be of assistance.
>
> Anthony Spadros

Even with everything that had happened, it was seeing that line in his handwriting that almost broke me. He hated his name so much.

I can't always be your Tony. These days, I must be Anthony, heir to the Spadros Family. And that man must be cruel if we're to survive.

After a long time, I wiped my eyes. Tony loved me. Somehow, some way, he'd forgiven me for everything. He loved Jonathan as a brother, and he wanted to help.

In all of the possible ways I might have foreseen this round of my life dealing out, I never saw this happening.

My heart felt so full I thought it might burst, both in wondrous joy and terrible grief. But I had to focus. I had to learn all I could about what the Families were doing, so I could help.

Tony didn't know what to do — he'd even said so. But through Sawbuck, he commanded the bulk of the Spadros Family's forces, thousands of men who'd die following his orders. If Jonathan had been brought somewhere in Spadros quadrant, we could find him.

My apartments were quiet. A rustle and a ringing as our street's messenger boy sped by. A couple across the street and down the other way talked, but I couldn't make out what they said.

I went to my dresser. The writing-box Tony had given me on our anniversary two years past sat there. What lay inside it had entirely changed, as supplies ran out and new ones bought. I don't know why I'd kept it, when I'd sold everything else.

I retrieved his letter. *Anthony Spadros.*

I saw then that once I'd gone, this role he'd forced himself into was the only thing he'd had left.

Yet he didn't realize his power.

I wrote:

> Tony,
>
> I'm sure the Four Families are doing what they must to find Jon. Yet to duplicate our efforts risks missing something vital.
>
> Learn what you can. The Acting Keeper has given permission to search the records there. Your man Master Rainbow has been a true and loyal help, and has put aside all

else to assist us. I will focus upon those scoundrels Jon helped imprison who might wish him harm.

There was so much I wanted to say. Tony knew as well as anyone the urgency of finding Jon, as the last drops of his medication ran out. But to say so would only distract him.

I love you beyond all bearing.

It frightened me. But Tony had to receive an answer.

Any pain I felt today was in my heart, and of my own doing. There is nothing to forgive.

Jacqui

The clocks struck noon. When I first sat, I'd intended to write to the Families, my informants, everyone. But before that, I must make the list Tony wanted. I left out anyone who'd said they didn't want the Family to know of our association: I wouldn't contact them again.

This list I put with my letter, sealed it, then put it and my cigarettes in my pocket. Then I put on my long elderberry-colored shawl and walked towards the Backdoor Saloon.

I hadn't gone more than ten yards before Theodore Sutherfield walked beside me. "Going for a stroll? I hope you'll not visit an alley today."

I smiled to myself. "Good day, Mr. Sutherfield."

"Might I assist you?"

I considered the matter, including my mad thoughts the night prior, and I suddenly didn't want to go inside the Saloon. Yet none of Tony's men stood outside the doorway. "You might."

We continued on down the street. Tony's scent still lay upon me: the musky smell of his body, his cologne, his deposit to my account. And I marveled at Mr. Sutherfield's ability not to ask the questions he must have most wished to. When we arrived at the Backdoor Saloon, I took out a cigarette, let him light it for me.

The questions lay in his eyes, yet he said nothing. I could see why Tony gave him such trust. Mr. Sutherfield's whole purpose for being here was to assist me, not to ask what must be burning inside.

I handed him the letter. "Would you bring this to Mr. Eight Howell? It must go to my husband. His eyes only."

Mr. Sutherfield nodded gravely, his dark eyes searching my face. "Be right back."

I turned away, taking a deep drag on my cigarette, savoring the peace it brought me. I stood there a while, watching the birds pass inside and the clouds float far outside the faint shimmer of the dome, until my cigarette was done.

Mr. Sutherfield emerged. "They've expected you; a man stands ready." Hoof-beats rang out from around the corner, trailing away fast. "May I escort you home?"

So Tony came here next. "You may."

***

The clock struck one, yet I had no desire for luncheon. I wished I had something to do, some way to strike a blow for all the people who the Red Dog Gang had murdered simply to torment me.

Wait, I thought. Etienne Hart.

I paced about, suddenly furious. *Charles Hart swore he'd get to the bottom of this. And now Jon's gone missing and yet another of my friends has been murdered?*

Mr. Sutherfield stood across the street, leaning on a wall, apparently reading the newspaper.

I waved him over. "I want to visit the racetrack today to speak with Mr. Charles Hart. Can you call my plain carriage?"

"Well," he said, "I could. But it'll take a while to get here. And even if we left right now, it's a four hour drive at least. It'd almost be faster to take a taxi-carriage to the train. We wouldn't get there until tea-time. Did you have an invitation?"

"No," I said, deflated. "But I must speak with Mr. Hart."

Mr. Sutherfield nodded. "Let me send someone to the Hart bridge on Market Center. They'd know where he is today." He gave me a kindly smile, as a man might give his little daughter. "No sense going all the way to the racetrack if he's here in town!"

That made sense. "Thank you."

I went inside, looked in the mirror. What had I been thinking? If I needed to leave, I couldn't get into one of my walking dresses without help: there were too many buttons I couldn't reach. And I didn't dare go in front of a Patriarch at his home wearing a house dress!

But he might come here, which I found equally daunting. I was alone in the house, and he might command Mr. Sutherfield to wait outside. Why had I asked for him?

I could prepare in either case. I bathed, changed my dress, did my makeup and hair. If he sent word that I might meet with him, I'd ask for it to be tomorrow. If he came here, well, I'd be as presentable as I could, and insist on Mr. Sutherfield staying inside.

Finally, I had to force myself to sit, stop pacing and worrying. It was unlikely that even if they found him on Market Center that he'd be allowed to come into the quadrant without Roy's permission. And I had no idea where Roy might be.

My heart pounded; I shook inside. When Mrs. Crawford unlocked the kitchen entrance and came in with the shopping, I almost cried in relief. "Let me help you get that," I said.

"Why thank you, my Lady." The old woman curtsied, eyes wide. "You're very kind."

Blitz and Mary arrived shortly before dark, their cheeks pink, their voices merry. Little Ariana slept in her basket, not even waking when it was set upon the table.

"I take it you enjoyed your day," I said.

Mary beamed. "Ever so much so."

Blitz placed a newspaper-wrapped bundle upon the counter. "Bought this from a fisherman before we left. Trout for dinner!"

I realized I was hungry. Morton wouldn't be so pleased, but I felt sure they could find something for him to eat instead.

Mrs. Crawford had been watching me. "You're dressed and everything. Were you able to get some rest?" She hesitated. "I hope your day went well."

Did it? "I'm not sure. It was eventful, at any rate."

"Oh dear," Mary said. "Hopefully nothing bad."

Recalling Tony in my bed, I felt my cheeks grow hot. "No," I said. "Nothing bad."

The Connection

Early the next morning, the front door-bell rang, and I heard a heavy tread go past. Blitz walked slowly, as if weary. I smiled to myself: they'd no doubt had as eventful a day as I did.

A few minutes later, Mary came in with my tray: a pot of morning tea, toast and jam, my tonic, and a letter, edged in red and marked with the Holy Symbol of the Hart Family. I opened it: an invitation from Mr. Charles Hart to luncheon.

So Mr. Sutherfield's men were able to reach Mr. Hart after all.

Mary still stood there.

I handed the invitation over. "I'm to have luncheon with Mr. Hart on Market Center."

"I'll let my husband know," was all she said, then hurried out.

Ariana fussed in the distance, and Mrs. Crawford moved into the hall, murmuring gentle words I couldn't make out. Then she came back, with a light tone meant to be encouraging.

I recalled back home in the Pot, the way babies fussed and were comforted. It seemed all babies were alike until we tried to unmake them, form them into things who knew if the Dealer intended.

I thought of Mr. Hart and Roy's feud, one seeming to span decades. Then I thought of what Tony wrote about Jon: *He and I share a bond.*

How unlikely that would seem upon examination of the facts — the hate Jon's father and eldest brother had for Tony, the endless war their two Families shared. How did this happen?

I chuckled to myself, drank down my tonic, which unlike my morning tea, still tasted just as bitter. It seemed everyone had their secrets. Then I looked at the glass in my hand. Jon's medication had to have run out by now. How long could he last without it?

Grief, fear, worry all seized me. I had to do something, but I didn't know what else I might do. Running into the street without an aim would do nothing to find Jon.

The kitchen door-bell jingled as Amelia came in, rushed about. It didn't surprise me when she burst in panting. "I'm so sorry to be late, mum, but —"

I raised a hand to stop her. "It doesn't matter, Amelia. I won't inform to my husband on you."

This stopped her in her tracks, and she curtsied. "Thank you, mum." She seemed flustered. "I'll start your bath."

"Yes, do." I took a bite of my toast. Morton would be up soon, and would want to leave as soon as he could. I hoped to ride onto Market Center with him.

Amelia turned on the water then returned. "Your carriage should arrive by nine."

"Oh?" Generally, we didn't have the carriage until ten.

"Yes, Mr. Anthony asked me to tell you. You and Master Rainbow may use it as often as you wish until Master Jonathan's found."

I sat back, surprised.

"I take it we'll be at the Courthouse again today, mum?"

I nodded.

"I'll bring some mending then."

I smiled to myself. "Good idea." That workroom in the Keeper's office had barely room for me and Morton, with all the boxes in it.

"Up you go, then. Breakfast will be ready soon."

***

Morton didn't seem surprised at the early arrival of my plain carriage, and I wondered if Tony had contacted him. He sat on one of the bench seats, myself and Amelia upon the other. And I considered the pact Tony had made with Morton after he appeared unconscious on the doorstep at Spadros Manor two years past.

It seemed odd at first, Morton moving into my apartments after my trial, but as we'd worked together I became more accustomed to it. Yet I never stopped wondering if one of the reasons Tony allowed him in my home was to report my doings.

Morton never once tried to become familiar, nor to pry, nor to work at anything other than my cases and his perennial search for his informant Albert Sheinwold. He'd been a faithful friend, risking his life more than once on my account. But I got the sense at times that while intently busy, underneath he waited for some sign to make his next play. "Have you heard from your man Clover recently?"

"I haven't," Morton said. "Why do you ask?"

"It's nothing; a news article I read about a man by that name."

Morton shrugged. "If I hear from him, I'll let you know."

I had Zeus drop him off at the Courthouse. "I'm going to look into this 'LB' business."

Morton said, "What 'LB business'?"

"Oh." I'd forgotten he hadn't been with us at the Courthouse that day. And he hadn't seen the card when I showed it to Beloty.

I handed him the card through the carriage window. "Do you recognize this? I found it near where the carriage which took Master Jonathan was parked."

Morton peered at it, turned it over, then handed it back. "Never heard of it."

"Well, I thought that if this refers to some business venture, they might have a record of it at City Hall."

"Good idea!"

"Give my regards to Mr. Beloty," I said. "I have a luncheon date, so don't wait for me."

Morton tipped his hat and went inside. We continued on.

City Hall had white walls with thick, dark wood borders around each of its equally dark doors. A floor of black tile led to a set of black wooden stairs with black banisters, edged in brass.

The City Clerk's office was down a flight of stairs. While the front area was small, sporting a few chairs on either side of a narrow counter, the view behind two small bookcases full of ledgers showed rows of cabinets, stretching back the length of the building.

The widow woman behind the counter stood reading one of the many tabloids which plagued the city, a silvered bell beside her. The placard in front of her read:

Mrs. Brenda Trex

City Clerk, Bridges

She glanced up as I entered. "Can I help you?"

"Yes, I'm looking for a business called 'LB.'" I showed her the card. "This is all I have, and I need to contact the proprietor."

Surprise crossed her face. "What kind of business doesn't put their information upon the card?" She scoffed. "Amateurs."

Handing back the card, she went to a bookcase, going along it until she found a large, thick ledger, which she brought back to the counter. Upon it was the letter "L." After opening it, she began going down the lines of written word. "There's no company called simply 'LB' ..." She went to the beginning and started again.

"I'd be happy to look through it myself, if you're busy."

She let out a laugh, holding up her copy of the *True Story*. "About run off my feet. But sure, be my guest." She went back to reading.

I leaned upon the counter and went through the list of "L" names until I came to Laughing Boy Enterprises.

LB.

Amelia said, "Have you found something?"

I'd completely forgotten she stood there. "Perhaps so." A line of boxes with various notations appeared after it, which I wasn't sure how to interpret. I turned to Mrs. Trex. "What can you tell me about this one?"

She turned the ledger round to read the listing. "Let's see ... Laughing Boy Enterprises. Says here it's owned by a second company, with the initials HR — it's like those dolls, one inside another."

I nodded. "Why would you do that?"

She shrugged. "You don't want anyone to know who owns the company. But if it's on Market Center, the taxation rate is better."

"Taxation? Is that like property tax?"

She gave me a glance, a hint of amusement in her voice. "More like Family fees, but once a year."

Hmm, I thought. "Does it give an address?"

"No. See this notation here? It means, 'same as parent company.' So I'll have to look up the parent first. It's got a catalog card code, which means I'll need to go into the back to search the card files. It could take a while. Do you have an address I might contact you at?"

I handed her my card:

Mrs. Jacqueline Kaplan Spadros

Kaplan Investigations

2917 East Thirty-Three and a Third

Spadros, Bridges

The woman's eyes grew wide, and she curtsied. "My Lady. Forgive me, I didn't recognize you."

I smiled to myself. "I'm very pleased to hear that."

We returned to the Courthouse, where I found both Morton and Mr. Beloty Diamond hard at work. I don't know why it surprised me: surely Jon's brother would be as invested in finding him as anyone.

But I stood a moment, touched by the sight of them there, jackets off and sleeves rolled up, perusing the boxes of files around them.

Morton glanced up. "There you are! Were you able to learn much?"

"The 'LB' stands for Laughing Boy Enterprises. It's —"

"Wait," Beloty said. "I've heard that name before." He pressed his hand to his forehead, then let out a breath, hand falling to his lap. "Cesare's been looking into why Jon's medication shipment didn't come this month. It was supposed to arrive the day he went missing, but it never did. The Customs Office says that the address on the package was for a Laughing Boy Enterprises. Quadri went there but the building was empty."

Quadri was the nickname of one of Jon's older brothers, Hector Diamond II, who'd been named after their grandfather. "Can you get me that address?" Whoever was there might have left something Quadri might not have thought to look for.

Beloty nodded, going to his office and returning with a pen and notepad. He made a notation. "I'll ask him about it tonight at dinner."

So it could be that Jon was still getting his medications. Why hold him? "The real question is who diverted the shipment."

Then it struck me: this wasn't the first time this had happened. "Did you ever learn who had diverted the shipments the last time? When they went to the Country House, or your Manor, instead of to his quarters as the Keeper?

Beloty got a blank look on his face. "No." He stared at me, eyes wide. "Do you think it could be related?"

"I don't know."

Morton said, "If they're being addressed wrong, then our problem could originate upon Azimoff." He looked at us both. "Isn't that where his medications are sent from?"

"Right," Beloty said. He rose. "I must speak to my father about this. We'll have to investigate the matter."

"Might I see one of the packages first?" There were any number of ways a package might be diverted, some as easy as slapping a false label over the true one. Before going to the enormous expense of sending someone to Azimoff by zeppelin, it seemed wise to investigate what we could here in Bridges first.

Beloty shrugged. "The shipments come monthly; I'm sure the packaging has been thrown out by now. But Jon still had several days' worth left of his last shipment. I'll look in his rooms for it — perhaps there's something you might learn."

I'd never seen Jon's rooms at Diamond Manor, and after searching his office, I felt intrigued at what I might learn. Did I dare ask his brother Beloty about the woman's portrait in his desk? Why had Jon never told me of her?

Then I felt ashamed at the thought of rummaging around in Jon's bedroom. If Jon wanted me to know these things about himself, he would have told me.

Yet I'd known Jon since I was eleven. He'd always listened to me, known what I liked, the details of my life. He'd been up to then my best and closest friend.

And I knew so little about him as a person. Why?

It's because I never asked. The thought dismayed me.

Morton handed me a file, and Amelia a notepad with a pencil.

I sat there, the file upon my lap. I'd been so childish, so focused on myself and my problems that I never once asked about his life. I'd learned more about Jonathan Diamond in a dozen minutes in his office than I had in a dozen years with him at my side.

Morton handed me a handkerchief. "Perhaps it's still too soon for you to return to this work," he said, and his voice was kind.

I shrugged, a great gulf of fear opening up within me. Who else would take and hold a man but the Bridges Strangler? Could we find Jonathan before the man tired of his sport and killed him? "Too much is changing, too many parts to this puzzle, and most we don't even have. With each bit of information comes a dozen more questions."

Morton nodded. "It's overwhelming, to be sure."

Yes, that was the word, I thought. He'd described it perfectly.

"But we can do this part of it, yes?" He gave me a fond smile. "Or we could go slogging through the rest of the Spadros Pot with your husband's men." At that, he let out a laugh. "I prefer it here."

He did have a point. While it would be good to see Benji and little Tim, formerly of the Keycard Cafe, no one would welcome it if I went there, particularly in daylight, dressed as I was.

And my great-grandmother had me banished from the Cathedral. So even if I did go there to learn what they might know about Jon, I wouldn't be received.

"Constable Hanger heard of what we were doing and came here," Morton said. "I gave him what we'd learned so far about Sheinwold, and a list for the detective on Master Jonathan's case about the men who'd wished him harm."

Beloty's eyes met mine. It was incredibly dangerous for Morton — or any of us, for that matter — to be seen talking with the police, even on something with as clear benefit to the Families as this one.

And though the Court disagreed, Jon's case had been deemed a Family matter.

"Take care, Master Rainbow," Beloty said. "You mean well, but I'd hate for the Families to take offense."

The Patriarch

We went through file after file, continuing to make notes of who might wish Jonathan harm. When it came close to luncheon, Amelia and I left the men there for my meeting with Mr. Charles Hart.

Mr. Hart wished to meet at the Kournikova again, and I wondered at his choice. Did he simply like the food, or was he sending me a message? This was a place the Families met at, men high in the Business, as well as those who wished to court them. The Chief of Police came here, as did the City Council.

Did Mr. Hart mean for me to become used to this place of power?

Mr. Hart already sat waiting, with his men along the walls around him. And as before, he had me send Amelia to eat with the servants.

But this day, I brought Honor in with me. He stood ten paces behind where I sat, and Mr. Hart didn't send him away.

The food was set before us, and we ate. Yet I sensed a certain amusement in his eyes. "How may I help you, Mrs. Spadros?"

Why was Anna killed? Why make it look like Roy did it? "What have you done about the matter we last discussed?"

Mr. Hart's eyes widened. "Did your husband not tell you?"

He did show up at my home for a reason. "No, he didn't." We'd gotten more than a bit sidetracked. The thought amused me.

"I've questioned Etienne about the matter. He claims he had nothing to do with your home being attacked."

All he'd done was question the man? I couldn't believe what I was hearing. "Well, now Jonathan Diamond is missing and another of my friends has been murdered."

"You think Master Jonathan's disappearance is -?"

"Yes. Everything that has happened has been to dismay and frighten me, to keep me from investigating the Red Dog Gang's crimes — and your son is at the heart of it. Jon is my best friend and now he's gone. If he doesn't get his medication soon, he'll die. And my friend who was murdered," at this, I faltered, trying not to cry, "was like a mother to me. She was cut up to make it look as if Roy Spadros did it." I stood. "Why are you Harts trying to separate me from my Family, turn me against my people? Do you hate and despise Roy Spadros so much that you'd torture **me** instead?"

"What?" Mr. Hart held his hands up, shaking his head. "I had nothing to do with this!"

"But you do nothing about those who torment me. You act as if you have some regard for me, yet do nothing to protect my interests." I sat, yet my chair was now too far from the table for me to lean upon it. "All I see here is a fraud and a coward."

Mr. Hart's men glanced at each other, hands upon their holsters.

Mr. Hart snapped, "Young lady, things are going on that you know **nothing** about."

For a moment, he sat unmoving. Then his manner turned fierce in a way I'd never seen before. He scowled, slamming his meaty fist into the table. "I'm going to get to the bottom of this."

Fear surged through me at the blue-hot rage in his eyes. I knew now how this man had held onto a quadrant.

"If Etienne is involved with these matters in any way," Mr. Hart growled, "he's going to regret it."

I had to get out of there. I rose, hands shaking, and curtsied. "Thank you, sir."

I hurried off, Honor flanking me. It wasn't until I was inside the carriage that I could breathe.

Honor leaned on the open window. "That could have gone better."

Tears came to my eyes, yet a laugh burst from me. "Something about him frightens me." Something about him wasn't right. "There's too much going on, in too many ways. I don't understand any of it."

Honor nodded. "Where to now?"

I raised a hand. "One moment." I had to think. Had I learned anything? Then I realized I'd forgotten something. Well, someone. "Get Amelia. Then pull us over to the park near the Courthouse. I don't want the Harts finding us still here."

Honor paled. "Right away."

After a few minutes, Honor and Amelia emerged, both appearing shaken. We drove a few miles until we reached the park I'd described, and Zeus parked the carriage under the shade of an apple tree. The apples had been picked by now, yet a few sat upon the ground, piles of golden mush sinking into the ground below.

Just like my life.

Something about Mr. Hart wasn't right. He seemed to care deeply about Jon the times I'd seen the two of them together. But I couldn't trust Charles Hart to do the right thing when it came to his son.

Jon being taken and Anna being killed had to gain the Red Dog Gang something. But what? And why now? It had to have been sparked by something. But how could I deduce what that something might be?

I now felt certain the two were linked.

Tony depended on me to advise him. While Jon possibly had his medications, we had no proof of it. Where could he be? Why take him in the first place?

The fact that Jon might be held somewhere both eased my mind and frightened me that much the more, when I considered that Frank Pagliacci, the Bridges Strangler, might have him.

It made no sense. Why go from holding and killing men just past boyhood to confining a man almost thirty? The other men who'd been strangled in their beds — the stable-master, Major Blackwood — had been much older, well past fifty.

And as for Anna's murder ...

While others had been killed — presumably by Frank's associate Black Maria — they'd all been shot, not stabbed.

Did Bridges have four murderers loose?

"Mum, what's going on?"

I shook my head, unable to speak.

Amelia took up the brass tube. "We need to take her home; this has been too much for her."

"Right away," Zeus said, his voice sounding tinny.

It didn't matter where we went. Until I could get more information on what was going on, I had no idea what my next play should be. But I did need to let Morton know where we were. I took the tube. "Zeus, the Courthouse first."

"Yes, mum."

I sent Honor in to notify Morton of where we'd gone. Then I let them take me home. As I went, my mind cleared, my heart slowed.

We stopped a few doors before my apartments. "A carriage is up there, mum," Zeus said.

The small window behind me opened. Honor said, "I'll find out who's here and have them move."

He passed my window to the right, and some discussion occurred out of my ability to make out the words. Then he returned. "I've asked them not to park on the street here." He stepped up onto the sideboard as the carriage moved forward, then down again.

"Who was it?"

He opened the door. "Mr. Anthony, mum. He's inside, waiting to speak with you."

The Snare

Tony sat on the sofa in my parlor, rising when I entered.

"Please, sit," I said, and it reminded me of when Joseph Kerr sat there, in almost the exact same spot. I sat in my armchair across from him. "How may I help?"

The door shut, and Tony slumped forward, his face in his hands. "Oh, Jacqui ... when I received your letter ..." He took a deep breath, sat up. And he looked different somehow — in control of himself, yes, but he hadn't forced his face into his usual public mask. He seemed hesitant to speak. "I'm not certain where to begin."

I must admit I felt the same. Yet I didn't dare ask about my letter; it seemed I caused him a great deal of grief. "How goes the search?"

He nodded, eyes on the table between us. "We should be finished with the Pot today. I lost twelve men —"

The Family was, for the most part, family: those who lay dead were probably his cousins.

"— but thank the gods, we should be able to begin the quadrant." He seemed daunted by the size of the task.

"One street at a time," I said, giving him a smile I hoped was encouraging. Yet at this rate it would take weeks, if not months, to search the city proper. And there were almost three hundred miles of countryside. If Jonathan was even being kept in Spadros quadrant, as his brother Cesare implied.

At times, Cesare was quite the fool: what possible motive might we have for holding Jon, of all people, here?

"Have you learned anything that might help us? Anything at all?"

I let out a breath, annoyed. "I want to find him as much as you do."

He sat up, hands raised in surrender. "Yes. I know. Forgive me."

Tony, asking me for forgiveness? I took a deep breath, trying to calm the wild bird fluttering desperately to escape my chest. "Master Rainbow and Mr. Beloty Diamond are compiling a list of men who may have wanted to harm Jon, and are not currently at the Prison."

Tony nodded.

"Also, I found this by the carriage which took him." I handed over the card. "So far as I can tell, the LB stands for a company called Laughing Boy Enterprises. This is also the name of the company which Jonathan's medications have been sent to this month."

Tony let out a relieved sigh.

"Mr. Beloty told me they went to the address, yet it stood empty."

Tony's mouth hung open, eyes wide. Then he frowned a bit, blinking. "So ... this was planned well in advance!"

"Jon told me he had a decision to make. And if anything should happen to him, I was to go to you for help."

"He **knew**." Tony looked incredulous. "What the hell is going on?"

"It's clear to me he suspected his life was in danger. And ... but why you? Has he told you something which might help?"

Tony shook his head. "Nothing out of the ordinary." Then his face changed. "Wait." His eyes narrowed. "He's told me more of your cases lately." He gave his head a little shake, bit his lip. "I don't know if it means anything, but during the past few months, he's spoken almost entirely of your missing persons cases."

I shrugged. "It **is** my specialty."

Tony chuckled, smiling fondly at me. "And has it gone well?"

"Since the age of sixteen, I've always found who I search for." Obviously, I'd yet to find Mr. Albert Sheinwold. And Jonathan ... I would find him if I died trying.

He gazed to one side. "That's good to know."

I really wanted to lean forward, put my chin in my hands. Yet with two corsets on, it was impossible to do so. "Someone has plotted against the Keeper of the Court. They know a great deal about him, because they had his medications diverted and created a false carriage and men." I glanced at him. "They had false Spadros livery on."

Tony let out a groan, gazing up to the ceiling.

"Well, our only witness — a guard — says they wore black. But he didn't see much because a group of 'toughs,' as he put it, came trying to push in at the same time."

"Convenient."

"Yes, I thought so." Then I recalled what else he said. "He said the footman looked like a woman."

"Did you get a description?"

I felt dismayed. "Not really. Just 'the prettiest man I've ever seen'."

"Hmm," Tony said. "Not too terribly many of those in the city. Get me the name of your guard, and I'll have him look at those we find."

Might the Court feel upset by us questioning its guards? "Perhaps that request should go through the Court."

Tony nodded. "Of course. You're right."

We sat silent for a while.

Finally, I said, "Have the Families learned anything?"

Tony shook his head. "No one's seen him. He hasn't gone calling in some time, what with being ill and all. Just home to the Courthouse. And luncheons with you."

"Jon wanted us to try a new place that day. The day he went missing. What do you think it might mean?"

Tony shrugged. "Who knows?" He let out a breath. "All we do know is he's being held. Or at least someone wants us to think so."

"You think?"

"Why leave the card there otherwise? It reminds me too terribly much of what you told me about the boy you rescued."

"Oh." The comparison became clear. "No request for ransom."

"Exactly. What possible chance would a wealthy man from a powerful Family, the Keeper of the Court be taken, yet the scoundrels not ask for anything? And while you say you believe this man Frank Pagliacci to be the one who they call the Bridges Strangler —"

I nodded.

"— this is outside his normal age of man taken, just like the boy." Tony leaned forward. "I believe this villain wishes to ensnare you."

I felt astonished. "Me?"

"Yes," Tony said. "Who else would undertake this investigation as you have? Who else has the wit and determination to follow these," he gestured with the card, "small clues? Who has the motivation, not to mention the experience in finding lost men?"

He sent the card spinning onto the table. "This is a snare aimed precisely at you, Jacqui. And if you go running off, as you invariably do, you'll be caught up in it. And there may not be anyone to aid you this time."

"When I rescued David Bryce, Frank Pagliacci claimed he wanted to kill anyone who might try rescuing me. He spoke particularly of hunting each down as they arrived."

"Surely he can't mean to be trying that again?"

"I don't know. There must be something else in play." This reminded me of what Mr. Hart had said. "Do you know of something going on with the Harts?"

Tony blinked, his face going a shade lighter. "What do you mean?"

"Mr. Hart said just now that things were going on that I had no idea of."

"Jacqui, why were you with Mr. Hart today?"

Surely Tony couldn't be jealous! "If you must know, he invited me to luncheon. But I asked to see him about his son. I can't help but wonder if Etienne Hart had Anna Goren killed to torment me." The memory of Anna lying there dead swam before me; grief squeezed my heart tight.

Tony sat still, eyes downcast. "I don't believe Charles Hart intends you harm. As for Inventor Etienne ..."

"But why? Why would he kill Anna, take Jonathan —"

Tony jerked as if poked with a stick, then gaped at me. "Surely you don't think —"

I couldn't look at him. All I could focus on was to not cry. "Every time, every person I've lost in my life has been to torment me. Just as I thought when you were beaten so badly: it's a distraction, something to hide what they're really doing."

Tony seemed to ponder this. "If Mayor Freezout is up to something, I don't know what it is. He hasn't been seen in two days."

This startled me. "Oh?"

"Rumors have it he's terribly ill. His wife Delanie runs the city most of the time."

I recalled Mrs. Delanie Freezout at my trial. "I can't say that I'm sorry for it, not after what he tried to do to me."

"Oh, Jacqui ... what good has vengeance ever brought? To wish harm upon others eats away at you until there's nothing left inside."

I wanted to say: *You haven't lost everyone you love.* But it would be hurtful, as well as not entirely true.

"And that High-Low Split gang hasn't been seen in the Pot either." He glanced away. "At least, no one will speak of it."

I almost laughed. Of course no one in the Pot would speak to a Family man about it. "And the Red Dog Gang?"

"Not so much as a card dropped, or a stamp upon the wall."

Now I felt certain they were up to something. "We've spoken but of three quadrants. What does Clubb report?"

Tony seemed on stronger ground with this topic. "The Travelers' Board is aware of Jonathan's disappearance, and assures us he's not left the city. They continue to search everything, as they've done up to now. Mr. Alexander has ordered a ground search starting at the zeppelin station, to cover the countryside and sweep towards the city. He has hundreds of hounds out sniffing." Tony sounded in awe. "I'd never have considered that. We've been gathering our own sniffer hounds to search here."

He admires Mr. Clubb. Seeing as Tony's son could become the man's grandchild, it seemed a positive development — if not for the fact that Tony was besotted with the boy's mother, Jonathan's sister Gardena.

What needed to happen was for Tony to forget me and marry Gardena. But that was looking less likely with every day.

Why did I bed him? Now I was beginning to regret doing so. "That sounds good."

"Well, we don't have many. Our dog Rocket, of course, and my father's dog Spadrille. Some of the aristocrats have sniffer dogs, as well as a few of my men. But not nearly enough."

I smiled as I recalled our bomb sniffer dog Rocket. "I'm glad to hear Rocket is still well."

"A bit long in the tooth, but doing well. We're going to breed him and get some pups trained in case of future events such as this one."

It sounded wise. And I felt surprised they hadn't done this long ago. "This search sounds to be a long process."

"Well, whoever took Jon can't get him out of the city. He's bigger than me and unwell, so it'd be difficult to move him around much. They have to have a place where he's being hidden, with guards and lookouts. Anything like that is bound to attract attention."

Guards and lookouts? "Use the zeppelins from those nightly tourist shows! During the day, they could fly the city and see if there are buildings with these guards and lookouts. Those could be best seen from the air."

"Yes! They could quarter the countryside better than a thousand men." He gained a new energy, and rose, so I did as well. He kissed my cheek with vigor. "You are entirely splendid. I'll speak with the Clubbs at once."

As he hurried off, I felt unreasonably pleased with myself.

Entirely splendid. Such a change from his attitude towards me just a few days prior.

I had Amelia change me into a house dress and sat at my desk in my study. Took tea there. The whole time, I pondered what we'd all learned of this.

Jonathan knew whoever came for him the other day. He expected them: he'd opened the blinds so he might see them arrive. He sent his secretary on an errand: find him a particular book. A book Jon knew would take a while to find.

Jon did all he could so as to leave in secret, to go somewhere very close by, possibly hoping to return in time to meet with me before anyone was the wiser. That park, maybe.

Then some scoundrel — or perhaps group of scoundrels such as the Red Dog Gang — had seized Jon and held him, possibly supplying him with his tonics to keep him alive.

That in itself spoke of a deeper plan.

Yet they'd not asked for ransom.

Tony believed it a snare to capture me. And the longer I thought of it, the more I believed it to be true.

So we'd be ready. Whenever we learned of Jon's location, I wouldn't go alone, but with many men.

When I'd been in that shootout with Frank Pagliacci in Jack Diamond's Party Time factory, I'd never been so frightened in my life. If I would have shot him properly, this whole matter might've ended there. No, I'd let others shoot this man, ones more skilled than I, and if we took care not to kill him, we'd have our answer once and for all.

The thought of perhaps seeing the man who'd tormented me for so long excited me. I must be there when Roy drew the name of his master from him.

It might well have been a thirst for vengeance, but I believed it my right to face this man who had done me so much wrong.

Amelia said her goodbyes and went home to her family. Morton came in, and after washing up and changing, sat before us at dinner, with good appetite. "The files are done, the list sent to the Court's investigators. Mr. Beloty thought it best to let them handle the matter than for me to involve the police."

"I'm relieved." I bit into a chunk of fried potato.

"Well, yes, and he wanted me to tell you they'd been to the zeppelin station," he took a drink from his water glass, "spoke with the Customs office there. His brother's men, I mean." He leaned both arms upon the table. "Did you know that they keep record of every package shipped through there?"

He sounded incredulous, and I have to admit, I felt much the same. Thousands of packages went through there every day! "What did they say about Jon's medication shipments?"

"Those were many months back, and at least two shipments diverted." He leaned back. "It'll take some time to search the records."

I nodded. "The woman researching Laughing Boy Enterprises said it might take some time to find who owns it. But hopefully we'll have more to go on then."

There had to be other avenues of inquiry. Worry beat inside my chest: Jonathan had been missing for four days now.

Blitz and Mary were chatting about something else entirely — a new style of carriage she'd seen advertised in the evening news. Apparently it was larger and had a mechanism to prevent tipping. All Four Families had placed orders to replace their current ones.

Blitz said, "What will they do with the old ones?"

Mary peered at the paper. "They don't say. Gifts for their men, I'd imagine." She said to me, "I used to get the dresses when you outgrew them, mum. Back before you married, of course."

I never knew that.

"My mother'd take the finery from them, turn them, do some altering, let out the hem." She shrugged. "I could only wear your clothes when you weren't there, or when I was in my rooms. I wore one when the lot of us went to the fair." She turned to Blitz. "Remember?"

Blitz laughed. "Yes. You were just a girl."

They went on about all the young servants going to the fair. It sounded lovely. But my mind remained upon the carriage.

Jon's captors rode up in a carriage. But what color? The men wore black, not navy. How did that carriage, with those men, get into that alley? The way past the Courthouse was guarded ... wasn't it?

Morton hung on the discussion about the fair. Mrs. Crawford came in, took the plates, began to wash them. Ariana began to cry. Mary got up to see to her, while Blitz swept the floor.

"You're awfully quiet," Morton said.

"There's still a lot we don't know. What the carriage which took Master Jonathan looked like, how it got into that alley. But more importantly, where it went after that."

Morton nodded.

"Suppose this carriage was navy. Yet no navy carriage has gone missing. Someone had to build it. Someone had to make their uniforms. Someone had to sell them those horses and their tack." I set my teacup down. "The information is out there. We just have to find it." I considered the matter. "A navy carriage with men dressed in black inspires curiosity. Someone saw them after they left that alley."

Morton shrugged. "Most people see what they want to. They see a navy carriage, they think: the Court. Especially if it's labeled that way.

The men riding it could have been dressed in white, but men will say they saw navy, because navy is what the Court wears."

"Oh." I felt more than a bit dismayed.

"But of course, you're right," Morton said. "Someone saw it. We just need them to come forward."

"Right," I said. "I believe I know the best person for that job."

The Reward

When I first went to Spadros Manor, Roy had given me garrote wire with metal handles fashioned into flat butterflies. They were meant to be threaded through my under-corset, for use if I should ever need it. One of the butterflies could be unhooked to release the wire.

Roy had trained me in the garrote's use, yet I never could imagine actually using it on someone. So once Roy and Molly moved to Spadros Castle, I coiled the thing up in its box and put it away.

But the next day, I asked Amelia, "Do we still have Mr. Roy's gift?"

Amelia stared at me blankly for some time, then said, "Oh. Let me check." She began rummaging through my things, which didn't take long. "It's probably still at the Manor. Should I go fetch it?"

Tony thought the scoundrels who took Jon did so to snare me. And if this happened, I needed a hidden way to escape. I'd gotten myself, Morton, and David Bryce free with my gun, but we'd been very lucky. "Bring it with you when you come here tomorrow."

While Morton returned to searching Sheinwold's case files, Amelia and I made a visit to the *Bridges Daily*. The same thin man stood leaning upon the counter reading a tattered novel just as when I last arrived there, yet the years had grayed his hair a bit and the novel was much thicker. He peered up from his spectacles. "Not seen you here in some time."

"Good morning, sir. I'd like to see Mr. Blackberry, if I might."

He took up a brass tube beside him. "Mrs. Spadros for you, sir."

"Which one you got there?" Mr. Blackberry said.

"Mrs. Jacqueline," the thin man replied.

"Ah, yes! Send her over at once."

The man pointed across the room full of men busily typing away, stacks of paper on each side. "Door's labeled. Can't miss it."

I traversed the room, gaining a few curious glances. Yet most seemed intent on their work. The correct office was labeled as the man mentioned, black upon the wooden door's clouded glass paneling:

Mr. Paul Blackberry

Editor in Chief

I'd first met Mr. Blackberry when I was five: he asked me to pose for a photograph in the Spadros Pot. Afterwards, I tried — unsuccessfully — to pick his pocket. We'd been fast friends ever since.

When I opened the door, he rose, beaming. "Jacqui! How are you? Close the door there, and sit down." Amelia he entirely ignored; she stood by the door, hands clasped in front of her.

The almost twenty years since our first meeting had sagged the man's face and widened his formerly slender frame. His bushy sideburns were now entirely gray, as was his hair. Yet his eyes were bright as ever behind his spectacles. "Sit down. You want some tea?"

"No thank you, sir." I sat. "I hope you're well."

"Never better. What can I do for you?"

I told him about my observations regarding the carriage which took Jon, and my hope that someone might have seen something useful. "I'd like to get real information, not what we tell them or what people think they should say."

Mr. Blackberry nodded gravely. "I have just the thing." He took out a notepad and pen. "Carriage seen leaving the scene of Master Jonathan Diamond's capture. Information sought about its description and further movements." He glanced up. "Want to offer a reward?"

"Only if they deliver something useful."

He nodded. "Reward for information directly leading to the return of the Bridges Keeper." He glanced up. "How much?"

I had a hundred dollars still, plus a small amount of interest which I put towards our Family fees and running the house. "Ten dollars."

His eyes widened. "That'll get some takers."

In a city where people were paid in pennies a day, ten dollars was a significant windfall. I wanted to offer more, but I didn't want to commit too much in case more than one had good information. "I suppose I should give you my address."

Mr. Blackberry shook his head. "Not unless you want every crackpot in town at your door. No, we keep a rather large box at the Post Office for such things. I'll task one of my secretaries to it, and have him send you a daily listing."

I had no idea one might purchase a box there. "That would be so appreciated." Despite the frequent and vital use of messenger boys for the daily mail, a whole other cadre of workers took in packages and mail from the outside world directly from the zeppelin station onto Market Center, to be put upon horse-trucks to distribute to the quadrants. The boys brought any packages or mail for other cities to this spot, where they'd be marked and sent in a daily horse-truck to the zeppelin.

Anyone curious and intelligent enough to consider the matter would believe the request for information came from outside the dome, perhaps even Hub itself. "It's quite ingenious."

Mr. Blackberry gave me a fatherly smile. "Glad to see you looking well. It seems life these days suits you."

"Thank you, sir."

"Anything else I might help with?"

"I don't believe so."

"Go on, then. I won't take up any more of your time." He rose. "I'll get a man on this at once."

***

Once Amelia and I returned to where Morton searched the Archives, I sent a messenger to Mr. Blackberry, asking him to only send word if anything interesting occurred, as I feared my mail was being opened. Then we went down to the Archive room.

Morton sat there busily working, glancing up as we entered. "There you are! Any news?"

I sat. "The Bridges Daily will run a request for information about the carriage which took Master Jonathan, with a reward."

Amelia, as usual, continued standing, feeling it inappropriate to sit with "her betters."

Morton's eyes widened. "You got the Family to post a reward?"

I hadn't even considered it. "No, just me."

"Well, you should get Mr. Cesare or someone in his Family to stake it. He's **their** brother."

I wasn't sure I wanted to have that conversation with Cesare, particularly since I'd done it without asking. "I'll think about it."

"Not sure why they haven't done so already."

"You must admit they've had more than their share of turmoil in the past few months." First the entire mess with Cesare taking over, then the battle between their brothers, then the attack upon their Country House, and now the negotiations and massive search for the bones of those fallen in the last Diamond-Spadros War. "They must be all a-flurry."

Morton nodded grudgingly. "I suppose you have a point." He turned to Amelia. "Get her a box, if you please."

Amelia set a box full of files before me, and I set to work.

To my surprise, Cesare Diamond arrived at my apartments late that night, well after dinner. He stood in my parlor with the evening version of the *Bridges Daily* in hand, and pointed at my advertisement with a scowl. "What's this?"

"I'm sorry I didn't ask first. But it'll help if we can get information from the public about the carriage which took your brother."

"You see, that right there is the problem. We never told people of his 'capture.' Only that he was missing. My father has had messages from across the city all evening demanding answers. Our entire quadrant's servants and half the Bridges slums in all four quadrants are distraught and weeping, or furiously throwing things about."

"I don't understand."

"Rumor's run wild. I've never seen its like. They fear that Strangler has taken him, and that he'll soon be found dead. None will be assured otherwise, even when we deny it. They've seen it in the **paper** that he's been taken, and therefore it must be so." His expression turned fierce. "How could you do this without consulting us?"

"I only wanted to help." I felt rather dismayed at the outcome.

"You have not." He threw the paper on the floor and stalked out.

I paced and fretted for a good hour, expecting Tony to arrive next with angry words. Yet he never did so, and finally I went to bed.

The next evening, the *Bridges Daily* released a special edition about Jon's disappearance with a press statement from the Diamonds.

They took questions, and "by chance" one came regarding the Bridges Strangler. "That culprit has been caught, tried, and hanged as his reward," said Cesare, according to the paper. "Our best hope of finding Master Jonathan is calm watchfulness. If you'd like to offer assistance, contact your street captain."

The Memorial

Hundreds came to Anna's memorial, the crowd flowing into the street. Inventor Call and I stood together at the ceremony. He wore dark spectacles, yet it couldn't hide the wetness of his cheeks. "She knew everyone, loved everyone. My only regret in life is not marrying her."

At her graveside, after most had gone, I asked about their betrothal.

He sounded old, tired. "It was sixty years ago, but I remember it like it was yesterday. Her hair was dark and her skin smooth, but she really never changed in all that time," he tapped his chest, "not inside. She said she wouldn't have it. Not me, you understand. She said she was quite fond of me. But marriage? No. She felt it beneath any woman to be ... how did she put it? 'Chained to a man.'" He shook his head. "But I never stopped loving her." At that, his nose reddened and he turned away.

"So how is it you're still betrothed?"

He let out a soft laugh, then took a deep breath. "I think she felt compelled to sign the betrothal papers, either by her mother or perhaps me. But one day she said she wouldn't do it. She never signed papers of release, and I never found anyone to match her. Nor any reason to lose that last bit I had, a signature upon a form. Then I learned of the Magma Steam Generators, and they fascinated me."

He pushed his dark spectacles up on his forehead, his tear-filled eyes far away. "I knew then her refusal was a gift: neither Apprentice nor Inventor can ever marry."

He fell silent for several seconds. "She'd trained under many Tinkerers, but when she was offered Apprentice and saw we'd be there together ... I wonder to this day if that's why she turned it down, so as not to cause me pain." He took out his handkerchief and wiped his spectacles. "It would be in her character."

"Pardon me, Inventor, but I thought betrothal here to be more binding than that."

He smiled. "Yes, I suppose technically we were 'pre-married,' if you will. All the obligations — financial, protection — yet none of the rights. No home, no care, no bed. Yet she never asked for anything, and I hadn't seen her until —" The man actually blushed!

Then I realized the truth. "You were going to see her the day the Family caught you leaving the quadrant." It'd been before I was sent by the Spadros Family to meet with Cesare Diamond.

"I was. After you told me she lived, and where, I had to see her." He peered towards the ground. "I don't regret it."

"If there's anything I can do for you, sir, please let me know."

He nodded, eyes upon my face. "You loved her too."

"As a mother." Grief swelled within me once more. "And as a friend. I never met anyone more alive, ever."

Pain filled his eyes. "And I failed her."

"You mustn't blame yourself, sir." I knew who was to blame. Anna Goren was one more on the list of those dead because of me. "What will you do now?"

"Return to work, I suppose. There's only the matter of her shop."

"I don't understand."

"I have neither the time nor the knowledge to run an apothecary, even if I had the desire to. Yet ... the thought of selling the place she'd worked so hard for to strangers ..." Grief twisted his lined face.

It seemed altogether too much of a burden for this man, old as he was. "I could help you, if you'd let me."

He jerked a bit as if startled. "You? What do you suggest?"

I bit my lip, unsure of what I might offer. "I have ninety dollars. Is that enough? If I purchase the building, I could keep it safe. Surely there's an apothecary I might rent it to so her tools and equipment aren't lost."

He nodded slowly, eyes far away. "Would you take care of her things for me, then?" His face fell. "I don't think I could bear to do it."

I took a deep breath. "I will." I didn't know if I could bear to do it, either, but there was no need to rush the matter. "I'd be honored to aid the Spadros Inventor."

He smiled to himself. "Never thought I'd hear you say that." Then his face changed, as if some thought had come to him. "See if you can find anything in her notes about the Generators. I don't recall any disturbance in her rooms, and the police have released the building to me. But see what you can find. Anything at all could be useful."

***

Amelia and I took a week off to go through Anna's things. Photographs of what looked like her parents and a very young Anna. The parents, elderly even then, were surely now long dead.

Books lay everywhere in her tiny living area. More boxes lay in the basement below. Apothecary formulas, scientific treatises, mechanical diagrams. Dozens of books on the city itself, news articles going back a generation, notebooks full of her spidery hand containing ideas, thoughts on a wide variety of topics.

Then an old brown leather notebook full of what appeared to be some kind of code. I took that with me, thinking I might be able to decipher it.

No one ever found her keys. The only explanation I could see was that whoever murdered her took them, using them to lock the back door. I had the locks changed.

A package in her room addressed to me held my spyglass, perfectly fixed. Yet search as I might, I found no trace of the samples Anna had been working on. Not even the tray they sat upon might be found. And none of her files referenced them.

Could one of the samples she worked on have caused someone to hurt her?

Constable Hanger came by as we inventoried the shop. "Just checking on you," he said. "I have this patrol. So if you need anything, please call."

I nodded. "There was a tray of samples for her to analyze sitting there," I pointed to the counter where the tray once lay. "Were they taken for some reason?"

He shook his head. "Not that I know of. I'll ask the Detective Lead Constable on the case about it."

"I'd appreciate that. She'd been doing some work for me, and I hoped to have her answer by now."

"What sort of work?"

"Analysis of a tea blend. I wanted to know how to reproduce it." I smiled, feeling sad that I had to deceive this man. "I have to make do. Times aren't very easy outside the Family."

His face said he'd run into trouble with the Families on his own.

Amelia held a clipboard, and pointed to a row of bottles, each filled with fluids of varying colors. "What are all these?"

On the bottles lay labels: phenol, chloroform ... "She produced chemical compounds, supplied most of the hospitals in the city." Out of curiosity, I opened the chloroform bottle and sniffed it. "Whoo," I said, quickly replacing the stopper. "Strong stuff." I felt a bit woozy.

Constable Hanger chuckled. "You know they use that for surgical anesthesia, right?"

I fanned the smell away, moving into fresher air. "I can see why!"

Remembering my discussion with Madame Biltcliffe's former shop maid Tenni several weeks back, I kept Anna's clothing. Altered, her purple dresses would be perfect 'half-mourning' garb, and for a while they'd be something to remember her by.

I found a locket with Anna, twenty and smiling, standing beside the Inventor, which I returned to Maxim Call along with her books. He wept when he saw it, clutching the locket to his chest as if in tremendous pain.

I could understand how he felt.

Amelia and I cleaned Anna's living quarters and disposed of the dozens of dried-up wilted flowers outside the shop. Anna's books, notes, and the cards and letters in sympathy were sent to Inventor Call, the shop interior dusted and swept.

All I needed now was for the papers to go through for the sale, so I might find someone to rent it out to.

The Hunt

When I returned to the Courthouse, Beloty had troubling news. "The rest of my brother's medications are gone. The staff claims they don't know where they are." He considered this a moment. "His manservant said that Jon would take the larger bottles then distribute them into his vials on his own. He'd never allow anyone else to do it."

"Really?" That seemed strange to me: Mary always set up my tonic and morning tea.

"Indeed, ever since that manservant of Jack's was killed."

The night I was sold to the Spadros Family twelve years back. I didn't know what to make of it. "There's something you might look into. The guard on duty the day your brother was taken said something strange: that the footman of the carriage he got into was, and I quote, 'the **prettiest** man I've ever seen.' My husband might have mentioned it, I don't know. But he remarked that there might not be too many men in Bridges with that description."

"Right," Beloty said. "I'll talk to the guard."

"There's something else. Has anyone spoken with the main postal office upon Market Center?"

"I don't know."

"Well, if we might let the next shipment go through, and set guards upon it once it leaves the zeppelin station, the next place it'll go is there. Perhaps we might catch the scoundrels when they try to intercept it."

"Good idea," Beloty said. "I'll have my father speak with the Clubbs about it."

As the leaves turned golden, then red, then began to drop, our next few weeks set into a pattern. Morton, Amelia, and I would leave early to continue our search for Albert Sheinwold, returning for tea. After tea, I'd read the daily letter sent from Mr. Blackberry's secretary, along with any communications from Tony or the Keeper's secretary about what they knew of the search for Jonathan Diamond. Then Morton and I would eat dinner and make our plans for the next day.

At first, our mornings were taken up in the Archives room, as we continued to search the files there. Later, our travels took us to speak with someone on the list we'd developed of those who might have wished Mr. Sheinwold harm.

The daily letter from Mr. Blackberry's secretary held lists of observations, mostly nonsense about carriages of gold or silver. Some of the people in Bridges had vivid imaginations: the horses drawing the carriage which had taken Jon spit blood or their eyes were red. "For heaven's sake," I said once. "This one claims they saw wings on the horse's hooves, and the carriage glowed."

Blitz laughed at that one. "Probably took too much Party Time."

That night, to my utter surprise, my father Peedro Sluff showed up at my door.

He refused to come in, so I went out to my front steps holding a lantern, my shawl pulled tight against the cold. "What in the world are you doing here?"

He looked well — what little hair he had left was combed, and he'd gained enough weight to look the same as any other man. His clothes were clean and his eyes clear. "That boy of yours, the one they call Clover. The one with the eye-patch? He comes to my store every week to buy beer. No one's seen him in three." He rubbed the side of his nose. "Police don't care. Thought you should know."

I felt amazed. *Peedro's actually worried for him.* And I remembered the news article. "Thanks for letting me know."

As he set off down the street, I marvelled at how the man who claimed to be my father had changed in the years I'd known him.

Then I thought of Clover, that young man who we'd threatened and used for information, that man who'd saved Morton's life. I went inside, woke up Morton, and told him of my fears.

All he said was, "I'll look into it," then closed the door.

***

The next morning, my Queen's rite appeared. As yet it was just a spotting, and I felt well, but it seemed best to be cautious. I sent word that I'd not meet anyone that day, and did some work around my study. Papers needed filing, bills needed to be paid.

Yet I recalled that day on the sofa beside Jonathan just four weeks prior, and the grief and fear which came upon me caused me to return to my desk and sit weeping.

Would I ever see Jon again? Or was he dead too?

That evening after dinner, Morton asked to speak to me privately. So we stood out on the front steps, just as my father had.

Morton's jaw tightened, his eyes moist. "It's difficult to believe, but Clover's dead. They say he was strangled." He shook his head. "He was a good lad: the boy only wanted to help. He saved my life, and I led him to his death."

"Surely you don't blame yourself?"

"Who else? Now two of the three boys I had charge of are dead, and there's been no sign of the third." He gazed out over the darkened street. "I won't be with you tomorrow at the Archives. I need to find my former employer and give him the news."

I nodded. "I understand."

"And I need to find that little boy, Mrs. Spadros, assuming he's still alive. I feel certain the Red Dog Gang's hunting him."

The Business

It took another week for the papers to go through for the purchase of Anna's shop. When I got the notice that I now owned the building, I placed an advertisement in the *Bridges Daily*:

Apothecary Business For Sale Due To Death Of Owner

Long-standing Market Center Establishment

Excellent Good-Will

Customer List And Current Supplies Included

Equipment And Building For Rental

Includes Living Quarters

Serious Inquiries Only

That accomplished, all I could do was wait. So I returned to my search for Jonathan and for Mr. Sheinwold.

Occasionally, Tony would visit my home with some news: a sighting of a man fitting Jon's description, or some building they'd searched. None of them produced any real leads, but Tony always would say, "I thought it might help," or "I didn't want you to learn of it from someone else."

I encouraged him to visit. I liked sitting with him, and he always had some view or approach which differed in a way which gave me insight, a new item of information to search for.

After one such visit, he had men going to each of the many riverfront villages to set up watches in case anyone should try taking Jonathan across the river by boat.

Another time, he hurried off to have the tunnels under Market Center searched, something the Diamonds hadn't thought of. Several strangled young men were discovered, the bodies many months old, yet no sign of Jonathan was found.

When I heard of this I became certain of Amelia's belief that the Bridges Strangler was still at work.

After several inquiries about Anna's shop, I chose an energetic young man, a Master Mike Pok-Deng, who'd been serving under one of Anna's competitors in Hart quadrant and wished to strike out on his own.

When I gave him the tour of Anna's shop, he gazed about in awe, clasping his hands to his chest. "This is more than I could have ever imagined. And upon Market Center! I'll take it."

I have no idea where the man got the money, but I grudgingly returned to my 'former' lawyer Mr. Doyle Pike to have him make up a lease document.

I'd always wanted to own property, and to see the joy in Master Pok-Deng's eyes upon being the proprietor of Anna's shop made me feel as if something finally went right in my life.

***

It took several weeks to hear back from Mrs. Brenda Trex, the woman at City Hall, who merely wrote asking me to visit.

So on a blustery November morning, Morton, Amelia and I stood in the little office to await her answer. "The card had been misfiled, sorry to say, but I stumbled across it doing another search."

"I appreciate your work," I said. "What have you learned?"

She leaned upon the counter, card in hand. "Laughing Boy Enterprises is owned by another company named Hector Roland, Incorporated." She took out a ledger labeled "H" and opened it at a bookmark. "Again, it has the notation 'same as parent company.'"

"You mean this Hector Roland, Incorporated is owned by another firm as well?"

She nodded. "I'm still looking for the card on that one." She let out a sigh. "The last clerk here was incredibly sloppy." She tapped her temple. "Too old for the post, from what I've heard."

"Sorry to hear that," Morton said. "Do you have any other information on this company?"

She went along the ledger line. "Type of business ..." She checked at the legend at the bottom. "Shipping and receiving." She continued on. "Established ..." Her eyes narrowed. "Wait a minute."

Mrs. Trex hurried to the shelf, taking out the ledger marked "L," then opened it, paging through. Then she stared at me, mouth open. "Both these companies were formed last year."

I pushed forward. "What date? Does it say?"

"June 21st. On both. The same day."

The day after the gun battle at the Old Plaza. I'd broken my foot and become a murderess, if not in truth but in intent.

Seventeen months past, yet it seemed like yesterday. "Do you remember who set up the accounts?"

"No, I wasn't here yet. The man here before me retired a few weeks later. I was hired shortly thereafter. It took me a month just to get the place in order!"

"Thank you," I said. "See what else you can learn."

I left feeling empty, bleak. Somehow, what I'd done that night led to this seizing of a man who I held dear.

Although I knew people named both Hector and Roland, thousands of others with the same name lived in Bridges. The names themselves were as common in Diamond quadrant as a name might possibly be.

Which made me think: could a **Diamond** have taken Jonathan? But if so, why?

Outside the carriage, I stopped, turned to Morton. "We need to have the Court investigators question those living in Diamond first, particularly those with means to begin a business."

Morton nodded. "That'll take talking with Mr. Beloty. The Courthouse isn't far."

As we rode off, I said, "I should've asked the former clerk's name."

"We can come back after we speak with the Keeper, or his secretary," said Morton.

But when we returned, the clerk's face fell at our question. "I'm sorry, I should have told you: he died just a month ago."

***

I sat in the kitchen picking at my dinner. The one person who might identify one of the men who took Jonathan, now most recently and conveniently dead.

Tony had been right: this business had been planned, and likely the planning had begun well before the shootout at the Old Plaza.

Yet I felt sure that if Jon were dead, we'd know: the Bridges Strangler never kept the men long after killing them.

For some reason this disturbed me as much as it eased my mind. Each day, I'd felt fearful of learning in the morning papers that they'd found Jonathan's body.

The next morning, I woke after a dream of glass breaking. Hoof-beats retreated down the street.

The main curtains were open, the inner sheer ones still shut. Bleary-eyed, I put on my robe and peered out of my window, yet saw nothing to indicate what might have happened.

It was a dream, I thought.

I went into my bathroom. When I came out, I heard a carriage ride up, someone alight to the street. Then a horrified gasp.

It sounded like Tony!

I rushed to the front door, flung it open. There indeed stood Tony, staring mouth open at my front steps.

The shattered remains of Jonathan's vials lay there.

The Puzzle

I clasped the front door-frame, feeling faint. Was Jonathan dead?

Then Tony stood beside me, holding a box.

I'd seen this box before. In his room, the day I picked the lock to the side table drawer in his bedroom in Spadros Manor.

The drawer containing all he had of his son Roland.

Tony said, "Can you stand?"

I took a deep breath and nodded.

He opened the box in his hand. Inside were more of Jon's vials, also smashed. And I pictured Tony running upstairs, dumping the mementos of his son upon the bed, rushing here in a panic.

To me.

Mary and Blitz stood by the door, both staring at the broken glass. Blitz looked like he was just wakened, shirt tail out, hair wild. Mary gasped, hands to her mouth.

Tony stumbled, almost fell. Blitz helped him inside, then went back out front.

"I can't bear it," Tony panted, "to think they might've killed him."

Mary and I sat Tony upon my sofa, pale and shaking, and I sat beside him, clutching his hand.

Blitz came in. "They want to prod you into action." In his hand was a card, the same card as I found in the alley. Upon it was typed, "LB."

Tony stared at it, then reached into his pocket. "I found the same."

I gaped at the card in Tony's hand. "Action? For the past eight weeks, we've done nothing but search for him!"

Tony shook his head. "They grow tired of waiting to capture you."

Blitz took a step back. "Is that what they're after?"

Tony nodded. "I feel certain of it."

Realization dawned upon me. "It was never intended to be a search. It's a puzzle. And when we solve it, then Jonathan's ... our reward? What kind of madman are we dealing with?"

"Wait," Tony said. "Vienna Diamond came to call last night."

One of Jonathan's older brothers: the second of the seven, if I remember correctly.

"His brother Beloty told him of your theory that a Diamond might have taken Jon. First, he wished to assure us that the Family had nothing to do with this —"

"I never would have thought so."

Tony nodded. "But something strange had occurred that day. They got word from Azimoff that all packages had been properly labeled, to be sent now to Diamond Manor. They set men to watch the zeppelin station as you suggested. Yet this month's shipment never arrived. So they went again to the Customs office. The package for Jonathan had disappeared from the holding area."

"What?" This scoundrel had someone in Clubb quadrant itself? Then I recalled the split in the Clubb Family, the ones who'd plotted to assassinate Mr. Alexander and his son Lance.

Maybe the Red Dog Gang was behind this after all.

"Fortunately, they'd marked down the address first."

"Let me guess what the address might be: Hector Roland, Incorporated? And the building's empty?"

Tony gaped at me. "How did you know?"

"It's the company which owns this," I pointed to the card, "Laughing Boy Enterprises." There was something else which had kept tickling the back of my mind ever since I'd seen the name upon the ledger.

"What is it?"

"Something ... I don't know. It'll come to me."

Tony snorted in disgust. "Laughing Boy. This Frank Pagliacci now stoops to taunting us!"

"You still think this is the Red Dog Gang?"

"Who else?"

"I'm not convinced it's the Red Dogs doing this."

Tony seemed confused. "Whatever do you mean?"

"Have they ever left these 'LB' cards anywhere?"

"Well, no ..."

"And I never found any of **their** cards at Anna's home, nor in Jon's office, nor in the alley where Jon was last seen. No stamps either. They always do one of those."

"But if this Pagliacci is the Bridges Strangler —"

"He left a stamp in the alley where David Bryce was taken."

Tony fell silent.

"He either doesn't want this connected with him, or he's not the one doing it."

"So where do we go from here?"

I pointed to the box with its shards of glass. "Track Jonathan's medications and we find this kidnapper. That's what he's saying here. He knows we're on to him, and he wants his prize."

Tony snorted. "You."

"I suppose." But something about it bothered me. Not Amelia, nor Honor, nor even Morton could protect me from an organized gang bent upon kidnapping. "I still fear some deeper intent than simply to capture me. Or he would have done so already."

"In the midst of Spadros quadrant? In sight of a dozen men?"

Tony had **that** many guarding me? "I must see these addresses. Perhaps they left clues for me that we can exploit to our advantage."

***

The next day, Tony and I left Amelia at my apartments. With a letter from Beloty allowing us into Diamond quadrant and escorted by a dozen Spadros men, Tony and I went with Jonathan's older brother Moretti to visit the first of the addresses a shipment had been sent to.

The third of the brothers, Mr. Moretti was perhaps seven years my elder and shared Jon's dark, dark skin, yet more resembled his father. As a Diamond Heir with a wife and sons he must have been entirely busy. Yet that day, it seemed he preferred nothing better than to follow along.

We pulled up to a tired warehouse in the Diamond slums. Rooms of dust upon old rotting boards, rusted nails sticking up through them. A bit of wire here, a scrap of paper there. Nothing that in any way gave clue to where Jonathan might be.

I collected each item I could using tweezers into a small paper bag brought for that purpose, examining the walls, the floors, as Tony watched. Then I went outside, looking round the building.

Weeds grew high. Trash lay strewn about, decaying into the soft soil. A playbill had been recently plastered upon the front of the left wall, and I took down the inscription:

Meeting For Enterprising Traders!

Jacksonville Hall

Fridays, 11 AM

Admission Free

After Tony sent one of his men to let the Diamond men for that block know we were done there — and report to Roy, I suppose — we went to the next building on the list.

Hector Roland, Incorporated lay upon the other side of the Main Road, in equally poor condition. But when I stepped into the room, my foot crunched upon glass: the shards of a large medication bottle. I tried to read the fragment of label, yet the letters had been rubbed off.

"That's the sort of bottle Jonathan's medication comes in," Moretti said. "Before he puts it into those vials of his."

Tony said, "What does it mean?"

I knelt to sniff a shard. No scent remained, and the inside was dry. I stood, looking around. "It must've been put here recently; surely Mr. Vienna would have mentioned stepping upon a medication bottle."

Tony and Moretti both nodded. Then Tony said, "The scoundrel wishes us to find him."

Upon one wall, the boards jutted out, just a bit. I recalled the closet in Anna's home, and pressed upon the board. A portion of wall swung out with a click. A handle was fixed to the inside. What the area contained: the remains of a man, long dead.

The Clues

I jumped back. "Ugh!"

Garments of a working-man's fashion perhaps thirty years past lay in tatters upon dried skin and bones, covered by crumbling newspaper. What remained of his right hand clutched an empty bottle of whiskey.

"Been there for decades," Tony said.

Moretti shook his head. "Some poor sot using this closet as his bedroom who fell dead in their drink. You find these often, this close to the Pot."

Tony drew back, staring at Moretti in horror.

I marveled at how unaware Tony was of the realities of life.

Tony said, "Shouldn't we have him buried?"

I clicked the panel shut. It was unlikely anyone still searched for him. And we didn't need to spend the day dealing with the police. "That resting place is as good as any."

We turned to inspect the rest. No further bodies nor any clues lay in the building. But the glass indicated that our villain had been here, and recently. I turned to Moretti. "Where is this Jacksonville Hall?"

Moretti nodded. "I'll show you."

Jacksonville Hall looked like it had been a small theater in its day. Yet the floor tiles were cracked, the paint peeling. The stage had moldering red velvet drapes and a sign reading "KEEP OFF".

Rough wooden tables stained by years of use stood at intervals. Elderly folk sat here and there at them, mostly women. Faded paper decorations hung on the walls. A table off to the left held a chipped teapot and a plate of cookies. A clipboard hung on the wall nearby.

Two older women wearing widow's brown poured tea for those seated. A third widow woman in her middle years wearing a tan apron came over to greet us. "Are you here for mancala?"

"No," Moretti said. "What goes on here?"

She smiled. "Entertainment for the aged." She lowered her voice. "It's a good place for people without young families to bring their elderly when they need to do their shopping. You know, the ones who tend to wander." Her tone became bright. "A different game every hour. Sometimes young people from the local groups come to sing." She peered at Moretti. "Do I know you, sir? You look familiar."

Moretti held out a hand. "Moretti, Diamond Heir, madam, at your service." He didn't introduce us, which seemed for the best.

The woman gaped at him, then took his hand, curtsying low. "An honor, sir, a true honor. What ... how may I serve you?"

Moretti said, "We're investigating the Keeper's disappearance. At a place we were looking into, we found a recent playbill advertising a business meeting here. Fridays at eleven?"

She shrugged. "The only thing we have here right then is Derrah. That's a popular one."

I said, "Derrah?"

Moretti turned to me. "Another game." Then he smiled at the woman. "Thank you; you've been most helpful." He made as if to leave then stopped. "How's this place funded?"

"Through the Dealers, sir, and charitable contribution. But I'm a volunteer, we all are." She reached into a pocket of her apron and brought out a card. "If you'd like to make a donation, here's the address."

Moretti said, "Thank you, we'll certainly consider it."

The sky outside was hazy blue. "So the playbill was false."

Moretti nodded.

"May I see her card?" I couldn't think of any other reason the men who took Jonathan would want us to come here.

The card was cream-colored with black lettering:

Jacksonville Hall Fund

11 Fish Hook Lane

Diamond, Bridges

"Preserve The Past, Preserve Our Future"

Number Eleven Fish Hook Lane was a tiny storefront with the exact lettering as the card upon the door's glass upper panel and an elderly man behind a desk. "Good day," he said, "how may I help?"

The room smelled of coffee. "What is it you do here?"

"Collect and record donations to the Jacksonville Hall Fund. Answer inquiries and order supplies. I go once a week to make sure enough volunteers have signed up."

Moretti said, "And where do you get your volunteers?"

Disinterested in the old man's answer, I gazed around the tiny room. A stack of brochures about the history of the Hall lay upon the man's desk. An ancient poster about a show called "The Messenger" hung on the wall neatly framed behind glass.

"The Dealers help us tremendously," the old man said. "We'd not be able to keep open without them. We're hoping to have the building declared of historical value."

We'd been sent to that place for a reason. And then here. Why?

I glanced over at Tony. He'd been watching the old man and Moretti Diamond converse, his face fondly amused.

I'd expected him to be bored or even annoyed, feeling this discussion and scrutiny all too tedious. Yet he seemed content to stand there forever.

I pointed at the poster. "What's that show about?"

The old man replied, "That one? A young man goes searching for his missing lover. It's quite exciting! One of my favorites."

A missing persons case. The comparison seemed a bit too close to home for me.

"Thank you, sir," Moretti said, reaching for his wallet. "I'd like to make a contribution to the fund."

Afterward, Moretti led us outside. "Did you find anything which might help?"

Laughing Boy Enterprises. Hector Roland, Incorporated. Jacksonville Hall. A show about a missing person called The Messenger. Number 11 Fish Hook Lane. A lot of "jack" references, as in the Holy Cards. Which reminded me of when Joseph Kerr called Jonathan a "spare jack."

Were the scoundrels trying to remind me that Jack Diamond had been captured as well?

But why? Was that supposed to dismay me? Or were they angry that nothing about Jack's disappearance was in the papers?

Perhaps that had dismayed **them**. I felt pleased at this thought.

Then there was the dead man behind the wall, most likely a coincidence. The broken glass, all from medicine bottles. The glass seemed important, but how? "I don't know."

Tony let out a laugh. "And this searching ... it actually helps you?"

Normally, Tony speaking like this would annoy me, but looking at the day from his perspective, I could see how he might doubt it. I doubted it myself, many a time, until the last piece of the puzzle fell into place. "Most of what I do is talking to people, looking at things. Something that no one else thinks is important is often what helps me find someone."

Tony nodded, face thoughtful.

Moretti said, "Would you care to go anywhere else? If so, I'll need to send a message. I promised my boys I'd be home for tea."

This touched me. "That won't be necessary, sir. Thank you."

On the way back to my apartments, I pondered Tony's question a bit more. What could I glean from what I'd observed so far? "About what you said earlier. Someone took Jon for a reason. You believe it's to entrap me."

Tony nodded.

I touched the metal butterflies now decorating my over-corset. "This may be true. But it makes no sense to be so obvious about it. Does he think I'm just going to hand myself over? And why now? What happened to cause him to undergo all this effort to take Jon in the first place?"

"I have no idea."

"If he merely wished to kidnap me, why, Amelia or Honor or even Master Rainbow couldn't stop him. Your dozen men couldn't stop a true effort." I frowned, shaking my head. "I can't see how it's merely about kidnapping." I sighed, trying to put the information I had together somehow, and failing. "Kidnap Jon, to gain ... me?"

"Then me, I suppose, when I came after you."

I shrugged. "Then why not just take **you**? It would be more difficult, true. But not impossible. Why take a sick man who needs medications which can be traced and tracked ..."

"There's something about you in particular he wants," Tony said.

A chill went down my back at his words. Some man who thought that because I stood separate from the Family that I was vulnerable to attack? Or a delusional fiend, some pitiful creature who fancied that this capture would prove his love for me?

For an instant, I felt grateful for my boot-knife, pistol, garrote wire, and morning tea.

But no: the idea was too simple, what he did, too complex. "Then why not capture me and be done with it?"

Tony shook his head. "This man ... men, you said two were with the carriage, so at least those two ... they play a dangerous game. All Four Families and the Court search for them, not to mention the police. How can they hope to escape with their lives?"

"Perhaps they don't. If their leader is some deluded fool, he may be desperate to make some final gesture." I shuddered. "I best not think of that: it frightens me."

"Jacqui, have you considered coming home? Just until we find Jonathan. If these men's goal is to capture you —"

"I'm perfectly fine where I am."

"— they might tire of this game and seize you directly. That's what frightens me."

I stared at him, surprised. He often seemed nervous, or afraid. But he seldom actually said so, and never since I'd left him.

"You think you're fine there, but you're not. This whole thing ... it's wrong. It's a poor example to our women, our quadrant's children." He pointed at my threadbare skirt, where yet another hole was forming. "And you'll be better at the Manor, Jacqui." He sat, elbows to knees and head down, hands clasped in front of him. "I was wrong to give you so little to live on. I felt angry and hurt, and ... back at the cottage, I lied. I did want you to suffer."

I swallowed, unsure what to say.

"But it was hateful. It was unkind. You've suffered so much already." He turned his face towards me. "I just want to make your life better. Not harm you or ... or cage you. Help you. You've helped so many people. Won't you let anyone help **you**?"

Jonathan had said the same thing, many a time. "It's not that. I just couldn't stand it there. Every bit of my day was planned — I had no life of my own. I felt I couldn't breathe."

"Oh, Jacqui ... can you not make your life anywhere? Why must you do it there?"

"Because I own it. I can be myself there. I'm not pressed into someone else's mold. I feel free." I gazed out of the window. He just didn't understand. "I do appreciate your coming with me today."

Tony smiled to himself, just a little, but he seemed sad. "I'm grateful to see a bit of your work. It's much different than I imagined."

"What did you imagine?"

"More ... dramatic somehow."

I chuckled to myself. "You've been reading too many novels."

His cheeks colored, and he smiled to himself once more.

"Would you like to see my spyglass? Anna managed to fix it." *Before she was murdered.* I felt more than a bit melancholy.

"Of course."

So I moved to sit beside him, retrieved the little case from my handbag, showed him how it extended, the various forms of magnification.

"This is exquisite," Tony said. "So this is for very small clues."

I closed the spyglass, stowing it away. Then I placed my hand upon his, feeling fondness for him. "I just try different things and see where they lead me." The carriage pulled up to my door, and Tony's footman Alan opened it. "But you'd be surprised how something very small can solve a case."

The Constable

I went inside my apartments, thinking of Jonathan and Sheinwold, and where they might be.

I'd never met the former Detective Constable Albert Sheinwold, and apart from a portrait done by the police department, had no image of him in my mind.

But Morton had paid me to find him and by the gods, I would. After dinner, I asked Morton to sit with me in the parlor.

Morton seemed surprised, almost wary. "What can I do for you?"

He didn't often sit in the parlor, other than to read over by the bookcase, so to see him on my sofa seemed odd. "I feel as though we've been conducting our own separate investigations on Mr. Sheinwold. Is there anything you've found that you perhaps haven't told me? It might be best if we go over the entirety of the matter."

I wanted this man found, this case out of the way, so I might better search for Jon. Yet I knew that to Morton, this man's recovery was just as vital to him as finding Jonathan was to me.

Morton nodded, leaning his elbows on his knees. "Well, the matter started ... it must be four or five years ago now. He'd been doing work for the Spadros Family for a while, and was getting as much into Party Time as he was that."

I nodded, remembering the story Mr. Jake Bower gave me of my father Peedro Sluff's descent into Party Time addiction. In spite of Mr. Bower working with Frank Pagliacci, I hoped Mr. Bower had managed to give Cesare Diamond enough to gain his release.

If Mr. Bower had fallen into Jack Diamond's hands, well, Mr. Bower was probably dead by now.

"What Sheinwold told Constable Hanger was that he met Zia Cashout at a bar while with a horse-truck full of Tommy-guns."

"The ones they used to kill our men."

"And the Diamond men as well. In any case, she took him to her place and he was Timing right in front of her. Long story short, she got the shipment, and he had to work for her or she'd take him to Hub to stand trial for cultural contamination."

"The Tommy-guns."

"That's how he learned she was one of the Feds."

"Well," I said. "That's a situation." If the Family even thought Sheinwold was informing on them to the Feds ...

Morton gave me a startled glance, and for a moment, it seemed as if he'd lost his train of thought. Then he shook himself, focusing upon me. "Yeah. So he's doing that for a couple of years then she tries to kill him. And all her other informants, apparently."

"Just like with yours."

Morton glanced away. "Rumor has it she killed her own partner."

"Good gods." What could drive a woman to such murder? Betraying your own kind was one thing, but ...

Then I recalled she was in love with Frank Pagliacci. "I suppose she felt she had to make an entire break with the Feds. Not one person could connect her to them."

Morton froze, eyes narrowing. "I just had a disturbing thought. Even in Bridges, if someone hears a rumor you're with the Feds, well, it might make the Family not trust you, but ..." he shrugged.

"It could get you killed if the wrong person heard of it."

"But what I mean to say is: for someone not in the Family, who merely hands over their Family fees each month, a rumor's no great matter. There are any number of places one might hide, or even live out a perfectly normal life. In the countryside, perhaps, or if you know someone, upon Market Center. But for someone intending to be in the public eye ..."

"You think Zia aspires to some great office." Then I made the connection: Mayor Freezout was old, sick. "Frank Pagliacci wishes to run for Mayor."

"And Zia wants to be at his side when he does so."

This made the notion that Frank Pagliacci was behind Jonathan's capture even less likely. Why chase after me, going so far as to seize the Keeper of the Court, if his alliance with Zia stood firm?

Unless this alliance was firmer in Zia's mind than his. "So she must keep her spot secure if she's not to become a liability to them."

"Yes," Morton said. "If what you've told me of this Black Maria is true, anyone no longer useful to them ends up dead."

Something occurred to me. "They know you're here. The Four Families like you, for the most part. Despite Zia's attempts to smear your name, you're well received. She knows you're the one person who might be believed if you were to accuse her. Why did her '"goons,"' as you call them, not just —" Then I saw the error of my logic and fell silent.

"Just throw a bomb in the window when I first moved here and be done with it? Beats me."

"Forgive me: I know why. Two years past, before I left my husband, I managed to decipher a note I found in my friend's hand as she lay dying. It was the night before the zeppelin explosion, you recall, when that woman Birdie shot at you." We'd later learned 'Birdie' and Black Maria were one and the same.

Morton nodded.

"Well, the note said, 'he wants you.' Apparently this is why they've not just shot me and been done with it."

"He who?"

"Well, that's the thing. It could be anyone: Pagliacci, Freezout — although I can't see that, the man hates me."

"Anyone else?"

Did I dare say it? "Mr. Charles Hart has been most persistent in his attempts to win me to his side."

Morton raised an eyebrow. "So while the rumors are true, they're not entirely accurate."

"What rumors?"

"Of Mr. Hart arriving at all hours while I was away, sending roses, gifts ..." He appeared abashed. "I thought them scurrilous gossip, particularly that you might encourage this sort of behavior."

"Well, that's good."

Morton gave me a wry smile. "He doesn't quite seem your type."

That amused me. "He **is** rather old."

We sat like this as the fire cracked and sputtered. And I thought: if Zia is trying to remove everyone who knows she's a Fed, yet she can't remove Morton as long as he's around me, then the first thing she'd want to do is to separate us. Could this have been behind Charles Hart urging me to leave my apartments? To create an opening for them to attack the apartments and drag Morton away?

Whilst Tony's motivation for asking me to return to the Manor had been clear, Roy's was even more so: he'd only ever wanted me so Tony might have an heir.

At first, I believed Charles Hart to be so besotted with me as to perform all the scandal Morton mentioned. Yet he'd seemed taken aback at the shooting, Anna's murder.

And the thought that his son might have been behind Jonathan's disappearance sent him into a rage.

The Harts are divided, I thought.

Perhaps at first, Charles Hart had thought the beating of Tony and the theft of our Party Time would strike a blow at his enemy Roy. But with his son Etienne becoming involved, it seemed to have gotten out of Mr. Hart's control.

Morton leaned back. "I've thought for a while that the issue hasn't been Zia killing Sheinwold, or this Frank Pagliacci holding him, but rather him hiding from us all." He let out a breath. "I fear the more publicly we search for Sheinwold, the more wary he'll become."

Hiding from everyone, for over two years? How had he been living? "He's got to have help. Someone has to have given him a job, or a place to stay."

"Yet no one will say so." Morton seemed glum. "Either they're all excellent liars or they truly haven't seen him."

And the last time Morton had gotten word of a sighting, it'd been a trap he'd barely escaped from.

Morton said, "But I suspect Constable Hanger is helping him, or at least has done so in the past." He shook his head. "The man's too honest for this place."

"Can the Constable not persuade him to help? Sign some paper or ... perhaps the Feds would take him from the city to testify." I couldn't believe I was encouraging someone to cooperate with the Feds, but if it would help Morton's case, it seemed reasonable.

"I'll ask. The man denies seeing him. And he's helped a great deal."

I snorted. "Getting yourself into an investigation is a fine way of knowing the direction it might take. If Mr. Sheinwold truly doesn't want to be found, it's the best way to do it."

Morton clapped a hand to his forehead. "I've been a fool. I should have explained the situation to the Constable at once."

"You never told him that the Feds are after you? That Sheinwold is the only man who can testify about Zia's murders?"

"He knows that last part from Sheinwold. No, I never told the Constable **why** I wanted to find Sheinwold, just that I was a friend who needed to speak with him." He hesitated. "I wasn't sure who I might trust, then later, he seemed to be grateful to help so I never thought there was a need to say more. I see now I was wrong."

Constable Hanger probably suspected Morton was working for Zia, particularly with their similar accents.

Zia had a very strong accent, which I'd been told was from an area of Dickens. "Little Island," or some such thing.

Morton's accent only ever came out when he was excited, or upset, or injured. But it'd only take once to make a man who was already wary, decidedly mistrustful. "You must tell Constable Hanger the truth. All of it. And if something happens to me, you're not safe here. Find a place to flee to now, before you have need."

Morton nodded. "If something were to happen to you, Miss Zia Cashout would be the least of my worries."

The Lawyer

Mr. Hambir Dashabatar came to call the next day. A lawyer friend of Major Blackwood's, I suspected that he wished to inquire once again about the letter I'd received from the Major before his murder.

My suspicions were correct.

"Mrs. Spadros, I know that the Major investigated your friends."

"Oh?"

"Yes. The detective on the case contacted me yesterday and asked that I see you."

Hmm, I thought.

"I understand now why you were hesitant to show me his letter. I assume it mentioned your friends by name."

I said nothing.

"If I might see the letter?"

"Who exactly was he investigating? Before I subject anyone to further inquiry, I'd like to know if the letter has any relevance."

"Well, that's one of the questions he has. You see, the only person registered using the surname in question is a five-year-old boy."

I stared at him, startled, recalling the little boy with Joseph Kerr's eyes that Jonathan showed me over a year back.

Mr. Dashabatar sounded surprised. "You know of whom I speak."

Wait, I thought. Joe, Josie, their grandfather — they weren't registered using their real names?

Jonathan had told me: *Not even the boy's great-grandfather uses his real name here.* And now what he'd said next made perfect sense. Why **would** she name her son this, if Joe hadn't urged her to do so?

"Mrs. Spadros?"

His voice startled me. "Yes, sir?"

He spoke kindly. "Might I see the letter?"

He knows.

"I could possibly get a court order, but of course, your Family would make it disappear. Why don't you save yourself a lot of time and trouble?" The man cast about, as if searching for what to say. "I mean your people no harm. I just want to learn who killed my friend."

That felt too close to home. "Of course, sir — let me get it for you." Leaving him sitting in my parlor, I found Major Blackwood's letter amongst a pile of old mail. And I read it once more:

> ... news has come to me that you have allied yourself with the Kerr family. I must beg you to reconsider.
>
> You may not understand the depth of information I have gathered on this topic, but I have just sent a package which will enlighten you.
>
> My dear, do not be dismayed; we all make mistakes in our choice of allies. But for your sake and the sake of your Family, reconsider. For I fear a storm approaches, and I don't wish you and those you love to be caught up in it.

Something wasn't right. I put the letter in my pocket and returned to him. "Do you know a man named Frank Pagliacci?"

By the startlement upon his face, it seemed he did.

I'd been right. "I suspected you had the *True Story.*"

The man's face moved from horror to confusion to dread. He leaned forward. "Who else listens?"

"My people are trustworthy, sir. And believe me, I wish no repeat of our friend's fate. But if you prefer, we can have that conversation elsewhere." I handed him the letter. "Tell me about Frank."

"He looks pleasant, but in reality, he's a scoundrel! I dare not say more. In the year before his death, Major Blackwood had particularly sharp disagreement with the man." Mr. Dashabatar looked over the page. "I don't understand his interest in this, though."

"The Major never spoke of it?"

"No." He seemed dismayed. "Why did he never share it?"

"Possibly to keep you from harm." This man was one of the few still alive who'd seen Frank Pagliacci. "Are you with a Family?"

"I live on Market Center."

"You must go at once to the police station on Market Center and ask for Constable Hanger. Don't leave until you've spoken to him, no one else. He's the only one I trust. Tell him — and only him — that it's about the Bridges Strangler."

Mr. Dashabatar paled. "What?"

"Tell him everything. Insist on having a portrait done of Frank Pagliacci, now, tonight."

He blinked slowly. "You believe Mr. Pagliacci to be the Strangler?"

"I do, and you may tell the Constable I said so. But you must go at once. You're one of the few who can identify the man, and nothing must happen to you."

He rose quickly. "I will. Thank you, madam." He made to go to the door, then stopped. "Do you know what name the Kerrs might be registered under?"

I considered the matter. "Their uncle was named Shigo Rei." There was another name, but at the time, I couldn't remember it. "If I think of anything else, I'll let you know."

He grabbed my hands in his. "You have helped me immeasurably." And with that, he rushed out.

After the door was shut, I said, "I hope so." I had a sudden deep fear that this would be the last I saw of him.

Blitz came strolling up the hall, and I turned to him. "Mr. Dashabatar. He came in a carriage, right?"

Blitz nodded.

That made me feel better: at least the man had some protection.

A lawyer who could identify Frank Pagliacci! With this man as a witness, we could post his portrait, see who else recognized him.

Maybe we might finally learn who the man really was.

The Changes

The next morning, I felt tired, and my head hurt.

The morning paper read:

PREPARATION CONTROVERSY

Mayor Denies Yuletide Quadrant Funding

This year's request from the four quadrants for funding to decorate the city next month for Yuletide has been denied.

Hart quadrant merchant Mr. Spotter King, president of the Bridges Merchants' Society, told this reporter, "These funds hire cutters to trim the Hedge for yew and holly, as well as artists to craft our Yuletide decor. We've received no word as to why the funding request has been rejected."

A source in the Mayor's office quoted the Mayor as saying, "Let them get the money from those scoundrels, if they need it so badly."

With Yuletide only two weeks away, merchants across the city would have been scrambling to secure funding but for the help from their neighborhood benefactors.

I chuckled at "neighborhood benefactors." A rather nice way to refer to the Families!

Why would the Mayor do this so close to Yuletide? Was the city really so short of funds? Or was this a distraction, like all the rest, to keep people from the city's lack of progress at finding Jon?

Mary came in with my regular tea and toast. "Will you be needing the carriage today?"

Ever since I'd drunk my morning tea and tonic, I felt a bit queasy. "I don't know. I'm not feeling entirely well."

"Perhaps you should rest then," Mary said. "Would you like breakfast in here?"

I smiled up at her. "That sounds lovely."

Then I remembered. "Has Mr. Dashabatar sent any message?"

"I'll ask my husband when he gets up." She made to leave, then stopped. "He did mention something: when he went to see your friend ... I believe his name was Vig. Is that right?"

"Blitz talked to Vig?"

"Yes, mum, he did. He said to tell you he was ever so grateful for the piano. Mr. Roy's men brought it to his saloon yesterday. They tuned it and everything."

My eyes stung, both at hearing from Vig and from Roy's gesture. *Maybe Roy really has changed.* "Mr. Roy sent it? Truly?"

Mary smiled. "He did, mum."

I felt stunned.

"I'll leave you to your paper, then," Mary said, and left.

Why was Roy doing this?

***

Amelia arrived and began fussing over me. Morton left for the day.

After my breakfast, and lying down a bit, I felt better. I got up, bathed, dressed, put my coat on, went to the hall. "I'm going out front." I wanted to smell the air, feel the sun upon my face.

"Very well, mum," Amelia said from my bedroom.

I took the key from its hook, put it in my pocket, then opened the door. The day was sunny and cold, a few clouds high above the shimmer of the dome. I leaned on my railing, looking out over the neighborhood.

A noise to my left startled me: Joseph Kerr came out from the alley, cigarette in hand.

"My goodness, Joe, whatever are you doing there?" He'd never stood out here like this before, so far as I knew.

He shrugged. "I hoped I'd see you." He seemed somber, pensive.

"Would you like to come in?"

"I prefer it out here."

Silence fell, but it didn't feel awkward. It reminded me of those days back in the Cathedral, when we'd talk beside the steps there.

Joe reached out his hand holding the cigarette, and I came down a few steps to take it, smiling at the memory of how often we'd done this before. I took a drag from it, handed it back.

I sat on the stair, patted the step. "Sit with me."

He sat, perhaps a foot or so away, and we shared the cigarette.

The street was quiet. A bird flew overhead. "I hope Josie's well."

"She is." Joe sounded bleak. "Planning her wedding."

I snorted softly. "Sounds about right." If I knew Josie at all, she'd have it planned to the second.

Then I felt bitter. I had very little to do with mine: Roy and Molly orchestrated it.

"I miss you, Jacqui."

I nodded, not sure what to say.

"That's all I wanted to tell you." His shoulders slumped. "I love you so much. I tried so hard to help my family. But now I feel as if I've ruined everything." He glanced over. "Between us."

I gave a small shrug. I wasn't sure I believed him when he said he loved me. How could he love me and do the things he'd done? But I understood the feeling of having ruined everything. At times, I felt much the same. Yet things had changed so much between us that I wasn't sure if there was anything left to ruin.

He leaned forward, arms upon his knees, holding his cap in both hands. The patch of brown curls upon his chin glinted golden. "You're different." He let out a breath. "I suppose we've all changed, with everything that's happened." His head drooped over his clasped hands. "I don't even know what's happened to make you this way."

I felt amused. "And what way is that?"

He gave a small shake of his head. "I don't know. I don't want to argue. It's just ... it hurt so much to hear you speak of someone I barely know as your dearest friend. I feel so alone." He hesitated. "I wish I were your friend once more."

A touch of fond pity, and on impulse, I rested my hand on his back. "You are." I moved my hand to my knee once more. "But you're right. So much has gone on. Most, I can never speak of."

Joe nodded. "Family business. I understand."

"We're not children anymore, Joe." I sighed. Oh, that we were. "I learned something strange yesterday."

"What?"

"You're not registered in the city."

"I don't understand."

"You, Josie, your grandpa. There's no record of you here."

Joe's eyes met mine, and at his steady gaze, a bolt of electricity went through me. "I don't understand. I thought Mr. Hart took care of all that when he sponsored us into his quadrant." He glanced away for an instant, then back. "Is that bad? Are we in danger?"

I watched him carefully. "So you don't use any other names?"

He didn't flinch, or glance away; his gaze was innocent as a child's. "I've never even considered it. Why would I? What name would I even use? I have nothing to hide."

Relief washed over me: Mr. Dashabatar had to be mistaken.

He sighed, leaning his elbows upon his knees. "Josie wants to know when you'll be coming to call again."

I smiled to myself. "As soon as I can." I stood, stepped on the cigarette. "I best get back to work."

The Questions

While I sat in my study setting up my Family fees for November, a letter arrived from Mrs. Trex at City Hall. "Amelia!"

The clack of her boots came up the hall. "Yes, mum?"

"I'll need to go to Market Center after all."

"Yes, mum." Amelia closed the door.

I went back to the matter of Family fees. Thirty-three cents for my street, then ... I looked through my bank statements. Ten percent of the first and last months' rent from that apothecary ... and that was it.

I hadn't gotten any clients that month, or the last month either. Or, I suddenly realized, since before Jonathan Diamond disappeared.

It wasn't entirely strange — I did sometimes go a spell without new clients, but I hadn't gone almost three months without one for some time. I might have to consider new ways to gain clients.

I got out my handbag and put the money in an envelope for Blitz to bring to Mr. Howell in the morning.

Amelia came back in. "What are you doing sitting here?"

"It'll be a while before the carriage arrives."

"No, it's at the corner! They've been by that saloon since they returned from Market Center."

I hurried into my bedroom to change. Then I brought the envelope to Blitz, who walked Amelia and me to the carriage, which, as she'd said, sat upon Scoop Street.

At the carriage, Amelia said, "Mum, I got word my daughter is sick again, very much so. Might I —"

"Of course, Amelia. Go see to your little girl. I'm just off to Market Center; I should be fine."

When I got to City Hall, Mrs. Trex said, "Oh, it's you! I have the information you wanted right here." She piled several ledgers upon the counter. "After we last spoke, I went through everything to see what businesses were formed upon that same day." She pushed a sheet of paper towards me. "I made a list."

All Fours Realty

Cribbage Textiles Co.

Hector Roland, Inc.

Johnson Brothers, Inc.

Knaves Shipping

Laughing Boy Enterprises

Included with these were the addresses for each of the buildings. "Thank you," I said. "This is most helpful."

"Well," she said, "you won't believe what else I learned. The interesting thing about these is that when I researched Hector Roland, Incorporated, I found it was owned by Johnson Brothers, and so on. All these companies are owned by one of the others!"

I realized my mouth hung open, and closed it. "And the owner of the top-most one?"

"Why, let me see ..." She rummaged through the cards she held.

"A Mr. Kajiso Oyn, mum. I have an address here, but it's the same as Cribbage Textiles."

"That's where he'll be," I said, almost to myself.

Kajiso Oyn. What a strange name. I wondered who this man was, how he played into all this. Was he a collaborator in Jonathan's kidnapping, or the kidnapper himself?

Or was he just being used as someone to pin the blame on should things go astray? Nothing in this town surprised me anymore.

"I would imagine, mum."

I looked over the list, feeling excited at finally getting some new clues. "You've been most helpful!"

"Well, it's been a bit slow, and the tabloids just don't appeal to me as they used to." She pushed aside the one she'd held, which still lay upon the counter. "It's no trouble at all."

I found Morton and Constable Hanger at the Archives Room and told them the news. "I imagine the Diamonds will want to approach this Mr. Kajiso Oyn on their own. But Knaves Shipping is in Spadros."

Constable Hanger said, "Oh? Where?"

When I gave him the address, he said, "That's an old warehouse. Several of them over there. It was just outside my beat, but I could see the buildings from 6th when I patrolled." It seemed that the memory was a fond one. "Nobody's been there for years, so far as I know."

Most likely another abandoned building. I turned to Morton. "Well, it's on the way home, so I'll take Honor and investigate."

"Sounds good," Morton said. "Want to work on some files now, or have lunch?"

Lunch? I almost laughed at making the word short like that. Morton could be so inventive at times. "Let's eat."

We ate luncheon at the Badugi bistro nearby, one of many in the city. Morton set up the tab. While Morton and I had tea, the Constable had himself a small mug of ale with a satisfied grin. "I'm off-duty, and since you're buying ..."

When Morton went to the Men's Room, I said to the Constable, "Why are you hiding Sheinwold?"

The man froze. "Who says I am?"

"You do know he's a Family man, don't you? They can protect him from this woman Zia, or whoever might be hunting him."

"Perhaps there's something you should know."

I said nothing, just watched him.

"Your in-laws were at Anna Goren's shop the day she died."

"They were?"

"Yes, not an hour before."

That was why Roy looked so alarmed at news of her death. Why was he there?

"There are a lot of questions, Mrs. Spadros, but no one seems to want to offer any answers."

"Like what?"

"What were in the samples you mentioned your friend working on, for one. Who cut her after she'd died."

So he knew at least something of her case.

"Roy Spadros would frighten anyone. Yet this woman Zia scares Sheinwold more. Possibly the only thing in this world that does. I doubt he'd even consider it."

Sheinwold didn't trust his own Family to protect him?

And I recalled when Zia chased me through that alley, I hid in Anna's shop. Could Zia have killed Anna as revenge for hiding me?

But that was two years ago. Why hurt her now?

"And your husband?" The Constable shook his head. "He's little more than a boy. Even with that thug at his side, he's no match for what I've seen so far."

Me and Tony were the same age, so I suppose this should have offended me. But the Constable was so old — at least forty — that perhaps we looked like children to him. "I can't see this going well if Mr. Sheinwold refuses to be helped." I leaned forward. "At least have him give Master Rainbow some statement of what he knows. For insurance, should they find him. Perhaps it might keep him alive."

"If I should somehow see him, I'll give him that advice."

I let out a soft snort. *Men.* "You can trust Master Rainbow. He works for them all, but I don't think he's aligned with anyone."

"That's exactly what I'm afraid of."

"What do you mean?"

"The fact that you don't know his loyalties after all this time is what concerns me." He leaned back, relaxed. "Me, I'm a cop living on Market Center. You know where I stand. That's important in a place like this."

"Yet you're sitting here with the Lady of Spadros."

"And that you name yourself so tells me all I need to know."

The Warehouse

As we strolled back to the Archives Room, I wondered at what the Constable had said. Clearly he still didn't trust Morton, despite all assurances to the contrary.

We got through the rest of the files, and I stacked the last one in its box with a sigh. "Now to find all these men." But could we even help Albert Sheinwold, all at cross-purposes as we were? Feeling weary, I handed Morton the list. "Good luck."

One look at Morton's face told me that he hadn't spoken with the Constable yet. "Thanks," he said. Then he said to Constable Hanger, "Might I have a word?"

I said, "Home for dinner?"

Morton glanced over his shoulder. "Yes, I'll be there."

I went to the carriage. "The Courthouse, if you will." I needed to give Beloty the list and have him speak with his father about how best to approach this Mr. Kajiso Oyn, to learn what he knew.

By then it was almost tea-time. Beloty was still in court, so I waited there in Jonathan's office for him to finish.

Mr. Hardeman brought tea and sandwiches from the Courthouse cafeteria just as Beloty arrived. Beloty and I took tea at Jon's desk as we discussed what I'd learned.

After I went through everything, Beloty sat still for several moments. Then he rose. "Your instincts are good. I'll recommend going in force, yet speaking gently. Mr. Oyn is likely to be a businessman who rented the buildings out and knows nothing of Jon's capture. But he may be willing to offer up the names of those behind this outrage," at that, he winked at me, "in exchange for his life."

Amused, I went back out to the front steps. The day had turned overcast and night had fallen. I handed the Spadros warehouse address to Honor. "Let's look at this place on the way back."

"Yes, mum."

I got inside, he shut the door, and we went moving along.

I expected this warehouse to be no different than the rest. Beloty's talk with Mr. Kajiso Oyn was very likely to be a dead end. But there might be some item at this Knaves Shipping, some clue which we could use to get us closer to whoever had taken Jonathan.

As for Morton and Constable Hanger, I'd gotten every scrap of information I could. And who knew if it even meant anything?

If Morton couldn't get the Constable to trust him enough to pass the message along, or if Sheinwold couldn't be made to see reason, then I didn't know if there was anything more I might do.

I found the situation frustrating. But I did understand why Mr. Sheinwold might feel this way. Being betrayed by one of the Feds, then hunted by a madwoman, then told a man he'd trusted had betrayed him? It would make any man wary.

But Constable Hanger had been hiding something. Perhaps a personal matter that Sheinwold had revealed to him?

We all hide things, I thought. *The real miracle is that anyone speaks.*

The carriage started over the bridge to Spadros quadrant. The fog rose over the water, hiding the moon. I shivered, closed the window.

Even for late November, this seemed a dismal night. I planned to go through this warehouse building quickly. Then home, warm and comfortable, with dinner and a book to end my evening.

After crossing, the carriage went down Main Street past the Pot, the lamp beside my driver shining murky over the darkened Hedge.

I wished I knew what was happening in the Pot. While I felt glad to hear that my mother and great-grandmother were alive, having been banished from seeing them pained me.

Yet it was more than that. How many of my people were now working for the Red Dog Gang?

I wished I might learn what they were planning. What they wanted from me.

Benji — a man who was like a brother to me — had said once that they wished to destroy the quadrants the way the Pot had been destroyed.

But this didn't make sense to me. What purpose would that serve?

Then I recalled Tony's words: *what good has vengeance ever brought? To wish harm upon others eats away at you until there's nothing left inside.*

Zia and Frank, by all accounts, sought fame and glory. The woman calling herself "Black Maria" who'd captured the Spadros Pot wanted vengeance. But I sensed that the Director of this conspiracy against the Families — an older man for certain — wanted more. Power? Control?

When we reached 6th Street, Zeus turned right, the carriage's front and back lamps illuminating closed shops, signs appearing ghostly through the fog. Here and there, a street-lamp shone dim, as if turned low behind closed draperies. Even the hoof-beats up ahead sounded muffled, gloomy.

The carriage turned left, then after a few blocks, right. Finally, it stopped, and Honor's face appeared at the door.

He held a lantern of his own, and it lit his face from below. "We're here, mum." He helped me from the carriage. "You sure you want to do this now?"

A street-lamp cast a pool of light upon the ground perhaps fifty yards down. No one was on the street, and we had a lantern. The lights might even be working here. "Why not? If it's like the others, I doubt it'll take us long."

"Very good, mum." He handed me the lantern and drew his revolver, going forward to the door. It opened at his grasp, and we went inside.

Like the others, the door opened onto a small hallway, which passed what looked to be an office area. Honor found a switch, and to my relief, the lights came on.

An ordinary front office, full of dust. Desk, cabinets, shelves, all rusted, all empty. By the time I finished searching the office, Honor had returned the lantern to the carriage and turned the lights on in the main area.

The main room was brightly lit and twenty yards square, its vaulted metal ceiling stretching high above us.

Dust lay thick upon the wooden floor. Along the brick walls lay old bricks, boards and moldering papers. No glass appeared here, nor any stamp-marks, nor cards of any kind.

A wide hallway ran along the back of the building, its windows high on the wall, with three workrooms to our left. As before, dust, rusted furnishings, old trash. No clues in any of them that I could see.

The only notable thing in the third workroom was a box of six-inch candles the thickness of my thumb and a few loose matches on a shelf.

While we were in this third workroom, the lights went out.

I fumbled around for the candles. Honor struck a match from his pocket. After lighting my candle, he lit a second one. "Wait here, Mrs. Spadros: I'll find the fuse-box." His footsteps went down the hall.

Candle in hand, I peered out.

Around the corner to my left, another wide hall stretched forth towards the street. Light streamed in through a large broken dome-like window from the fog-obscured street-lamp beyond, the one I'd seen when we arrived.

Fog filled this hall; glass glinted dimly upon the floor at its end.

I stood in the intersection of the two hallways, facing that window. Far to my left, I heard a gasp, then a thump, then the heavy click of metal upon wood.

It was then I realized I could no longer hear Honor's footsteps.

I turned to the sounds, casting my candle's glow along the hallway he'd just gone down. "Honor? What happened? Are you well?"

No answer.

Just then, I heard a noise to my right. Some twenty yards away, the figure of a man stepped into the foggy light from the street-lamp, just a silhouette framed by the open window.

Cane, top hat, overcoat ...

I moved towards him. A gentleman, here? "Hello?"

As I came closer to him, the light from my candle gave me a faint glimpse of his face. For an instant, I couldn't breathe. "Jon?"

He smiled, relaxing. He looked ... well.

Relief flooded through me. "Oh, gods, Jon!"

He took a heavy step forward.

Hand shaking, I moved towards him. The scent of Jon's cologne washed over me, the breeze blowing out my candle. I dropped it and ran to him. "Jon! Oh, dear gods, you're alive!"

He reached towards me. But instead of taking my hand, he raised his to my face. The other encircled my waist. Something wet pressed against my nose and cheeks, and I smelled ... chloroform.

A deep voice said, "I'm not Jon."

The Panic

I couldn't move.

A small, round room, brightly lit, a few paces in any direction.

Not entirely round: hexagonal, each section of gun-metal gray joined to the next by a stout steel bar.

The section before me had a metal counter in the same gray, bearing a panel. The panel held an array of buttons and levers and lights, all dark. A large window stood beyond that.

A wooden armchair around me. A bare bulb high overhead.

The room spun; I felt sick.

My hands behind me rasped against rough fibers. My waist was bound by hemp as thick as if three of my fingers pressed together. And as hard as I tried, my ankles wouldn't come free from the chair.

I thrashed, pulled against my bonds. I heard nothing but my ragged breathing and the pounding of my heart.

I had to get out.

The chair wouldn't move.

I had to get out.

Pulling my hand, trying to free myself, gritting my teeth to keep from making a noise. I stopped then, dizzy, exhausted.

My hand hurt a lot. But a part of me didn't care. I had to get out. I'd have cut my hand off right then if I had to, if only to win free.

I had to get out before Jack Diamond returned.

I am not Jon.

My vision blurred. "Oh, gods." Jon's face, his precious, beloved face ... but not his voice!

Was Jon alive? Or had his monstrous twin murdered him?

Jack Diamond told me more than once what he would do if he caught me: I would die. Horribly. Painfully.

Everything I'd worked so hard for would be lost.

No one would ever learn what happened to me.

I'd never see Joseph Kerr again.

I cried, raged, sobbed in anguish and fear. How could I have been so stupid? I'd let myself be trapped by the one man who'd sworn to torture me to death should he capture me.

All the clues had been there: all the Jack references: Laughing Boy, the Messenger, Fish Hook Lane, Number 11.

Then the businesses:

Johnson Brothers, Inc.

All Fours Realty.

Cribbage Textiles Co.

And here at the end, Knaves Shipping.

J-A-C-K.

He even mentioned his family: Hector, Roland. And all those addresses in Diamond!

I'd been a fool, an utter fool.

But I had to focus. I had to escape.

I glanced around. We weren't in the Knaves Shipping warehouse anymore. How did he get me here?

It didn't matter. The room was silent. I was alone.

I had to get out before Jack Diamond returned.

I took a deep breath, gathering up my courage.

Then I pulled at my right hand, screaming at the pain of joints loosening, dislocating, skin being scraped raw.

I wrenched my hand free. Spots of blood welled up upon the throbbing red flesh of my hand. I sobbed in pain as my left hand came round, the thick rope still dangling upon my wrist, to push the tortured bones of my right hand back into place.

The back of my right hand was a burning, oozing sheet of blood, every move a sharp pain in the joint of my thumb. I grasped the rope which bound my waist, pain going through my arms and hands as I worked the rope round so I might unloose the knot.

I forced myself to pull, bit by bit, at the thick knot which held me, mostly using my left hand. At first, the rope seemed cast in steel for all it moved. Yet I worried at the knot with all my strength, ignoring the pain in my hands. Fingers raw, nails giving way.

I don't know if my blood on the rough hemp helped or hindered, but after what felt like forever, the knot around my waist won free.

I bent to untie my left ankle. Dizziness struck, and I breathed deeply, fighting not to vomit. The chair was bolted to the floor.

I had to get out.

Every move an agony, I worked the left knot free, then the right. At the end of it, my nails on every finger were broken, bloody. Yet at last, my legs won free.

Once unbound, I lay my head upon my knees for a moment, gasping for air. Other than my hands and wrists, I didn't feel injured.

I sat up, waited for the room to stop spinning, then stood.

All was silent.

My mind felt hazy, but gradually my vision cleared. I staggered to the wall, off balance.

Surely Jack would return soon. Frantic at that thought, I placed my right shoulder to the wall, moving along every panel searching for a doorknob. But I found none.

How could I get out?

I yelped at a sharp pain in my right hip, and for an instant, my vision darkened. I'd gone round the room and hit the panel.

I clung to the metal counter, gasping at the pain until my vision cleared. A streak of my blood ran round the room at hand level, making the dull gray only that much more horrifying.

The glass was six inches thick. Outside it lay only blackness.

What function did this place have? I studied the panel's many controls. What did it do? Might it have some mechanism to let me out?

No lights appeared upon the dusty panel. Pushing and turning the controls did nothing but worsen the pain in my hands.

Holding onto the panel, I squatted to examine the underside. The mechanisms were stripped bare: not even so much as a wire remained.

I stood, and dizziness struck once more. Gasping, I steadied myself by leaning upon the panel.

Other than the chair, the room itself was completely empty. A door stood past the chair with a latch sunk into the door.

This must be how it opened. How did I miss it?

I glanced back at the window and shrieked: Jack Diamond stood on the other side.

Jonathan's face, yet this man was not Jon.

Head shaved, all in white, Jack Diamond held a small notepad in his left hand, turned so I couldn't see whatever writing might lay upon it. A silver ring decorated his smallest finger, a clear smooth stone glinting there.

His deep voice rang from a grate in the ceiling, "Ah, you're finally awake." He surveyed me and gasped. "Good gods! Your hands!" Then he blinked, his face horrified. "How could you have possibly gotten free?"

Even though the thick window separated us, I shrank back in fear. "Where's Jon? What do you want with me? And where's my footman?"

Jack chuckled. "My brother is safe and well, or soon will be. Didn't you decipher the message he sent?"

I thought I might faint: Jon was safe. "What message?"

Jack laughed. "Eventually you'll figure it out. And I'm sure your servant will be just fine." He let out a sigh, and shook his head. "But I'm disappointed in you. You took much too long to join me. You were much too easy to capture." Then his gaze turned thoughtful. "And you're much too dangerous to let roam free."

I rushed to the door and pulled at the latch, fighting a sudden urge to vomit. Locked.

A lock was set into the latch's mechanism. When I reached for my picks, hands shaking, Jack laughed. "Even if I hadn't taken your picks from you," he said, "you couldn't open that door. So don't try."

My gun and boot-knife were missing. The butterflies were gone from my corset. I turned to face him, my back against the door. "How dare you imprison me? How dare you take my belongings?"

"How dare I?" Jack said. "How dare I **not**? You had garrote wire, and knives, and a pistol upon your person!"

My hands and wrists hurt terribly. But other than what at the time I guessed were the effects of the chloroform, I didn't feel injured. And I didn't feel like I'd been violated.

But ... this was unthinkable. "You put your **hands** upon me?" I gasped, drawing back in horror. "What have you done?"

Jack burst out laughing. "Done? **I**?" He shook his head. "I've done nothing. Your feminine flesh," he paused, gazing aside, as if pondering some puzzle, "lovely as it is, holds little attraction for me." He faced me with an air of bravado. "I had something I wished to tell you, and I didn't want to be killed while trying do it."

He was **afraid** of me? "You could have sent a letter."

Jack gave a fond laugh. "I can see why he loves you. But I have little time. Eventually whoever you told you were coming here —"

I couldn't help but jump at his words. I'd told Morton and Constable Hanger about Knaves Shipping, and Morton knew that I planned to stop by the building after leaving him. Zeus was still outside with the carriage. But where was Honor? I remembered his gasp, the thumps afterward. What had they done to him?

"— ah, you see, I don't underestimate you — in any rate, they would soon become alarmed, and send word to your husband, or whoever it is you're consorting with —"

Outrage filled me. "Now, see here —"

He held up a hand. "I apologize. I would not argue. Leave it at this: there are things you must know, and I had no other way to tell you. Even if your mail was not being intercepted, this sort of thing is too delicate to say other than in person. My brother will be furious at the way I tricked you, but he'll soon forget that." He gestured to the chair. "Please, sit down. We don't have much time."

I returned to my chair and sat looking at him for a moment, feeling weary. He was nothing like his brother. "What do you want?"

"From you? Nothing. I've never wanted anything from you. My life has been dedicated to discovering the truth of what happened the night we first met, and why. Yet at every turn, the answers come back ... to you!" He waved his notebook in the air. "I'm not your enemy, not really." This seemed to spark some thought in him, and he leaned the notebook against his lips for a moment. "But there are those who are, and it would be wrong for me not to tell you why."

Jack didn't want to kill me? But then I realized what he was trying to say. "Who?"

"First I need some answers. Why was Daniel in the Spadros Pot the night he died?"

The name sounded familiar, yet I couldn't place it. "Daniel?"

"For gods' sakes, woman, my manservant!"

I gasped, my mind going back to that frigid night.

I was little, small. In an alley, crouched behind an old rotted barrel, my best friend Air at my side. Snow glittered on the ground.

Peedro Sluff — a man I barely knew — stood out in the street, in the intersection of Shill and Snow. He stood across from Roy Spadros, both cast in strange shadows by the full moon.

A much younger brown-haired man I didn't know at all ran towards them. His face so kind, yet so desperately terrified.

He didn't do anything wrong! And my father shot him anyway.

The grief for him and all those dead in my life began to crush me.

But I had to focus. I had to get out.

Maybe if I told the truth, Jack would let me go.

I blinked tears away, pushed them back, forced myself to breathe. "I don't know. He was shouting. Warning someone."

"Who?"

"I don't know!" At the flash of anger that crossed Jack's face, I forced myself to breathe, fighting to regain my calm.

And as I did, I recalled the discussion on this topic that I'd had with Tony, before I left him. "I think he was warning Roy Spadros. Your man seemed frantic. Desperate to warn him."

Jack frowned. "You want me to believe that a Diamond-sworn manservant, my bodyguard, left me and my brother and sister alone with our enemies because he was desperate to go to the Spadros Pot and warn ... **Roy**?" He shook his head, his face incredulous. "Why?"

The room wavered, my vision blurred, and I fought not to cry. "I don't know. But I think ... I think my father Peedro —"

Jack let out a bitter laugh.

What could possibly be funny? "— I think he'd been hired to kill Roy. But it seemed like he was scared to do it. I don't blame him — I'd be scared, too. But I think if your man Daniel hadn't arrived, hadn't given my father a way out, he might have done it. Killed Roy, I mean."

At this, Jack sobered, eyes downcast. "This would make sense."

"I never understood. Why ... oh, I suppose many people had reason to kill Roy Spadros."

Peedro Sluff — who told me and Roy that night that he was my father — why did he want me to be there to see it? Just so I was close by when he sold me?

Or had I been lured away from my mother because he couldn't get me out of the Cathedral otherwise?

What had I done?

Jack Diamond's voice startled me. "It was ten at night and freezing cold. You were what, eleven?"

"Twelve. Just turned." All this — my capture by Roy, my best friend's murder — had I been the cause of it all? "My birthday is Yuletide Center."

"So you were just turned twelve out in the street in the middle of nowhere at ten at night during Yuletide. Why were you **there**?"

"Peedro told me if I went there he'd give me a dollar."

Jack let out a disgusted breath, shaking his head. "So you were just there for **money**? You lived in the Cathedral! Your mother owns the place. You were fed, warm, and safe there. Why'd you need a dollar that badly? What does a child need with **that** much money?"

All the anguish of that night came pouring back. "My best friend Air was sick! He coughed blood! The doctor said he needed money for med'cine." I remembered what his mother Eleanora said later: that his father had sent the money.

But I didn't know.

Dismay filled me, and a bitter regret. "I thought I could help." And it had only gotten Air shot and me chained to the Spadros Family.

Jack shook his head. "That's always it with you, isn't it? You never think. You just blunder about 'trying to help.' I don't even have to put spies on you! I simply follow the chaos and I know exactly where you've been. For example, that lawyer who visited the other night —"

Terror struck. Mr. Dashatabar! "What about him?"

"He never made it to the police station."

"What?"

He pointed at me. "You should have called your Family to protect him! Instead, your 'help' only got him killed."

"But he came in a carriage. His men were with him."

"He had his **family** with him. His wife. His children! And you sent them to their deaths. His driver was a spy who led them straight into an ambush."

I couldn't think. "Mr. Dashabatar is dead?"

"Everyone who rode that carriage is dead."

His family rode with him?

"Don't you see what you're doing? How long will you go on like this? Three children are dead! You may as well have pulled the trigger. How many more are dead because of your 'help'?"

I knew Jack stood across that thick window, but Jon's face speaking to me so hurt.

Yet it was true. I'd killed them all: Air, Herbert Bryce, Stephen Rivers, Dame Anastasia, Madame Biltcliffe, Maria Athena Spade ... the list went on and on.

A deep despair came over me, the likes of which I'd not felt since before I almost died from drink.

And, for an instant, I wanted to die, just to make the pain stop.

Then rage filled me. "You gods-damned murderous beast. Who have you ever helped? All I hear about are the men you've maimed and tortured and killed."

Then a horrible thought struck. "Did **you** kill my friends? Did you kill Anna Goren and make it look like Roy did it?"

Jack's eyes widened. "Me? I've never killed anyone in my life."

But then he turned grim. "I **am** about to kill a man, though." In his eyes was an almost childlike fear. "Do you think my cards will be burnt for it?"

At the tone in his voice, I felt taken aback. "I don't know."

He recovered, focusing upon me. "And you never learned why Daniel felt the need to warn Roy."

A shock of surprise hit me. *He wants to understand.* I gazed into his dark eyes, feeling a connection to him I never imagined.

I never understood most of what happened that night, when the life I'd known was murdered along with my best friend Air. And I wanted to.

Jack let out a breath, then spoke as if he truly felt disappointed. "I suppose this hasn't been an entire waste of time."

"This can't have been all. What is it you want from me?"

Someone began banging on a door far behind me.

"So it's begun," Jack said, as if we were on a stroll by the river. "Yes, there is something you can do: leave my sister alone."

"Gardena? What has she to do with this?"

"Stop interfering with her. Stop pushing Lance Clubb to do things you know will cause trouble between them."

The banging got louder. "How do you know about any of this?"

"Do you think I don't talk to my own sister? None of us can fathom why you want to be rid of your husband so badly."

Tony. Would I ever see him again?

It was then that I realized I wanted to live. I had to get out. "Please, just let me go. I promise I won't tell anyone."

He let out a laugh. "First stop this nonsense with her betrothal."

"Fine."

"But do your promises even mean anything? I don't know."

I felt outraged, then I had to admit, he had a point. I'd promised Regina Clubb the same thing in exchange for her help during the trial, then after the trial was over ... "We're not in the warehouse anymore. Where are we? What kind of place is this? How did we get here?"

Jack only smiled as one might at a child. The shouts of men came from behind, muffled, and then the shouts fanned out, as if the men searched for another way in.

I had to ask: it might be my only chance. "Who's the blonde girl Jon keeps a portrait of? What is she to him?"

Jack snorted, his face amused. "All this going on and **that** is what she wants to know." He lowered his notebook, shaking his head, and began to fiddle on a panel of his own on the other side of the thick glass. Tiny lights appeared behind him, and the forms of machinery came into view.

This is a Party Time factory, I thought. "What are you doing?"

A humming sound began, and grew a bit louder with each passing second. And I remembered a conversation I'd had with Tony about his Party Time factory, long before.

A few of these reagents can be explosive if mixed in large amounts. If the men who attacked intended to kill me, they could have set the factory to explode when we entered.

"They won't be here in time to rescue you," Jack said lightly, his face thoughtful. "When I consider the matter, it feels poetic. We'll be together at the end of it all, just as we were when it began."

I stared at Jack in horror. "Are you mad?"

He smiled to himself. "That is my one great fear: that I am mad, or will become so in truth. But this," he waved his arms, strolling around the barely-lit room outside, "this has been a grand charade, don't you think? A 'madman' can do so much, talk to so many, and no one ever questions it. 'Black Jack' Diamond: the perfect disguise!" He came close to the window again, speaking to me in a conspiratorial tone. "And a madman can learn the answers to his questions, where a sane man cannot."

I shook my head. "What answers?"

Jack snorted. "Far be it for me to burden you with my problems, dear girl. Besides, we don't have time. You have problems of your own. First of all, your father."

I sighed. "I wish he'd never killed your friend. I wish to all the gods that Roy Spadros had died instead." Then Peedro would've let me alone, never killed Air. None of this nightmare would have ever happened. "I'm truly sorry."

Jack looked at me sorrowfully. "Peedro Sluff isn't your father, Mrs. Spadros. Your father is Charles Hart."

The Blow

For a moment, the words made no sense. "What?"

The humming sound grew louder, as did the shouts of the men, now once again behind me. At least a dozen gunshots rang out, some ricocheting around the room, and Jack ducked down.

Jack's voice came forth as if from nowhere. "I should've anticipated this." When he appeared again, he rose slowly, his face twisted in pain. A red blot spread bit by bit over the outer left shoulder of his white jacket. He spoke softly, as if to himself. "It wasn't supposed to go this way."

Then Jack looked at me, and spoke with difficulty, teeth gritted. "What I've told you is true, Mrs. Spadros. Hart and your mother were lovers. Probably still are. He helped her buy the brothel. So you both would be safe. He loves you. Well, as best as that twisted mind of his knows how."

I could only stare at him, stunned. Mr. Hart ... my father?

Everything Mr. Hart had said, everything he'd done — it all came rushing back, and all with new interpretation. Why he let me and Tony into his quadrant, no questions asked. His obsession with my safety. How he felt so compelled to see me. The red roses. The necklace which once belonged to his mother.

His tears at my wedding, a marriage he knew was forced upon me ... by his worst enemy.

"It's difficult to believe Charles Hart, of all people, could be your father. I realize that. But I'm not the only one who knows it, and that puts you in danger."

I stared at him, aghast, the room wavering. "Who else knows?"

Who knew all this time and never told me?

Jack sounded annoyed. "Surely you can reason it out yourself." He leaned on the glass, lips pale, sweat upon his brow. "Who would **have** to know?" He stopped for a moment, panting. The red blot on his jacket's arm had widened. "And who might wish you harm is just as clear. Who benefits if you die? Who might be swayed if you were a hostage?" Then he shook his head. "My brother thinks so highly of you. I expected more."

I felt as if in a fog. "Okay, so there's Judith Hart." She'd hated me for years — and now I could see why. No wonder she wouldn't look at me: every time she saw me, she must have seen my mother. Would have been faced with her husband's betrayal. "That seems obvious."

But why wish me dead? I was nothing, a bastard Pot rag! I had no power; I posed no threat to her whatsoever.

Jack stood leaning upon the glass, his breath shallow, his eyes boring into mine.

I tried to think. "Roy Spadros hates Charles Hart — this is true. But Roy's had me with him for years now."

Roy's beatings, his blind hate for me, his rants, the names he'd called me, the years of torment and control ... it all made sense now. Charles Hart had done something Roy felt unforgivable. And that made the small girl I'd been Roy's mortal enemy.

That was why he wanted Peedro to find me, to lure me to that intersection for him.

When Roy looked at me, he saw not my mother, but Charles Hart. Not only could he take out his rage at Mr. Hart upon me, he could torture Mr. Hart that much further by telling him in exact detail what he'd done.

But for Roy to kill me made no sense. If he were gaining pleasure from my torment or extorting something from Mr. Hart, he had reason to keep me alive, not kill me.

This did explain some of the things Roy had done over the years, though. Why he'd taken such pleasure in harm coming to me.

Yet he'd regretted it. I remembered his face as we sat in his parlor. He regretted how he treated me. What had changed?

I shook my head. I couldn't think. Charles Hart was my **father**?

I pictured that fat old man and my Ma together. It made no sense. I didn't understand. "I don't know."

Jack Diamond's smile mocked me; an edge lay in his words. "I don't know why I wasted my time. I suppose you'll have to learn the hard way. At least I've done my duty: you're armed with the truth."

I couldn't think. "At least give me some clue. I truly don't know."

He spoke as if to himself. "If she has so much trouble with this ...!" His eyes held a deep sadness. "This was a mistake: I should have known you wouldn't believe me."

"Master Diamond, please. You went to all this trouble to bring me here, at least tell me what this is about."

"Very well, the entire matter boils down to this: be wary of Joseph Kerr — he's not what he seems."

"What? No, I've known Joe since we were children. He'd never harm me." Perhaps Jack really was mad after all.

He let out a sigh. "Unbelievable. So the rumors are true."

"Rumors? What rumors? Please, I just want to understand."

A heavy thud shook the room, the sound coming from behind me.

Charles Hart ... left me and Ma there in the Pot all those years ... when he could have freed us?

Another thud sounded. Jack smiled, but it didn't reach his eyes. "That door will only withstand so many of those blows. It's a pity I didn't have it built better. But I mustn't be captured. And I can't keep running forever."

This startled me. "Running? But you're a Diamond heir! Why are you running? Who's after you?"

A much louder thud. He snorted. "Pretty much everyone." He put the notebook in a breast pocket, then held up a small control mechanism, like ones used with explosive devices. He tapped his chest with it. "And so now it's time for the mad, bad, Black Jack

Diamond ..." He gave me a broad smile, and this time it seemed real, filled with wild anticipation, a terrible fearful excitement. "To die!"

I felt horrified. "What? No!"

I remembered what Gardena said long before I left Tony, as we walked in my garden back at Spadros Manor: she feared Jack's end would be suicide. "Whatever is going on, we can help you. I swear, if your Family can't protect you, my Family can. We can keep you safe."

The thought of this man I'd just conversed with destroying himself right here in front of me felt unbearable. "Oh, gods, Jack ... no. Please. You don't have to do this!"

Jack cocked his head to one side as if instructing a small child. "But, you see my dear girl, I do. One day you'll understand." He smiled fondly at me. "Never fear, you'll be perfectly safe in there." He blew me a kiss. "Farewell, for now."

Another thud sounded, and with it, the cracking of thick wood. Tears filled my eyes. *Oh, Jon, Gardena ...* in spite of Jack's insanity, they loved him deeply. This would destroy them.

I sat there sobbing. "Please, Jack, don't do this." Then I rushed to the window, pain shooting through my hands as I touched it. "Think of your family!"

But he was no longer at the window, and my fear for his safety grew with each passing moment. Would another man die because of me? "Jack, for gods' sake, stop!"

A huge explosion rocked the room; I fell upon the floor at the blast. Flames billowed past the window, and even through the thick glass I felt the heat of that fire.

The pounding outside became frantic. A huge crash, and the shouts of men filled the hall. A man's dark face appeared at the window, and he shouted, pointing around to the side.

Smoke began to seep under the door. I crawled to my door, banging on it. "I'm in here!"

Clicking and rattling sounds came from the door-latch. I lay upon the floor, terrified, dizzy, sick.

Yet I knew that face.

Mr. Sutherfield, I thought finally, with some relief.

It's Mr. Theodore Sutherfield. Blitz is his brother.

He would help me.

Flames filled the window's view. Someone pushed the door, shoving at me, and I moved aside. The door opened near my head, smoke billowing into the room. Above the roar of the flames, a man's voice sobbed with great passion, "Oh, thank the Dealer, you're alive!"

Hands picked me up from the floor. Opened double doors lay ahead of me, men streaming into the smoke-filled room. I felt clasped in an embrace, but it wasn't Tony.

Disgusted, I shook it off, pushing toward the light and air. The man followed alongside me, shouting to the others.

It was Thrace Pike, of all people. What was **he** doing here?

Outside, a man I didn't know put a blanket round my shoulders. Others ran. Others shouted for buckets.

Women screamed, children shrieked. Lanterns were everywhere. Strange shapes lay in the fog beyond.

I kept coughing, clutching at the blanket, my hands bleeding and black with soot as I stood in the chaos, surrounded by people yet to my awareness, alone.

Tony ran up panting, terror in his eyes. I dropped the blanket, clinging to my husband with all my strength, weeping.

Jack Diamond was dead.

He had to be dead. No one could have survived those flames.

Why did he do it?

"You're alive, you're alive," Tony murmured.

I clung to him, gasping for air, sobbing over the horror I'd just seen, the terrible things I'd learned, grieving the lives wasted because of me.

Bells and whistles of the fire-men drew near as the building roared. I buried my face in Tony's chest, squeezing my eyes shut.

A hand touched my shoulder: Charles Hart stood there panting. "Thank the gods you're alive!"

A streak of light from a passing carriage illuminated just his eyes, the warm blue eyes of the Masked Man.

All those visits, the gifts, the pretense of caring about me as he hid behind that mask. All those years he'd left me and Ma in the Pot to suffer. Then when Roy captured me, Mr. Hart did nothing to stop it.

And now he wanted to be embraced as my father?

I punched Charles Hart in the face, there in front of everyone, and I was glad to see his blood run freely red. "Never speak to me again."

He stared at me, hands to his cheeks, hurt and pain in his eyes. "You broke my nose!"

"You ruined my life!" I turned to Tony, who stood there aghast. "Please take me home."

We walked to Tony's carriage, and there he drew me close. After several moments of holding me in silence, he said, "First, I'm taking you to the doctor."

***

After I told Dr. Salmon the story of how I found myself, he fussed over me for quite some time. He had the nurse remove my clothes and put me into a loose gown, after which time he checked every part of me most thoroughly.

A new pain stabbed the side of my tortured right hand when I tried to move it. So my hand was rayed, and after I lay back upon the examining bed, the doctor shone a remarkably white light inside me.

I'm certain that light was illegal tech, probably from Azimoff. It was too pure, too bright, and had round shapes inside the bulb that I'd never seen anywhere.

There was also the matter of the Tommy-guns, smuggled in from Chicago and now in the hands of the Red Dog Gang.

What else had the Spadros Family smuggled here?

Then he examined me again, one hand inside me, the other atop my belly. The whole while, Tony stood by my side.

I insisted there was nothing wrong — well, except for my hand, which hurt quite a lot from punching Mr. Hart — and could I please go home?

Then the nurse got me dressed. Tony and I sat together waiting for the doctor to return.

Tony never asked me any questions about anything, particularly about why I'd hit Mr. Hart, and his silence told me more than I wanted to know.

He knew Charles Hart was my father all along.

Why did he not tell me?

I had no answers. I'm not sure I wanted any.

But that meant Inventor Etienne Hart was my brother.

I'd done nothing to him, yet he tried every way he could to destroy me. And the man who'd birthed me stood by and watched it happen.

Finally, the doctor came in. "I'm sorry to take so long, but —"

Tony stood. "Is my wife well?"

"Oh, more than well. I mean, other than her fingernails, which you can see, and her right hand, which I'm afraid is broken. She punched someone, I take it?" Dr. Salmon's eyes twinkled in amusement. "But it broke clean; the nurse can lay it in plaster."

The doctor then turned to me. "My dear, you're with child."

I stared at him. How could I be with child?

Tony sat heavily, his face pale. "**What?**"

Dr. Salmon said, "Your wife's pregnant, sir. Congratulations."

The Aim

Dr. Salmon left. We sat silent for some time.

I felt so stunned I couldn't think. Too much had happened that day; it felt as if the mechanisms of my brain had turned off.

Tony said, "Once we're done here, I'll take you home." He paused expectantly, waiting for me to reply.

"I appreciate that."

Tony placed his hand gently upon my arm. "You don't understand. You must return with me to Spadros Manor."

I flung his hand off, pain shooting through my hand. "What! No! I refuse! You can't —"

Tony held up his hand. "Jacqui, I'm sorry, truly I am. This must seem terribly unfair. But it's not up to me." He took a deep breath. "You're with child. Who will you say is the father?"

I blinked. "Why, you. Of course!" I'd lain with no one else since I left him: surely he knew that.

Tony put his head in his hands. "The law is clear: a woman with child can't live away from her husband. You must either return to my side, or go to the Pot." He shook his head, not looking at me. "I — I won't touch you unless you wish it." He glanced up at me then. "Please come home. I'd rather die than see you return to that place."

The nurse came in then, trimmed my ragged broken nails, washed and bandaged my hurt hands. Cast my arm. Gave us instructions.

The whole time, I thought of what I might do.

The Eldest had banished me from the Cathedral.

Every time I met Benji, he told me not to return.

And the Spadros Pot was in the hands of the Red Dog Gang.

I could still go to the Pot. And I'd be free.

Yet without the blessing of the Cathedral or help from Benji, my freedom would be the freedom to freeze and starve on the street.

And once in the Pot, I'd literally be in a cage, my life forever bound by the Hedge.

"Pot rags" could own nothing in the quadrants. I'd lose my business, my properties, my bank account, even my belongings. Without papers to allow me into the quadrants, I wouldn't be able to learn who killed my friends. Worst of all, I'd lose the Spadros Family's protection: the Red Dog Gang could kill me and no one would lift a finger to prevent it.

There was an alternative to going to Spadros Manor: I could stay in my apartments for a few months more. No one in the Family would rat me out, I felt sure of that. But soon I wouldn't be able to leave my home for fear that someone would see the obvious. And if the news ended up in the tabloids ... everyone would assume the worst.

Who would they blame? Jonathan, most likely. Or Blitz, or Mr. Hart, or even Morton. They'd all be thrown into scandal and scrutiny. Every secret they had would be hunted down, every aspect of their lives fodder for gossip and speculation.

And Tony would be utterly humiliated.

It was then that I knew the truth: I had to go back. As much as I hated everything about Spadros Manor, I had to go back.

I felt bitter. One moment of pleasure in my wretched miserable life, and I'd been trapped.

But then I remembered the afternoon Tony came to see me. The way he looked at me. The way he made me feel.

When the nurse left, I adjusted my sling a bit, sat beside him and took his hand. "I won't sell my apartments. Or Anna's shop. And I won't stop being an investigator. Not for you or anyone else."

Tony kissed my hand gently, his eyes squeezed shut. "Anything, Jacqui. I promise. Anything you want. Just please come home."

I smiled to myself: I now had an aim. "Have the carriage at my apartments tomorrow morning at eight." Tony was always up earlier than I was. "I have some things to take care of tonight."

He had to be suspicious: I would've been. What would make him believe I meant this? Then I took a deep breath, let it out. "I think I'll redo the Manor."

***

It was late by the time Tony brought me to my apartments. Mary had obviously been told everything: she helped me undress and get into bed without even asking about my cast.

Everything hurt, and I kept coughing. But after a restless night and much thought, I was ready.

The next day, I bathed as best I could with Mary's help, got into my least threadbare dress, and went to the carriage.

Mary claimed Blitz still slept, but something in the way she said it made me think perhaps he didn't want to see me off. And although she usually was there around seven, Amelia never arrived.

The day was clear and cold, the sun just peeking over the buildings. Honor stood holding the door. Although subdued, he seemed none the worse for wear.

I took his hand with my left one, my nails still bandaged. "I hope you're well, sir."

He glanced at my sling. "Better than you, mum, from the looks of it." He seemed embarrassed. "I was somewhat taken by surprise."

"Let me guess: by someone holding chloroform?"

His cheeks darkened. "Yes, mum."

After he closed the carriage door, I let down the window. "Did you get a look at him?"

He gave a puzzled frown. "Whoever it was seemed shorter than me. They held a cloth." Then he looked startled. "Perhaps a woman?"

"What makes you say that?"

"I don't know. Before I turned, I heard something. The footsteps sounded familiar." He squeezed his eyes shut, shaking his head. "I don't know. Just a feeling."

"The guard said he thought the footman was a woman."

"Pardon me, mum?"

I waved him off. "It's nothing. Spadros Manor, if you please."

"Right away."

No matter how many man-lovers and pretty-boys they showed the guard, they'd never found anyone the guard said even looked close to the man he saw.

I gasped as the thought hit me: could this possibly have been a **woman** pretending to be a footman? Could a woman have dosed Honor with chloroform, there in the darkness?

Why would any woman **do** that?

***

My apartments were on 33 1/3 Street. Spadros Manor was on 192nd. So I had time to think as we drove.

I recalled the time I went to Spadros Manor around five months before in my mad search for Joseph Kerr, and how happy Tony's butler Pearson was to see me.

My terror almost two years back when I thought I was being taken to the Manor against my will was gone. If my plan went well, I had nothing to fear.

To my surprise, many of the servants applauded when I came into Spadros Manor's front hall, some with tears in their eyes.

There they were, all the people I'd missed so. John Pearson, the butler, with his pale skin and thinning brown hair. His wife Jane — the housekeeper — beside him. Our chef Monsieur Sabacc, and beside him the Mistress of the Kitchens. Maids, footmen ... they seemed glad to see me, in spite of all I'd done.

I stopped in front of a boy standing next to Monsieur Sabacc who stood almost as tall as I. If not for the pale blue eyes, I'd not have known him. "Is this my little Pip?"

Pip gave a small bow. "Yes, mum, Pip Dewey."

"What are you now, thirteen?"

"Next week, mum."

I felt quite surprised. "You've grown!"

He never looked me in the eye. "Yes, mum. Thank you, mum."

Tony and I sat at our breakfast table with the view of the gardens. I never realized how much I missed the gardens until I saw them again. The beautiful plates, Monsieur's delicious sausage, the fine tablecloth — I'd missed them all.

After breakfast, Tony — quite unnecessarily — gave me a complete tour of the mansion. Everything was the same — my room, my bed — as if I'd never left, never spent the past two years gone.

Yet I felt completely different.

"Let us know what you want, what you need," Tony said. "I've given the staff strict instruction. From now on, this house is yours. You are the Lady of Spadros, and they may neither defy nor correct you."

I sat in my bedroom. The tea-table was by the window, and the view of the graveled courtyard was just as before.

It all seemed smaller somehow.

I'd grown up here. I'd left here ... was it really for Joe, or was it just to be free? Then I recalled what Tony had said to me in my parlor: *can you not make your life anywhere?*

I could, true. But staying here would mean being drawn back into the Family, once again part of their schemes, their rivalries.

Not only that, I'd be pressed back into high society life with all its rules. Spending my days simpering at some empty-headed dowager's attempt at witticism with women who hated me was not the life I wanted for myself.

No, my plan would be best.

Amelia happily spent the day cleaning the closets. Every time she saw me, she'd say things like "A baby, here!" and "Who would ever have thought it?" until, feeling irritated, I snapped at her to be silent.

After luncheon, I sat trying to write with my left hand as I listed how I wanted to renovate Spadros Manor. Tony had to see a definite outline of work to be done, and soon, if my plan was to succeed.

I wasn't good at writing with my left, and my fingernails hurt. But it hurt much more to try and write with my right. The letters reminded me of that pitiful note Joseph Kerr had written me, more than two years past.

When I was almost finished, Pearson knocked. "Master Blaze Rainbow to see you, mum. I took the liberty of telling him you were 'at home.'"

I smiled warmly at him. I'd known Pearson since I was twelve. "Of course I am. Seat him in the parlor."

Morton looked the same as he always did, perfectly dressed in fine brown. He rose when I entered. "Good day, Mrs. Spadros."

I gestured for him to sit on the sofa, and sat in an armchair across from him. "It's good to see you. I hope all is well?"

He pointed to my sling. "What happened with your arm?"

"Didn't you hear? I broke Charles Hart's nose."

Morton made a choking sound.

"Don't worry; the scoundrel deserved it."

"If you say so."

"Would you like some tea?"

He shook his head. "Just came by with my last rental money." He placed an envelope on the low coffee table between us. "Sorry to see it end this way. But I know you didn't have much choice in the matter."

I smiled at him fondly. "You've been a good friend, sir, and a fine tenant. I'm glad you're moving on, just for your own safety. But I'm neither selling my properties nor closing my business."

Morton blinked. "You're not?"

I grinned at him. "Leave word with Blitz as to where you'll be, should a case come up."

He nodded, impressed. "I most certainly will."

***

That night, it began to snow. The evening edition's headline read:

LADY OF SPADROS RETURNS TO MANOR

All Quadrants Rejoice In Reconciliation

I closed the paper. The ramifications of what I'd done hadn't sunk in as yet. For a short time, it felt unreal.

And then the well-wishes began pouring in.

The Insight

The next few days were a blur of shock and congratulations. I mostly stayed in bed, or when the weather was good, sat out on the veranda bundled up against the cold.

I coughed often, but Dr. Salmon — who came to see me every day — said this was normal after inhaling as much smoke as I did.

Tony left me alone. Most days, I seldom saw him, until he came in late at night to slide into bed next to me and immediately fall asleep. From what the servants said, he'd been spending his days cheerfully making plans for "our new arrival."

I lay beside him each night as he slept, wishing to touch his hair, to tell him I didn't blame him for having to be here. I felt that perhaps he avoided me, stayed out late to exhaust himself, so as not to face our situation.

As I thought about my reactions to him that afternoon in my apartments three months before, I came to believe that something inside me was wrong.

I felt so close to Jonathan, yet while he obviously enjoyed my company, he refused anything more. Tony loved me desperately, had done everything but die for me, and while I yearned for his touch, I ... I didn't know what I felt for him.

Yet when I woke, he was gone; the day repeated itself once more.

I had Pearson tell everyone I was not at home, so we had no visitors. Even so, our maids did little but cart boxes around: letters, flowers, gifts.

But then it was time for Jack's funeral.

The sun shone bright that day. I peered out of the carriage window at melting snow as we made our way across the betters' bridge.

The Diamond quadrant was draped in black, yet thousands upon thousands stood in white for the funeral procession.

The whole quadrant must have come out for him.

Tony said, "Jon told me that the people refuse to wear black. But they do it to honor him." He sounded incredulous, yet sad. "They loved him."

So Tony had been to see Jonathan. "How is he?"

"About as well as one might expect. Quiet. Troubled. Grieving."

Poor Jon, I thought. I couldn't imagine what it would be like to have a twin, much less lose one.

Yet the more I'd considered things since my talk with Jack Diamond, the more this all began to make sense.

Jon had gone willingly, because his brother came to meet him.

I understood Jack being with the carriage which took Jon. It answered the mystery of how that carriage made it past the checkpoints around the Courthouse. If what Jack wore was close enough to Jon's uniform as the Keeper of the Court, the guards would have let the carriage pass, thinking Jonathan sat inside.

And if Jack came into the Courthouse through the front steps leaning on a cane and didn't speak, even if the guards weren't new, even if they had known Jonathan well, they might have been fooled.

I recalled Jack's face, lit by a candle in the fog. I certainly was.

But what did Jonathan know?

The day Jon disappeared, he knew Jack meant to take him somewhere: he was completely ready to go. And yet, in the center of the Courthouse, with the Security Office across the hall, he told no one. To me, this suggested Jon had been in on the plan to lure me to that meeting with Jack from the beginning.

That he'd sent me a message — one that Jack knew about — made things more unclear. Had he tried to get word to me and been stopped? But no, Jack thought I'd received it. Or had Jack told him to send the message in the first place?

Why would he do that?

The carriage took a side street, where we disembarked upon a black carpet edged in silver. Other dignitaries walked in front and behind, a few yards separating each group.

Outside Diamond Manor, covered box seating had been set up for the Families. Over the past few days my fingernails had healed, but people stared at my cast and sling as Tony helped me climb the silverwood stair to our seats.

Julius Diamond looked utterly devastated. His wife Rachel sobbed on his shoulder. Jonathan sat with them, along with his brothers, sister, and other family, yet he never once glanced our way.

The Harts sat many rows back. Charles Hart's nose was heavily bandaged. Neither he nor his wife looked at me, but Inventor Etienne followed me with amused gloating in his eyes.

I tried my best not to look at him. He might be my brother, but he still frightened me.

The Clubbs sat beside them, and more behind. I never realized how many of them there were. Rows and rows of them, none seeming to notice us at all.

We were placed many rows behind that, almost to the top of the seating. Roy and Molly weren't there, and neither was Tony's sister Katherine, but given the circumstances, none of that surprised me.

Tony and I sat silent through the prayers and speeches, then stood with the others when the procession passed.

Across the street, standing in the sun so far off in the sea of white that he was difficult to make out, I saw one man standing alone, dressed in black. His shoulders were stooped and rounded as he leaned stiffly upon his cane during the entire procession — unmoving, head bowed, a gray tweed cap of an older style pulled low. But when the coffin passed, he took his cap off and placed it over his heart, dark head shining through closely cropped hair.

He wore dark spectacles, a few days' beard, and a dark patch over one eye. If you'd have asked me then, I'd have sworn I never saw the man before. Yet something about him seemed familiar.

As the crowd showered white flowers upon the coffin, a glint came upon his cheek. The man turned away, shoulders shaking. He moved into the shade, leaning against the wall, overcome with grief.

My heart ached, and my eyes filled in sympathy, not only for the friends I loved so and their loss, but for this stooped lonely old man.

What power did Jack Diamond, this mad younger son, have over these people to make them love him so?

*****

Tony and I stood huddled in the corner of a vast hall amongst the crush of dignitaries, mostly from Diamond quadrant. To my relief, the Diamonds didn't drink alcohol, so we nursed glasses of fruit juice.

Two men stood talking behind me. "They say all they found once the fire was out ..." the man lowered his voice, "was his body."

"And they sure it was him?"

"Them shoes was most all that survived it. You know them ones he wears, that white patent leather."

"Lotsa men wear patent leather."

"But white? No one else I ever heard of wears white. And I seen them. Looked to be from the same store I get mine at, with them black soles and the silver stamp by the heel and all." The man's voice turned sad. "But what gentleman wears white? It's crazy."

"Such a shame." The two began to move off.

"Ya know, he musta had them made special ..."

Tony's eyes held sadness, and relief. "He can't hurt you anymore, Jacqui." He took my left hand, staring at my fingers. "Maybe the nightmares will be over."

I pictured Jack Diamond, that man with Jon's face, burned beyond recognition, and shuddered. I feared the nightmares were only beginning. "I completely misjudged him, Tony. He'd only ever wanted to understand why his friend had to die."

And yet he died never knowing.

Why did Jack feel **he** had to die? While his demeanor was odd, I'd detected no melancholy in him, no despair, nothing which pointed to some hopeless inner pain. So his death had to have gained something, or at least he thought it did.

He said everyone hunted him. Why? What alternative, what terror for the future, what potential harm to others had he tried to avoid by this act? What could he possibly have feared happening that was so awful to cause a Diamond Heir to take his own life?

Jon and Gardena stood stiffly, several yards to my left, their faces set and drawn.

Gardena was heavily veiled; Jon wore dark spectacles. They must have seen us, but they never once looked in our direction.

After the crowd began to thin, I went to Jon, handing him his umbrella. "I'm so glad you're safe."

Jonathan nodded, his eyes downcast.

I wanted to ask about everything: why he went with Jack, if he knew Jack planned to lure me. If he'd tried to escape, what message he'd sent.

Surely he didn't know his brother would try to take his own life!

But looking at the grief in their faces, it suddenly seemed wrong to speak of the matter. "I'm so sorry for what happened ... he never told me why he wanted to do it. Only that people were after him." I felt truly grieved, and it surprised me. "I tried to stop him!"

Through his dark spectacles, Jon's eyes were red. He put his hand on my upper arm, by my sling, but he never looked at me. "Don't blame yourself; it wasn't your fault."

His voice sounded distant, guarded. I'd never heard him speak in this way to me before.

He loved his brother so much! Jon had stood by Jack, helped Jack, defended Jack even to his family, though they didn't understand.

Gardena took my hand, her voice full of emotion. "Thank you."

Then Jonathan put his arm around Gardena and drew her away, as if unable to say anything more.

We watched them move off. What pain they must be in! And Jon ... poor Jon! He had to be blaming himself for going along with this madness, for everything leading to his brother's death.

I almost went to speak with them again, but Tony took my left hand. "Let's go home."

When I considered it, this seemed a better idea. But even though most of the people had gone, the room was still so full that it took us a while to get to Tony's carriage. The sidewalks and streets were worse, choked with people, and the carriage crawled along as it moved out of the quadrant.

Tony sat close by, his arm around me, and I put my head on his shoulder. He didn't speak. But it felt comfortable, if in a stunned sort of way. I had no words for what I'd seen and experienced.

It was many hours before we reached Spadros Manor. Without any fanfare, Tony and I ate dinner in our rooms, in silence.

Amelia got me undressed. I lay in bed.

After a while, Tony lay beside me. A half-hour later, his quiet breathing told me he slept.

I felt exhausted. But that night, I lay awake.

Ever since I'd escaped the explosion, I'd felt uneasy.

Something wasn't right.

Why would Jack Diamond take his own life?

I've never killed anyone in my life. I am about to kill a man, though. Do you think my cards will be burnt for it?

Jack Diamond's death had been all over the news. A whole edition had been devoted to it. There had been rumors, gossip, speculation. Yet none of them made any mention of finding Jack's ring.

He always wore a ring on his left small finger, silver with a clear stone. I had never once seen him without it.

And Jack never wore anything black. Ever.

No one wears white. And I seen them. Looked to be from the same store I get mine at, with them black soles and the silver stamp and all. But what gentleman wears white? It's crazy.

I carefully sat up so as not to wake Tony, putting the pillows behind me. I drew my knees up, resting my arms and chin upon them.

Not one stitch of clothing, they said. Everyone I'd ever heard talk about him agreed on that. Jack Diamond couldn't stand to wear anything of any other color but white. It was an obsession with him.

Not even the soles of his shoes.

Not even the soles of his shoes.

Not even the soles of his shoes.

I pictured the look in Jack's eyes, the way he moved.

Farewell, for now.

I began to laugh.

I laughed until Tony woke, and when I told him why I laughed so, he began to laugh as well, and we laughed there together, holding each other in the darkness, until we cried.

The Audacity

The next morning, none of it seemed funny, particularly when I remembered Jack's parents.

I took the plain carriage and went to my apartments.

When Blitz opened the door, he looked as if he'd seen a ghost. "What are you doing here?"

"I own the place, Blitz. Let me in."

He drew back, looking astonished. But then he recovered. "Very well. But quietly: we finally got the baby to sleep." We went into the kitchen and sat. "What's all this about?"

"Keep taking appointments for my investigation service. Only allow someone you trust with your life to have Master Rainbow's rooms. And don't rent out my rooms just yet."

He gave me a thin smile.

"I'm serious. There's more going on than meets the eye."

"What do you mean?"

Should I say? Jack Diamond had kidnapped his twin and faked his death for a reason. If a Diamond Heir had to go to such lengths to protect himself, then whatever was happening was much bigger than I imagined. "I'm not giving up."

Mary came in from the back hall, closing the door behind her.

Our eyes met. "And I won't be forced to bear a child."

Mary paled. "The morning after you left, we woke to find Mrs. Crawford gone."

Anger filled me. "She must have done this." The audacity of that woman! "I knew my morning tea hasn't tasted right." And it was all too convenient, everyone being out of the house the day Tony arrived. This pregnancy stank of Roy's scheming. "Find out where she's gone."

Mary's eyes reddened. "I'm sorry, mum. You let her in here on my word, and I failed you."

"Come, sit down." Once she'd done so, I said, "I'll take care of matters. It's a bit more expensive, but it'll be over soon. My husband will never know. I'll have a suitable time of mourning. Then I'll return, and all will be well."

Mary gasped. "You wouldn't!"

I leaned forward. "Mrs. Crawford didn't do this on her own." And no one could have forced Jack Diamond to do what he'd done. "I'm tired of these people trying to ruin me. I won't stand for it any longer."

Mr. Hart's cowardice had led to my own brother trying to kill me — whether out of jealousy or some other motivation, I wasn't sure.

And if Jonathan wasn't a part of his own abduction — the "decision" he'd had to make, the way he went so willingly, the way he wouldn't meet my eye — he must have at least suspected something. I certainly couldn't see Jack doing all this without a great deal of help.

Do you think I don't talk to my own sister?

Was Gardena Diamond the "pretty footman" that the Courthouse guard saw the day Jonathan vanished? Had she been the one who pushed the chloroform upon Honor the night I was captured?

Could the three of them have been in this together?

Jack Diamond's plan all along was to pretend to be mad. So Jon knew all this time that his brother Jack was not only reasonably sane, but meant me no harm.

So why had he never told me? Why let me live in fear?

Not only that, Jonathan had willingly disappeared after pushing me at Tony. Did he choose to frighten his family and his people, to set the entire city's efforts upon this farce?

Worse still, did he know this pregnancy would happen? Had Jon conspired with Roy in order to entrap me?

At that table, my table on my property, I didn't know who to blame. So I blamed everyone.

I would be free of them, their plots, their schemes, their control over me, once and for all, even if it meant my death. "This won't take long." I rose. "I'll be back in a few weeks, a month at most. You'll see."

As I returned to Spadros Manor, determination rose within me, and anger. I felt determined to learn the truth about what really was going on here. And I could no longer let my fear of the answers stop me from asking the questions.

These people, people who should have loved and cared for me, had instead conspired to ruin me.

At the thought, a bitter desire for revenge rose up inside my soul. And that day, I vowed upon my Holy Cards that by the time I obtained some real blood tea, I would have devised a way to ruin them as well.

~~ This ends Chapter 7 of the Red Dog Conspiracy ~~

The Three of Spades
Coming October 2021
Preorder now!

The Players
(those mentioned in this chapter)

Spadros quadrant

Jacqueline Kaplan Spadros (Jacqui)

Anthony Spadros (Tony), her husband and Spadros Family Heir

Blitz Spadros, the butler at Jacqui's apartments on 33 1/3 Street

Mary Pearson Spadros, his wife

Ariana Spadros, their newborn daughter

Roy Spadros, Tony's father and Patriarch of the Spadros syndicate

Molly Hogan Spadros, his wife

Katherine Spadros (Katie) their daughter; Tony's sister

Ten Hogan (Sawbuck), Tony's first cousin and right hand man

John Pearson, the butler at Spadros Manor on 192nd Street

Blaze Rainbow (Morton), Jacqui's business partner

Amelia Dewey, Jacqui's lady's maid

Pip Dewey, her son

Claudete Crawford, Jacqui's temporary housekeeper

Eight Howell, Spadros Associate; owner of the Backdoor Saloon

Theodore Sutherfield, Spadros Associate; oldest brother of Blitz

Diamond quadrant

Jonathan Diamond, Jacqui's best friend; the Keeper of the Court

Jack Diamond (Black Jack), his identical twin; the Keeper of the Prison

Gardena Diamond, his sister; she and Tony have a child together

Cesare Diamond, his brother and Diamond Family Heir

Beloty Diamond, his brother

Moretti Diamond, his brother

Hector Diamond II (Quadri), his brother

Vienna Diamond, his brother

Julius Diamond, their father and Patriarch of the Diamond syndicate

Clubb quadrant

Alexander Clubb, Patriarch of the Clubb syndicate

Lance Clubb, his son and Clubb Family Heir

The Players
(continued)

Hart quadrant

Charles Hart, Patriarch of the Hart syndicate

Judith Hart, his wife

Etienne Hart, his son and Hart Family Heir; an Inventor

Joseph Kerr, Jacqui's former lover

Josephine Kerr, his twin sister

Susan, their maid

The island of Market Center

Chase Freezout, Mayor of Bridges; former District Attorney

Delanie Freezout, his wife

Doyle Pike, Jacqui's former attorney

Thrace Pike, his grandson; works in the District Attorney's office

Cinco Hardeman, Jonathan Diamond's secretary at the Courthouse

Anna Goren, an apothecary

Brenda Trex, City Clerk

Mike Pok-Deng, an apothecary

Paix Hanger, a Constable

Geofrey Schwimmen, Chief of Police

The Spadros Pot

Fanny Kaplan (Ma), Jacqui's mother and owner of the Cathedral

The Eldest, Jacqui's great-grandmother

Benji, Jacqui's childhood friend

Tim Keycard, Benji's adopted son

Black Maria (Birdie), controls the High-Low Split street gang

At large

Albert Sheinwold, former Detective Constable and Spadros Associate

Zia Cashout, former Federal Agent

The Red Dog Gang, a shadowy organization

Frank Pagliacci, a scoundrel

Acknowledgments

My thanks to Julian White for his beta reading and encouragement. I'd also like to thank Erin Hartshorn for her editing and proofreading.

Thanks also go to my street team, The Commission, without whom this book might not have made it into your hands.

Special thanks go to my Patrons, whose monthly financial support helps make this series possible:

Julian White

Melissa Williams

Jennifer Eades

Cristina

Michaelene Alston

Eirlys Evans

Jane Kamvar

Aramanth Dawe

Rachel Heslin

Phoebe Darqueling

Laura Prime

Toni Mcconnell

Kelsye Nelson

James Mallison, Sr.

Follow the Red Dog Conspiracy on Patreon

patreon.com/red_dog_conspiracy

About The Author

Patricia Loofbourrow is a writer, gardener, artist, musician, poet, wildcrafter, and married mother of three who loves power tools, dancing, genetics, and anything to do with outer space. She also has an MD. Heinlein would be proud.

You can follow her at:
• Her website JacqOfSpades.com
• Twitter @Jacq_Of_Spades
• Tumblr red-dog-conspiracy.tumblr.com
• The Red Dog Conspiracy Facebook page

Note From The Author

Thanks so much for reading *The Two of Hearts*. If you liked the book, please contact me, or leave a review where you bought this!

For news, backstory, and more, visit JacqOfSpades.com